Bad Company

From the Casefiles of Detective 'Mal' Malone

Jen Flanagan

Bad Company

From the Casefiles of Detective 'Mal' Malone
Copyright © 2019 by Jen Flanagan

First Edition: April 2022
This edition was first published in 2022

Cover design: Haley Tenney
Editor: Moniga Bogza, Trusted Accomplice

Library of Congress Control Number: 2021916181
ISBN: 978-1-7377499-1-2 (Paperback)
ISBN: 978-1-7377499-0-5 (eBook)

Printed in the United States of America
Published by: Serenity Endeavors Press
https://www.jenflanaganbooks.com/

Contents

To all those who came before me: The storytellers who wove rich tales and caused me to dream, the artists who inspired me, and this beautiful world and its lesson to persevere.

Also, to my incredible support group, my friends and family who have encouraged and helped me along the way. I couldn't have done it without you. Particularly my parents, sister, husband, and my Rose who always believed in me.

To my readers, I hope you enjoy this introduction to Mal and her gang of friends. Be sure to keep an eye out for more stories about our friends in Roscoe Village!

Chapter 1

The stapler sailed through the air to hit the brick wall across the room with a loud, satisfying crunch, pairing well with the guttural scream echoing from my chest. I rarely resorted to throwing things, but I'd been working on the Mennon case for a full week with absolutely, positively, *no* successful lead. It was the most frustrating seven days I'd ever had. I had been *so* sure this last lead would go somewhere.

Collapsing in my chair, I shoved away from my desk and further office-supply destruction. I sat, defeated, slouching deep as it rolled to the wall behind me, reddish-brown hair floating around my twisted face.

After all that time, I had found only two people who had seen Suzanne Mennon the afternoon after she walked out for her lunch break. The gas station clerk and a contact the clerk said she spoke with. When I *finally* got ahold of the contact, Jeremy Jones, he gave me no further leads to follow.

All Jeremy had shared was that he bumped into her at the gas station near her work. After further cajoling, followed by some light harassing, he explained he had swung by on his way home from an all-nighter at the betting parlor for some Mickey's. I pressed him for more information, but he said he didn't remember what she was buying. No memory of anything strange about her mood or appearance. He didn't give me anything to go on. He said he only remembered Suzy because she had a big rack…*Cue the eye-roll.*

Over the past week, I had canvassed the neighborhood around Suzy's home and workplace, trying to find anyone who might have seen her or anything that might give me a lead to go on. I felt like I was circling the drain.

Trying to focus my thoughts, I took several deep breaths. I most certainly wasn't going to get anywhere by sitting in here, sulking, no matter how appealing it seemed. I had to figure out my next move. I shoved up from my seat, snatching up my keys and my leather jacket to head out for a walk. Maybe it would clear my head.

Stepping out of the old brick building where my PI office was located and into the warm spring morning, I slipped my jacket on. It was a beautiful day, and the sun was out. My boots crunched on the leftover road salt from winter, and the typical Chicago wind tossed my shoulder-length auburn hair around my head. I couldn't keep it straight to save my life, the constant gusts adding to its natural wave. I had long-since stopped trying and tucked a particularly pervasive chunk behind an ear. Crossing the street, I turned into Grounds, my favorite coffee shop. Earning that title because it was ten steps from my office and I really liked Maurice, the fifty-something shop owner.

Maurice looked up when I walked in and waved hi. "Good morning, Mal!"

"Morning, Mo," I answered, sliding to the counter. The fresh air—correction: the *coffee-scented* air improved my mood considerably.

"Working on a case?" Maurice asked thoughtfully. I noticed the slight gray on his temples was getting more pronounced.

I often talked out issues with Maurice for input, leaving out details to protect confidentiality. It helped me put perspective on things. He was a good listener, or so I'd discovered after many a late night at the café, notes and coffee in front of me.

"Yeah, but no good leads right now." I blew a straggler from my face and toyed with a coffee stirrer in front of me. "No leads at all, in fact. My last one just fizzled up."

"That sucks, Mal. But I know you'll work it out," Maurice said with a wink as he slid my usual to me.

I tipped a cinnamon shaker over the foam of the cappuccino to add a light dusting. "I guess," I murmured, taking a sip of the little slice of heaven. "I just need to get a different angle on it. I'm missing something."

I wasn't much of a girly girl, but I did like fancy coffee when I could get it. Caffeine being a main staple in my diet, I believed variety was good.

After paying Maurice, I pushed away from the counter and headed back into the sun. I stretched my long legs and turned down the street in a nice stroll. Breathing in, I took a long sip and surveyed the streets. It was still early, and there were a lot of people wandering in and out of the shops in downtown Roscoe Village.

I loved my little suburb of Chicago. It wasn't as crazy as downtown Chi-Town, and it had more charm, too. It was located in North Center and was just the right mix of cheap enough for me to afford, yet relatively safe enough to walk through the streets at dusk. I let the atmosphere roll over me, people watching and smelling the local pizza place across the street.

Sam Mennon had come into my office a week ago, eyes drawn, hair on end, and clothes crumpled. It was obvious he hadn't had much sleep. His wife, Suzy, had gone missing from work three days prior.

Suzanne, 35, goes by Suzy. The facts rolled through my head amid the distractions. Sweet face, long straight brown hair, worked as a teller at Heward Bank. She was seen on camera leaving the building around lunchtime and again by the clerk at the gas station down the street. The gas station clerk remembered Suzy checking out at the same time as a regular, Jeremy Jones. The same Jeremy Jones who had just told me he didn't remember anything pertinent about Suzy.

The cops had the case, but with no leads and others piling up, it was no longer being actively worked. According to them, Suzy's absence could be a simple matter of an unhappy wife leaving her husband. It happened all the time. There wasn't any sign of foul play, so the cops moved on to bigger fish. She had passed the critical forty-eight-hour mark. The likelihood of finding her had drastically decreased.

Sam was entirely distraught. I honestly couldn't see how a man so completely lost without his wife wouldn't have known if his wife was having an affair. I mean, it was always a possibility; people could be clueless. But I was leaning toward kidnapping or murder, and my gut didn't typically fail me.

Besides, Sam was the client and he didn't believe Suzy had left him. He was paying me to find her, not necessarily to spend my time pursuing a route that involved her voluntarily leaving him. *Some*thing had happened to Suzy, and I planned on finding out what.

I really hoped it wasn't murder, though. Murder cases sucked.

I took another sip of my coffee, enjoying the warmth before I noticed unusual movement down the street. It wasn't until I saw the smoke, that I smelled it in the air.

A couple of blocks down, two people came running out of a brick building, dark clouds puffing around their heads. Flames leapt out the upper-story windows.

I ran forward to help a blonde woman who was stumbling out. Helping her down to the curb to catch her breath, I pulled my phone out of my pocket and dialed dispatch to report the fire.

"Are you okay?" I asked her, searching for signs of a burn.

The blonde coughed and looked back, trying to see through the smoke. "Yes, I'm fine, but my coworkers are still inside!"

I relayed the situation to the dispatcher and put her on speakerphone.

"There's a fire in the kitchen. I don't know what happened. We tried to grab the fire extinguisher, but the fire spread too fast!"

The dispatcher sent trucks and asked me to keep the woman close till the ambulance got there.

Only a few more people came out, so I worried there were still others upstairs. Moving toward the doorway, I peered inside. All I could see was smoke pouring out in big, rolling plumes. I had to move back to the fresh air, biting my lip in indecision. I hated leaving anyone in there, but I didn't think I could make it inside. I wasn't trained for that sort of thing.

The siren announced the fire truck only moments later. It wheeled to the curb, men jumping off and grabbing axes before heading inside the building. Another two trucks and an official-looking SUV came around the corner immediately after. One hooked up to the hydrant across the street, and its crew went to join the others inside.

I went back to check on the willowy blonde. Her coughing had died down, but she was shaking from the adrenaline rush. I helped her up and walked her over to meet the arriving paramedics.

"I'll be all right," the blonde said, smiling. "Thanks for your help."

The paramedics got busy, checking over everyone who had escaped the building. Their work looked choreographed as they moved around the scene. I was impressed by how quickly and efficiently everyone responded. A firefighter in charge stood outside with his radio, shouting orders and keeping a keen eye on everything.

The sheer amount of black smoke coming from the building was startling, like diseased air crawling to the sky. I always figured fire would be bright and yellow, but everything about this building was dark, and black smoke billowed out of the doorway and windows. I was surprised at how difficult it was to simply look inside. *How could they even see in there?*

Suddenly, a loud explosion followed by a crash erupted from the building. Smoke flared out of the windows in an initial rush, then died back a bit to where it was before. The firemen and police officers ushered everyone, myself included, farther away. A few more headed in, and everyone stood in tense silence until they finally came back out again.

Two firefighters had someone slung over their shoulders, a woman and a man, while another looked to be hurt and was leaning heavily on his teammate as they made their way out of the building. I heard someone yell into his radio, but it seemed like the tension had somewhat abated.

The fireman helped the injured one to the side of the truck where I was standing. After stripping off his Air-Pak and helmet, he leaned over to help his buddy do the same. Checking the other fireman's eyes, he laughed jovially and slapped the other guy on the back in a brotherly way. The back of his bunker coat read "RHODES."

He was a big, well-built man with broad shoulders, average height, and a commanding presence. He was obviously in charge of one of the crews, and his incredibly intense gaze scanned the scene to take in every detail. It seemed he wasn't just a good-looking man; there was more to him than what was on the surface.

Rhodes seemed to be satisfied the other fireman wasn't too badly injured, because it sounded like he was teasing him for getting under falling debris. Still, when he sent him over to the paramedics anyway to get checked out, I could see a little worry crease his eyebrows as he ran a hand over his shaved head.

The air was still filled with smoke, and while it was spreading, it seemed like everything was under control. Not that there was much I could do to help.

As I turned around to go, I noticed someone skirting around the back of the onlookers. It looked like a kid, maybe sixteen years old, wearing a gray hoodie.

He was edging towards the paramedic's vehicle. The skin under his eyes was dark, and he looked sick. I couldn't tell what he was up to, but my gut said it wasn't good. Deciding to follow, I edged forward.

The kid was watching the paramedics closely, but they were busy with the fire victims, and he slipped into the back of the ambulance. I moved over to a female police officer nearby, nudged her, and nodded slightly toward the van.

Turning, she took in the situation immediately and moved into action. Catching up with the kid, she yanked him out. In the scuffle, the kid pushed and shoved the officer into the crowd, where she tripped on the curb and fell to the ground.

I jumped forward to catch the kid just as a large body came up behind me. Looking up, I saw it was the firefighter Rhodes. The two of us surrounded the young man each grabbing an arm.

My eyes met his over the kid's head: his intense, mine quizzical. I was surprised he had been paying attention to this part of the scene. I twisted the kid's arm lightly but firmly to secure him as the officer made her way over to us, dusting off her uniform slacks.

"Thanks," she said to Rhodes and me.

I knew quite a few of the officers from the local precinct, but she didn't look familiar. Her name tag said Mathews, and I nodded as she took the boy from me.

"Drugs," said Officer Mathews, pulling out a couple of vials from the boy's pockets. "Buses are stocked with drugs for emergencies."

"Buses?" I asked.

"The ambulance," Rhodes answered, still watching me intently.

"I'll take this one in," Officer Mathews said, walking the kid to her cruiser.

I looked back at the fireman. "What kind of drugs?"

"Morphine, typically. It's worth quite a bit on the street," Rhodes said, crossing his arms, assessing me.

"You jumped in there pretty fast," he added finally.

I turned back to him, one side of my mouth tilted up. "So did you." I hadn't even seen him come up behind me.

Rhodes stood eye level with me and a little close, so I stepped back to put some distance between us. Chemistry was sizzling unspoken in the air, but I had an afternoon meeting with a new client and had to get back to the office. Turning to head back, I noticed the fireman made a move to say something. I paused, but he looked back at his crew and turned to join them instead.

I got halfway back to my office before I remembered my coffee on the sidewalk, by the blonde. "Crap." I sighed. "Probably cold by now anyway," I muttered to myself as I trudged on, still without a new lead and no idea where to look next.

Chapter 2

My three o'clock was late.

I was just about to give up on him and revisit Heward Bank in search for another lead when Peter Mantovani walked in at 3:45 p.m. However, one look at me and he stopped in his tracks and looked back towards the door, hesitating.

"You're a woman?" he finally said.

"Just since last week," I replied without missing a beat. "Those surgeons really are impressive!"

It was pretty common for people to come in to meet with Detective Malone, then take off once they realize I was a woman. I got a lot of grief for my gender, but honestly, I was good at what I did and tenacious as hell. I supposed it would be easier to go by my first name, so it wasn't such a surprise, but then I'd get even fewer people coming to my office, and I needed the work.

Also, I didn't go by my first name. Ever.

Mr. Mantovani just stared at me like I was insane. *How would he know? The therapist was never able to prove anything.*

"Mr. Mantovani, yes, I am a woman. I also happen to be a damn good detective. If you have a problem with that, please feel free to leave now." I leveled with him as I came around the desk, arms crossed. I was tall for a woman and had about five inches on Petite Pete...*Man, I'm going to have to remember that one.* I had to fight a grin.

Peter stood there, frowning and shifting from one foot to another until he finally said, "Honestly, I'm not really sure what I'm doing here." He sighed and ran a hand through his brown hair, leaving it standing on end.

"What do you mean?" I asked, relaxing my pose.

"I wouldn't even know what I'd do about it!"

"If you'd just start at the beginning," I prompted him, guiding him to a chair. The space I rented included a small lobby with a private room in the back. Since I didn't have a receptionist, I left my door open and waited in the outer area if I was expecting someone.

It also gave me a little more privacy if I had multiple people present. Someday, I hoped I would have enough work to hire that receptionist. But for now, it was just me.

Another sigh escaped Peter. "Alright. It's just that I think my nephew is embezzling from me. I own Mantovani's Pizza, down on 8th."

"Okay," I started. "That happens. I can look into it. I should be able to find out if he's really stealing from you."

"That's not the problem," Peter said, frustrated. "I'm pretty sure it's him. I mean, *someone* is stealing from me. Money has been missing from the tip jar, and we've been bringing in less revenue than normal with the same customer activity. The sales are normal, but money is missing between the cash register and the deposits. Sometimes the cash register closes out short at the end of the night, and sometimes it's fine, but then the money is disappearing from the safe."

Peter sat dejected, hands on his lap, as he continued. "He's the newest and has the most opportunity. He works as a fill-in between the kitchen and tables. And I've been catching him sneaking around, acting guilty."

"Okay. If you're so sure it's him, why don't you call him out on it?"

"Because that's not the problem. The problem is that my nephew's father, my brother-in-law, is Domenico Poggiali."

Hmmm…That does complicate things, I thought, my eyes widening. Domenico Poggiali was suspected of having mob relations; he may even be one of the head guys. He was a scary dude and not one I'd want to piss off.

"And you didn't think about the complications of hiring his son when you did?" I frowned at Pete.

Peter began pacing the office. It didn't take him long; it was a small office.

"Well, yes. Of course, I did. But I kind of thought it'd be good for business, you know? Doing Domenico a favor and all by giving his son a job. But now…I don't know what to do. I just want to know if it really *is* Marco, stealing from me. If I have proof, then maybe…I don't know. Maybe I can scare him off or threaten to tell his dad or something. I really have no idea, but I have to at least know for sure."

"Well, I can come to meet him and feel the situation out. I could work as a 'fill-in' for a few shifts," I offered, leaning a hip against my desk and crossing my arms. "People are more inclined to talk to their peers. It also gives me a cover for poking around in the office and asking questions."

I did some work like this in the past, and the employees generally had an idea of what was going on in a company. They just tended to keep their mouth shut about it. No one wants to rat out a fellow worker.

Of course, there could be more than one of them in on the gig.

"Once I get a feel as to who's behind it, I can stay close and see if I can find out more information, like if they're working with someone else or maybe their motivation," I continued, walking back around my desk to get my price sheet and handed it to Peter. "These are my fees. I work on an hourly basis. Any fees I incur while under investigation will be passed on to you. I require a $1000 retainer. If you don't use it all, I'll reimburse you. Otherwise, I'll bill you the remainder." It was fair. I had tried to go without the retainer in the past, and it had bitten me in the butt a few times.

Peter was still listening, so I continued.

"I'll give you daily updates on the case, by email or phone call, whichever works best for you," I said, pulling my standard contract out of the drawer. "Although, I will warn you, sometimes it takes a few days to get any sort of lead to follow up on. If you decide to hire me, I'll need you to fill out and sign this waiver. It explains that you have hired me and for what purposes. It also states that you understand I will be looking into whatever information is necessary to solve the case, whether it's pertaining to you, your family, or your business."

I needed it in case a client changed their minds or didn't want to tell a spouse they had hired me. It was a little insurance that proved I had business looking into their business.

Peter frowned, still undecided. But he was still in the room.

"You can take your time. Take it with you, and bring it back if you decide you want to pursue it. I will tell you, though, if someone *is* stealing from you, they won't just develop a conscience and stop. People just get greedier." I stood to shake his hand and usher him out. I had given him all the facts. The ball was in his court.

"No, I'm ready," Peter said resolutely. "I want to get to the bottom of this." He filled out the form with grim determination, signed it, and fished out a checkbook for my retainer fee. "I'm not telling my wife that I hired you, so no one else will know about this. Shelly would be really upset if she thought I was looking into Dom's boy."

"That's not a problem," I replied, filing the fact away. "I can be discreet. When does Marco work next?"

"Tomorrow, but Friday is our busy night," Peter said. "If you want to pick up an extra shift then, it won't raise as much suspicion. Would you want to be making pizzas or waiting tables?"

"Probably wait tables. I can get more exposure to everyone and will have more excuses to be digging around." A rough plan was already forming in my mind. "What time?"

"The dinner shift starts at 5 p.m."

"I'll be there at 4 p.m. to familiarize myself with the place and the menu."

"Have you ever waited tables before?" Pete asked.

"Yes," I said. I had worked at a local bar and grill back before I entered the police academy. I wasn't there long, but I figured it'd be similar enough.

"Then, it shouldn't be a problem. I don't have any fancy computer system or anything."

I shook Peter's hand and led him out the door. Another job in the bag.

I hoped I would have better luck with this new case.

Heward Bank was only a few miles away. I couldn't start on the Mantovani case until tomorrow, so I jumped into my Jeep and headed across town to poke around a bit. I had already seen the video footage. The manager, Mr. Tomlin, was more than happy to share it with me when I took the case. He was worried about Suzy and had been very helpful.

Everyone seemed to like her and commented how sweet she was. In the video, she wore a bright purple blouse and gray slacks. She didn't look stressed or worried at all. She just strolled on out of the office, purse swinging from her elbow, with a pleasant smile on her face. As she walked out the door, she slid her sunglasses on and turned to look up as though to soak in the sun.

The other employees said it wasn't unusual for her to head out at lunch. Sometimes, she'd walk to a nearby restaurant. Other times, she brought her lunch and took a short walk around the block instead.

When Sam saw the footage, he confirmed that nothing looked out of place and she seemed happy.

Pulling up to the bank, I parked in the lot and walked in to look around. I had been in several times; the tellers knew who I was by now. I glanced up at the security cameras, following the path Suzy had walked as she came around the teller window and out the front door. Turning, I took the same route once again.

Walking back out the front door, I took off on foot to the gas station where Suzy had last been seen. I wanted to trace her steps as closely as possible, to see what she saw that day. Maybe I would notice something I had missed before.

Walking into the small dark store, I grabbed a water. No one could remember what Suzy had bought at the gas station; they didn't have a deli counter or packaged sandwiches. It was likely she'd either grabbed something small like nuts, fruit, or a drink. There was no record of her card being ran, so she had to have paid in cash.

I slid a few dollars from my wallet to keep up the pattern. As I walked by the beer case, I noticed they didn't have Mickey's beer in stock. Puzzled, I walked up to the cashier and asked if they were out.

"No, we quit carrying it."

"When?" I said, surprised.

"About a month ago," the store clerk shrugged. "The owner's been cutting back on inventory. Business has gone down with the economy, so we have less variety in stock. It's too expensive."

"Are you sure it's been that long since you had it?" I pressed him. Jeremy had said he bought Mickey's here last week when he saw Suzy. I had to be sure he wasn't just mistaken on timing. "Could it have been more recent?"

"No, actually, I'm sure. St Patrick's Day, we sold entirely out of Mickey's, along with any beer or liquor even remotely Irish." At my questioning expression, he added, "Mickey's is green…After that, the boss only replaced the best-selling brands."

I paid for my water and walked out slowly, looking around for any other clue.

He had confirmed what I'd heard about the gas station having financial issues. I hadn't been able to get any good footage from the video cameras as they only kept them on at the gas pumps. The owner claimed he wasn't going to run any more electricity than absolutely necessary, to cut costs.

But that was okay because now I had a lead again. A small one, but it was still a lead. Jeremy Jones had definitely lied, and I was about to pay him a little visit.

I found Jeremy's address in a database I paid for. It was an expensive monthly subscription but critical for tracking people down. It wasn't always the most recent information, but I could generally find who I needed, given enough time.

I had tried to visit him a week ago when the gas station clerk mentioned that Jeremy, a regular, had been there at the same time as Suzy. However, he was never home when I stopped by. After some persuasion, his roommate gave me Jeremy's number. Then, after another two days' worth of messages, I finally got him to call back...earlier this morning.

The same highly unhelpful phone call that had been the death of my stapler. I liked that stapler. I frowned.

Jeremy owed me a new one.

He lived in a pay-by-the-month motel in Hamlin Park. It was near the Julia C Lathrop Homes, not exactly the best part of town. Since I had been eluded so many times, I decided to make camp down the street and watch for Jeremy to leave, see what he was up to. It was likely he had been home a few of the times I tried to see him, so I doubted I'd be able to talk to him if I knocked. Unless I thought I could get a warrant, which was doubtful at this point, I had to try a different tactic.

I found a parking spot about a street down from the motel and pulled out my notepad to go over facts and make notes. I sighed, deeply regretting not grabbing another coffee on the way over.

It had been ten days since Suzy's disappearance. If she had been kidnapped for ransom, there would have been word by now. Had she been taken for information, she would have likely told them what they wanted by now, and they would have either let her go or killed her. She could have been kidnapped for the sex trade or by a stalker, I ticked off the list.

Then there was the fifth option: she could have been killed. It was the easiest solution and, at this point, most likely. There was little information to the contrary, and I knew the odds but wasn't ready to give up yet. Maybe I was just being stubborn, but I kept thinking a body would have turned up by now.

Chicago was busy, with lots of foot traffic. That was unless the body had been dumped or buried way out of town. I didn't have any leads pointing in that direction, and there wouldn't be much I could do about it anyway, so for now, I let that scenario go.

Option six was the most difficult. I had to consider if Suzy *had* left Sam. It was starting to look like a real possibility. Sam wasn't really paying me to pursue that route, but it was my job to track down Suzy. If I couldn't get anything else to materialize, I could at least find her to offer him some sort of closure.

Thinking through that, there were no clues that she was unhappy. None of her belongings were missing, there were no new charges on her credit card, and no credit cards in her name only. No one at work had reported any changes in her mood, and all had confirmed her commitment to Sam.

But still, stranger things did happen. She could have been planning it and saved up cash. Maybe she was quiet about it and keeping up pretenses because she was afraid of backlash. Sam seemed wealthy. Maybe he had connections I didn't know about.

My gut was telling me this path was a waste of investigation time, but I would be ignorant not to consider the possibility. I rubbed my forehead, frustrated. What if this woman didn't want to be found? *Am I chasing a ghost?*

About two hours later, I saw a heavy-set man emerge from the motel and lock the door behind him. *Jackpot.*

It didn't look like the scrawny roommate, and the key suggested he lived there. It was a good chance this was Jeremy. He headed south on foot, so I waited until he was almost out of sight before I slid out of my Jeep to follow.

I kept close to the buildings and let him get as far ahead as I could without losing sight of him. It had gotten dark, and I kept my right hand in my leather jacket pocket, curled around my expandable baton, scanning the area for trouble as I edged along.

The man walked into Al's Beef on the opposite corner, coming out a few minutes later with two takeout bags wet with grease. He continued down the street, munching on fries from one of the bags, wiping his hands on his jeans. *Eww.*

After several blocks, Maybe-Jeremy walked up to the entrance of a brownstone, unlocked the door, and entered. I couldn't tell if it was residential or commercial, but it looked run-down.

I waited a few minutes, then walked closer to get a good look at it. It was an offtrack betting parlor. Maybe-Jeremy had a key to the place, so he had some business with the shop, probably an employee or manager.

It didn't look like he was coming out anytime soon. I watched a few people come and go, presumably to place bets, but nothing significant. So I headed back to my apartment to do some research on Jeremy and the betting parlor.

I had a solid new lead. *What was going on inside that place?*

Meanwhile, inside the betting parlor,

"You were right about that Italian beef, Suz!"

"You know it!" Suzy replied with a fist pump. "What did I tell you? Al's is the best."

"I totally have to try the chili fries next time. They looked amazing, too."

"Definitely, but I have another favorite you've just got to try next time," Suzy replied. "You haven't lived until you've had the Bananas Foster crepes at Yolks. We totally have to do that next!"

"Ooh, I love crepes!" the pudgy man replied, wiping meat juices from his chin with a napkin. "So, did you get this week's numbers figured out? I can't push the boss off another day."

Chapter 3

I woke at my desk with a long line of "g's" on my laptop monitor. I had fallen asleep at my computer, forehead on my keyboard, yet again. My laptop had been left at the office the night before, so I went there instead of home. I really needed to get some office help.

What I really needed was a full night's sleep, but since I was too tight on funds to hire anyone, all the work fell to me. *Someday*, I promised myself.

I had found some interesting information, though. Jeremy Jones' driver's license photo confirmed that *Maybe*-Jeremy was really *Actually*-Jeremy. *Fist pump for that one!*

I also found out that the offtrack betting parlor was owned by Fabian Dessi, a well-known criminal in Chicago. He had ties to Pietro Marchi, a known member of an old, suspected mafia family.

What was up with the mafia connections this week? My cases were edging toward the bad-for-your-health variety. But I couldn't give up on it now; Sam needed to know what had happened to Suzy.

Turning off my computer, I checked the time. It was nearly 7:00 a.m., so I decided to forgo sleep and clean up for the day. I lived in an apartment on Henderson Street. It was small but had a decent kitchen and was only a few blocks from the office.

I liked being close enough to walk to work. Being stuck indoor was my idea of a bad day, and luckily, most of my time was spent on the streets, following leads. The research and bookkeeping part of my job was the only thing keeping me in the office. Bookkeeping always came last. My cases were always top priority, as they kept the money flowing in. It was also the easiest task to procrastinate on.

I let myself into my apartment complex, stopping for my mail before walking up the stairs to 4B. My neighbor, Noelle, was leaving, and I nodded a hello to her as I let myself in. I sighed as I realized how I must look coming in this early, wearing slept-in clothes, and hair more than a little crazy.

It probably wasn't the first time my neighbors had seen me dragging myself back in at such an early hour. Dropping my mail in by my dead ivy plant on the kitchen counter, I got a glass of water from the sink. I chugged it and poured the small amount left into the pot, absently hoping it would revive. I had never been good with plants.

I was hungry and really wanted some breakfast, but my need for a shower—*and a toothbrush,* I thought with a grimace—was much higher. Ultimately, my desire for caffeine outweighed both and I delayed long enough to start a pot of coffee in Mr. Bunn, my coffee maker, before heading to wash up.

The shower felt like heaven. I sighed with pleasure as I pulled on my robe and opened the bathroom door to the smell of coffee. Luckily the heavy cream was still good, so I added a large tablespoon to my favorite mug, which was proclaiming "I DRINK COFFEE FOR YOUR PROTECTION," before pouring the delicious life-giving essence.

Fried eggs and sausage in my favorite cast-iron skillet were next. I tried to start every morning with a good dose of protein and an even better dose of caffeine. I topped it with half of an avocado to add something green.

By the time I was heading out the door, I felt much more like myself. The local precinct was across town, on Belmont, so I walked back to the office for my Jeep. After such a brutal winter, the fresh air felt like a gift.

At the police station, I noticed all the officers behind the window, all decked out in their starched uniforms, and glanced down at my own jeans, V-neck tee, and leather jacket. I couldn't help but smile a little. It hadn't been an easy road on my own. Most people had no idea how many permits and licenses it took to be a private investigator, but I was happy with my decision to leave the police academy. Being my own boss had a lot of benefits.

I showed my PI badge to the rookie on duty and let him know who I was here to see, then waded through the desks.

"Morning," I said with a nod and a smile to the blonde in the evidence-room window.

"Hey, Mal! How have you been?" asked Jen, blue eyes smiling.

We had been friends since the police academy. As the only two women in training, it had cemented our friendship. We'd had each other's backs since then.

"I'm doing great. I just came by to ask you a few questions."

"Sure. How can I help you?" she replied with a smile.

She looked too sweet to be a police officer with her bouncy bob and heart-shaped face. She had been very popular with the boys back at the academy. But she was smart and strong when needed.

"What do you know about Fabian Dessi? I'm trying to find out more information about one of his employees who works at his offtrack betting parlor in Humboldt Park."

"Fabian Dessi? Who have you been hanging around? You know he supposedly works with Marchi, right?" Jen asked.

"Yeah, I've heard as much."

"Well, he owns quite a few betting parlors across Chicago. I don't know anything particular about the one in Humboldt Park, though. His goons roughed up a few guys pretty bad last week for not paying out on some debts." She frowned. "He's been brought in on charges loads of times, but somehow always walks. There has been some suspicion that he has someone on the inside, but who knows. He's bad company, Mal. I'd stay clear of him."

"I wasn't planning on dating him, Jen." I grinned. "I just wanted some info on him."

"Well, I've heard he's at the track on race days. You could find him there if you're looking for him. But I hope you aren't," she added, concern evident.

"I hope I don't need to, either. I just wanted to know what the word was on the street. I'll be careful, Jen. You know me," I said with a wink.

"Yeah, that's what I'm worried about," Jen said, eyebrow raised.

I laughed. "I'll be fine. Thanks for the info. We should catch up next week if you're available. Lunch, maybe?"

"Sounds good," Jen replied. "You should drop by Hungry's. I'm sure the guys would be happy to see you."

Hungry Brain was the local cop hang out. A lot of the officers stopped by after shift—until 2 a.m., that is. Then they'd move to Underbar. Both were within a couple of blocks from the cop shop.

"Uh, I don't know. It's been a while, and…" I trailed off. I hadn't been to Hungry's in years.

"You still avoiding Rodriguez?" Jen asked.

"Well, I'm not avoiding per se; I'm just not going out of my way to see him," I hedged. "I'm not avoiding the precinct, am I? It's a lot different, running into someone on their off-hours after a couple of beers."

Alex Rodriguez and I had dated for a while when we were at the academy. Rodriguez had been attracted to my ballsy nature, and we'd had a good time together. We were a good match physically and used to spar in our off time. It led to a passionate four-month relationship.

But he had a wandering eye and a wandering penis. *Not much to be done about that one*, I thought, forced penis-ectomy still being illegal, and all. Too bad.

"Fair enough." Jen nodded. "See you soon, then. I'll call you...and be careful!"

My next stop was PhishNett, Sam Mennon's IT business. We met at my office a couple of times and talked over the phone frequently, but I'd never physically been to PhishNett.

Sam and his team wrote software, created website marketing tools, and wrote computer apps. When I walked up to the door, I snorted at the tagline painted on it: "Serving Binary Brilliance!"

The place had an edgy modern feel with clean lines, bold colors, and minimal furniture. There was a creative and fun vibe, with movie posters and Star Wars cardboard cutouts decorating the office.

I walked up to the smiling receptionist, asking to see Sam. I wasn't sure what the team knew of his personal life. They may not know of his wife's disappearance or that he'd hired a PI.

The receptionist asked for my name and buzzed Sam on his intercom. However, instead of a response on the intercom, Sam burst through the office doors at the end of the hall and speed-walked to me. Not exactly worried about discretion.

"Any news?" he asked excitedly.

"Nothing big," I warned, hands raised. "I'm just following up on a possible lead and wanted to ask you a few questions."

Sam nodded, excitement filling him regardless of my warning, and ushered me down the hall. I glanced around Sam's office, noticing pictures on his desk and his bookshelf of Suzy and him together. They did look like a happy couple, smiling and holding hands. They were just a bit older than me, in their mid-thirties, and never had kids.

Sam's smiling face in the picture, arm proudly wrapped around Suzy, contrasted so much with the frazzled man in front of me. His brown eyes were rimmed red and puffy from lack of sleep. There even looked to be age lines on his brow from the constant worry. Sam had short, slightly curling brown hair and was of medium frame and height.

His knit vest over a button-up shirt and slacks, combined with his Batman watch and Star Wars belt buckle, cemented the techy-geek look. The wrinkled clothes and strained face told of his stress over the last few days.

I knew it was possible Sam was faking it, but it went against my instincts and observations. I trusted my gut; it had always served me well in the past. Even so, I was careful not to be blinded by pride.

He led me to a group of chairs placed in a circle and gestured for me to sit. The chairs looked to be used for meetings, set to put everyone at equal importance. It raised my opinion of Sam to see him value his employees' input.

We settled into our seats, and Sam leaned forward, entirely engaged.

"I just wanted to ask a little about hobbies," I started. "Do you or Suzy have any interest in gambling, like betting on horse races? Or maybe going to the racetrack?"

"Well, no. Not that I know of," Sam replied, frowning. "I've never seen her interested in gambling of any kind. You said you had a lead?" Sam prodded.

"Well, maybe," I hedged. "I heard back from Jeremy Jones and have reason to think he may have been lying about what he saw at the gas station. I'm still not sure why, but I wanted to know if you had ever seen him before or had any connections to betting parlors. I think he works for Fabian Dessi."

I showed my phone to Sam. I had taken a picture of the laptop monitor last night when I pulled up Jeremy's license.

Sam peered at the phone for a minute, then sadly shook his head. "Doesn't look familiar to me. I can't think of any reason why he would have anything to do with Suzy."

I shifted in my seat, disappointed there was no obvious connection. "I'm not sure he does. He may have been lying for other reasons. But it's the only lead we have. I've got to pursue it."

Sam's eyes drooped, the energy he'd had when I first arrived draining. Disappointment weighed his shoulders.

"Well, think about it. If something comes to you, give me a call. I'll continue to work this lead, just to see if it goes anywhere," I said, standing up.

"Okay. Thanks for stopping by," Sam answered, shaking my hand, but his attention was trained on the photo of Suzy and him smiling on the park bench.

"I'll let myself out," I said softly, slipping out the door.

I felt a little bad for leaving Sam in such a depressed mood, but I needed to find out if he knew of any connections between Suzy and Jeremy. Then again, just because he didn't know of any didn't mean they weren't there. I rubbed my forehead and slid my sunglasses back in place to block out the bright sunlight as I exited the building.

Driving back into town, my focus alternated between the case and my growling stomach. I swung into Mariano's Fresh Market to pick up something for the latter. At least dinner was something I could accomplish. Right now, I needed that.

I grabbed a basket as I walked in the door and headed toward the salad bar.

I was still concerned that Suzy wasn't alive. With the lack of evidence, that scenario was becoming more and more likely. No one matching her description had been admitted to any of the nearby hospitals. My mind swirled with possibilities, and the probability scale just kept tipping in a bleak direction.

Alternatively, Suzy might have had a gambling problem Sam didn't know about. If she owed a debt, the outcomes were the same. She could have been injured or killed. Still, there was no body. In a busy city like Chicago, surely, a body would have turned up after eleven days. Things weren't adding up. Generally, that meant I didn't have all the facts. I was missing something.

I headed to the back and picked up avocados and more cream for my coffee, adding them to the basket with my salad, saving myself a trip later. Making my way to the marked-down meat section, I saw a broad male back leaning over the meat case. I raised my eyebrows in appreciation of the outlined muscles. As he straightened up, he turned to reveal an equally wide chest and the face of the firefighter from the day before. Rhodes.

He stopped, recognition lighting his eyes. "Hi," he said with a nod.

"Hi, yourself," I replied, breaking away from my spiraling thoughts of the case. "Did everything turn out okay back there at the fire yesterday?"

"Uh, yeah." Rhodes shrugged. "A couple of guys got burnt, but nothing bad. They'll recover."

He stood there, watching me intently for a moment.

"You were pretty quick on the response with that kid," he finally said.

"Good instincts, I guess," I said.

"I guess," he repeated my words. "Captain Rhodes," he said decisively, extending his palm.

"Mal," I replied, shaking his hand. "You're a Captain? Was that your crew?"

"Yes, two of them are. Truck 12, Bricktown." He tilted his head, sizing me up. "So, what is it *you* do? Outside of taking down thieving kids, that is," he added with a wink.

"I'm a private investigator," I replied, raising an eyebrow at his question.

"A PI, huh? Why PI and not a cop?"

It was a personal question, but considering personal questions were my business, it didn't offend me.

"I tried that route." I glanced down, then back up at Rhodes with a smirk. "Let's just say I don't play well with others."

He let out a deep, throaty, down-to-his-toes laugh, which I immediately liked. I couldn't help but respond with a wide smile. Few people were so free. It was attractive on him.

"Fair enough," Rhodes finally said, still grinning. "I'm picking up pork chops for dinner at the station tonight, but," he said, pausing, that calculating look back on his face, "how about joining me for dinner tomorrow night? I cook a mean steak. I can even bend my normal rules and give the steak last rites if you're into well-done."

My smile dropped a notch. I hadn't expected a dinner invitation, not that it was entirely unwelcome. It was a knee-jerk reaction to back off. I didn't exactly have a lot of personal time and hadn't dated since Rodriguez.

Even when I didn't have a serious case like Suzy's disappearance, I didn't take a lot of time for myself. I had made myself a promise when I walked out of the academy, and away from Rodriguez, that I would find a way to make this work. I worked a lot, but I liked my job, so I was happy. I had some friends, just not a man in my life. A lot of people weren't in serious relationships, I told myself.

I did enjoy Rhodes' company, what little I'd been exposed to anyway. He was confident, but not cocky; a rare combination. He was intense and had an almost predatory way of looking at me, which I'll admit I liked, but he seemed to have a fun, lighthearted side, too. The man had a lot of contradictions, and I surprised myself by wanting to know more about him.

I settled on a, "Sorry, but I'm in the middle of a big case right now. It's kind of taking all my free time." I honestly couldn't spare a minute, even if I wanted to.

Rhodes searched my gaze, deciding if I was blowing him off or not. "Well, then maybe some other time, when your case is over?"

"Yeah." I nodded slowly. "Maybe."

He gave me one last size-up, nodded, and pulled out a notepad from his breast pocket. After jotting down his number, he handed it over with a slow smile. "Just in case you find some time," he said with a wink and sauntered off.

I glanced down at the paper; the name Marlon was scrawled at the bottom. *Marlon, huh?* I considered the note, then watched him walk away. Glancing back over his shoulder, he caught me in the act. The grin on his face showing his pleasure.

Unable to help it, I returned his grinned and shook my head, tucking the number into my back pocket and returning to the meat case to consider my dinner options.

Chapter 4

Meanwhile, across town,

"I have it all laid out for you," Suzy proclaimed, going over to the desk. "See? These ledgers show the bets. The next column shows the type of bet, and then the odds are here." She pointed to the ledger books. "I made some notes on how to figure out the odds for each type of wager. I can go over these with you each night until you've got it straight."

"That's great, Suzy," Jeremy replied enthusiastically. "I really appreciate your help. You really are a whiz with math!"

"I work at a bank." She smiled. "And you've got plenty of time to learn."

"Look, Suz. I really don't want to kill you, but I've put it off for two weeks now, and the boss is gonna get suspicious. He's gonna wonder why your body hasn't turned up yet."

"I know, Jeremy, but what's another couple of days?" asked Suzy with a shrug. "You need to be able to handle these numbers by yourself once I'm gone. I just want to make sure you have everything you need. It's not like they gave you training on this job. You're just doing what needs to be done. You're *resourceful.* That's what makes you smarter than them." Suzy finished her carefully rehearsed speech with a smile.

In reality, she was shaking inside, unsure how much longer she could keep up the charade. Suzy had hoped she would be able to break out when Jeremy was gone, but she hadn't had any luck yet. The place was locked up tight, with no phones, no windows. She had been trying to pick the lock from the inside.

She didn't even know how she got here. The last thing she remembered was leaving the gas station when it all went dark and she woke up in this tiny office.

A month ago, back at the bank, she had seen something she shouldn't have, something in the guest room for safety deposit box viewing. After forgetting her phone on the table, she stopped back in without warning. It had only been a minute, and she was running late for a dentist appointment, so she only briefly knocked and walked in to see the customer pulling passports and cash from his safety deposit box.

Honestly, she hadn't even given it a second thought. People have all kinds of odd things in safety deposit boxes. The passports might have been a collection of sorts or possibly belonged to family members. She hadn't put it together with the fact that one of the two men in the room was Pietro Marchi, a known mafia criminal. She knew now…

Her first day was spent in pure panic, mouth duct-taped, and tied to a chair at an office desk. From her seat, she could see a mini kitchenette in the corner and the door to a bathroom. Steel doors in front of her and at her back separated the office area from what she assumed was a small-scale betting parlor up front, due to the marked-up and scribbled-on ledgers on the desk and the large safe built into the wall. She wasn't sure what the door to the back led to. Maybe an alley? There were no windows at all around her. She had faintly heard a few people up front but wasn't able to make enough noise to notify anyone.

It had been hours before Jeremy came in to deal with her, presumably to kill her. She'd had time to think about the ledgers. She couldn't tell if someone was trying to modify them badly or was too stupid to figure them out. She'd hedged a bet and hit the payload, convincing Jeremy to let her help him out in return for a few more days alive.

Suzy was stalling now, still attempting to find a way out at night, but careful not to be too obvious. It was getting harder, though. Her single violet shirt was wrinkled and starting to smell, despite attempts to clean up in the bathroom sink. Luckily, after their deal that first day, he had agreed to untie her from the chair, leaving her free to walk around, frustratingly locked behind those steel doors.

The office was sound-dampened from the betting shop in front. Suzy was worried screaming would only piss Jeremy off, and other employees might be in on her kidnapping. She ran her hand over her finger-combed chocolate-colored hair held back with a rubber band.

"You're right, Suzy. They just don't realize what an asset I am," Jeremy replied. "I'm just worried I might make another mistake when you're gone."

"Damn straight, you're an asset," Suzy said with a smile. "I can help teach you, but it might take some time." She knew she couldn't keep it up much longer, but she had to keep trying. She couldn't give up hope.

"We don't have time. I appreciate you fixing the last two weeks' numbers, but I really gotta finish the job now. I can't wait much longer."

"Are you sure they'll be waiting for my body to turn up?" Suzy asked. "I could just keep helping you out on the side...Who would know?" She glanced up, afraid he'd see how nervous she was.

Jeremy frowned. "Now, Suzy, we talked about this. You know I have to kill you. Don't go getting any crazy ideas." Jeremy shook his meaty finger at her. His stringy, too-long hair bobbed with the movement. "It's not like I want to do it."

"Yeah, Jeremy. I get it. No problem. I was only thinking of you. They just ask so much of you." Suzy hurried to soothe his mood. "Now, let's go over these numbers together. I have notes all written out for you. Then I can tell you more about those crepes. They really are amazing!"

Sitting in my green Jeep with a steamy cup of coffee, I watched Jeremy come out of the betting shop. After an early dinner of pork chops from Mariano's, I had done some online research on Jeremy and Dessi. It had been a waste of time, as Dessi apparently covered his tracks well. Jerk. There were several police reports, but nothing ever charged, just like Jen had said. I had headed over to the betting shop in hopes of catching some movement.

Jeremy got into a small, rusty yellow car, and I slowly edged out after him, keeping several blocks behind. He turned towards Lincoln Park, then pulled off to the side of the road outside Yolks Restaurant on

Lakeview. After a few minutes inside, he came back out with a to-go bag.

I did notice the bag looked like it held two large containers of food. So, either he was a major pig, which would be no huge stretch, or someone else was working in that office with him. Someone I had yet to see come and go. I stayed in the Jeep, sitting outside the betting shop for another hour and a half with no other activity before deciding to call it a night.

Waking up in my own bed for the first time in days, I stretched and lingered under the covers for a few minutes to enjoy the morning. I had a good feeling about the day. Breathing deeply, I kicked off my covers to dress for a run.

After a few miles, my mind felt clear and I felt great. I had really needed to stretch my legs and work up a good sweat. Freshly showered, I made a quick breakfast, heavy on the coffee.

Driving into town to pay my office rent, I decided to grab a cappuccino, *'cause who can have too many cups of coffee?* Fate was smiling on me; as I turned the corner, I noticed a little yellow car stopped in front of HERO Coffee Bar. I grinned and parked to go in.

The little coffee shop wasn't one I had stopped into before, and looking around, I was surprised. They had a great selection of both coffee and food. A chalkboard menu hung behind the counter beside a large sign that said, "Every morning is a coffee morning!" *Too true, my friend.*

I spied Jeremy at the counter with two large coffees, pointing at large maple long johns, with what looked to be a long strip of bacon on top. After paying the clerk, his eyes wide with excitement, he grabbed the bagged doughnuts and coffee tray to leave, practically drooling over the food. It was disgusting. Not the doughnuts, the drool.

Stepping in front of him, I said, "Good morning! Looks like you've got yourself a nice breakfast there!"

Shocked, Jeremy stopped in his tracks, giving me a frustrated look. "Uh, yeah." He shifted to move around me, but I sidestepped in front of him again.

"Not so fast!" I said, holding my hands up. "I don't think we've been properly introduced," I ended with a sugary sweet smile on my face.

Jeremy glanced around the shop, clearly uncomfortable. I stuck out my hand. "Detective Malone, remember? I talked to you on the phone recently. About Suzanne Mennon?"

I watched his eyes closely for any emotion but wouldn't have needed the scrutiny. The man's face drained of color then lit on fire with rage. He was easier to read than a first-grader. And he *obviously* knew more about Suzy than what he'd said on the phone. *Bingo!*

"I told you I didn't know anything about that when you called," Jeremy proclaimed, waving his coffee in the air.

I dropped my hand and the act. "Yeah, so you said. But you see, I don't really believe you. In fact, I think you killed her."

I watched him get mad. "What? I didn't kill Suzy," he exclaimed, then looked around and lowered his voice. "You've really got some balls, accusing me like this!"

A deep-crimson bloomed further across his forehead and down his neck. I worried about pushing him too far. If he was holding Suzy hostage, he might hurt her if he thought there was a threat. But as I weighed my decisions, I realized it had been twelve days, and this was my first real lead. Inwardly, I winced at the risk, but I needed to see his reaction. He definitely didn't like the accusation, but I didn't quite get the feeling he was remorseful. My gut just read fear. But to be fair, he was working for Dessi and was likely into several illegal pursuits.

"I think you did. I know what you did, and I'm going to prove it," I bluffed, trying to shake him and see what he would do. I had already blown my cover. *Go big or go home.* I couldn't care less about the customers watching us, even though the guy behind the counter looked nervous.

"You don't know anything!" Jeremy snarled. "Lady, I don't think you know who you're messing with."

If looks could kill, I'd have been pushing up daisies. He stomped out of the store, his doughnut bag clenched in his fist.

I shrugged and turned to the front of the store. Quite a few of the patrons were looking around, eyes round. I finger-waved at them and walked up to the counter for my cappuccino.

I was having a pretty good day. Jeremy Jones confirmed he knew more about Suzy than he had previously said. He had called her "Suzy" this time, instead of "that lady," "the lady with the rack," or even "Suzanne" as I had. I had a solid lead.

It was a good day, indeed. Now I just had to figure out my next steps.

Meanwhile, back at the betting shop,

"I shouldn't have listened to you!" Jeremy shouted at Suzy, grabbing her arm too tightly. "I just ran into that detective, and she accused me of killing you! How would she know anything about me?"

"Jer, calm down. I'm sure she doesn't know anything!" Suzy said soothingly.

"I should have killed you a long time ago, and now with her watching me, it's going to be a lot harder to get rid of your body," Jeremy said, throwing her onto a cot in the back room. He was sweating more than normal in fear and starting to reek. "I've got to get rid of you immediately. I just have to find a place to dump your body. And I have to call Dessi and let him know that bitch detective is poking around again. He doesn't know I still have loose ends. He's going to ask questions, and I'm going to have to make something up about you."

Suzy shook with fear. "Jeremy, it's okay. She was probably just trying to gauge your reaction. I'm sure she doesn't know anything. You've been so careful. So smart! What could she know? You didn't actually kill me. She has *nothing*."

Jeremy looked down at her, calming a little. "You might be right. I didn't leave any clues behind. If you hadn't picked *that* gas station, there wouldn't have been any witnesses at all."

"That just made you the last one to see me. That's hardly a lead."

"Well, that may be true, but I still have to get rid of you right away. You've known that all along. Dessi doesn't know you're still alive. He might ask questions about where I dumped you. So, I'm going to have to come up with something."

"Okay, yeah, I understand. I'll just help you out with tonight's numbers and go over the cheat sheet with you one more time. That gives you a couple of days to make your plans," Suzy said, hoping it would give *her* a couple more days.

Jeremy looked at her with a frown. She wasn't sure he bought it, but he nodded and got out his doughnut. She knew she had to act fast. Tonight may be her last chance at finding a way out.

Chapter 5

The gates of the Arlington Racecourse were just opening when I pulled in. The hour-long drive to Arlington Heights offered plenty of time to come up with a plan and was in a good direction for dropping off a few monthly bills. *Score on the multi-tasking!*

Dessi hadn't arrived yet. And according to the waitress at his executive box, he wouldn't show up until closer to 2:30 p.m., as the first post wasn't until 3:15 p.m. So I wandered around a bit, placed a small bet, and got a Cactus Cooler at the bar. I kept my sunglasses on as I scanned the crowd.

By the time I made it back to Dessi's box, he had arrived. I could only assume it was him because I figured no one else would be wearing a full suit, complete with vest, in the middle of the day. Sure, others were dressed up, but none quite with the polish he displayed in his tailored dove-gray suit.

He was standing with a self-assurance that could come from none other than Fabian Dessi. I was surprised to see he was fairly young, maybe mid-to-late thirties, and quite attractive. Dark slicked-back hair and stark Italian features set well on his tall, fit build.

I wandered over toward where he stood outside his box, talking to an older couple, pretending to watch the pre-race crowd mingling. Dessi was expounding on one of the horses, Admiral Buttercup. He was going into detail about breeding and supplements, *blah de blah.*

As I got busy eavesdropping, pretending to look over the race program, Dessi said, "Who do you think has the best chance?" in my direction. I glanced over, surprised to see him looking at me, eyebrows raised in question. "I'm always interested to find out who people are talking about." The sly look on his face made me wonder if he meant the statement to be pointed at more than the horses.

"Well, I bet on African Queen. I always liked that movie," I responded, brushing down where the breeze had lifted my red curls. "I have a very complex betting formula. It was between her and Napoleon's Dynamite."

"I believe that's Natalia's Dynamite," Dessi clarified with a grin.

"Ah, well, then I made a good choice. Of course, Rum Punch sounded awfully good as well." I nodded sagely.

Dessi was smiling broadly, his eyes crinkling at the corners. "I wonder if I should change my bet. I put quite a large sum on Admiral Buttercup. My sources must have been wrong."

"Looks like it. I mean, had it been *Princess* Buttercup, he'd be a shoo-in. Or rather *she* would be."

"I like your sense of humor," Dessi said appreciatively. "I'm Fabian Dessi. These are dear friends of mine, Greg and Beth Hammond." He reached out to shake my hand.

"Mal," I offered, shaking his hand. "It's nice to meet you."

"Dear, have you ever been out to the Arlington Racecourse before?" Beth asked.

"No, I'm afraid it's my first time. I've been wanting to come out here for ages, but never got around to it. It's all very exciting," I lied. I had very little interest in gambling, not when I worked as hard as I did for what little I earned.

I eyed the field and those getting ready for the race. I couldn't imagine putting my hard-earned money on a chance. How easy it would be to just lose it all in an instant. I mean, unless you had detailed knowledge of the horse, the odds were really not in your favor.

"Well, you are in for a treat! It's all very exhilarating!"

"I can only imagine."

"Well, Fabian, darling, we must be off. Many more to mingle with before it starts," Beth said. "Enjoy the race!"

"Enjoy the race!" Greg added as they walked away.

"So, Mal," Dessi turned to me with a smile. "While it's wonderful to have finally met you. I'm betting you have other questions on your mind." At my confused expression, he added, "Oh, please, Detective Malone. Let's not be shy."

I had been made, and it took me by surprise. How had Dessi heard of me? Even if Jeremy had told him I was looking for Suzy, he wouldn't have my picture. I guess even criminals had search engines. Or people to run search engines.

"Mr. Dessi, I must say I'm surprised you know my name."

"Fabian, please," Dessi purred. "I know a lot of things about a lot of people. I hear you're looking for someone in particular."

"Yes, a woman named Suzanne Mennon. She went missing twelve days ago. She left for lunch one day and hasn't been seen since. Jeremy Jones was the last person to have seen her. I believe he works for you."

"Yes. Jeremy does, in fact, work for me. As do several dozen other employees. He manages bets for me at one of my offtrack betting parlors. I don't personally know him all that well, however. Has he been sufficiently helpful? I can only imagine what Mr. Mennon is going through, being left by his wife." Dessi shook his head sadly.

"I don't believe Suzy left her husband," I interjected, not believing his empathy for one minute. "I believe she was kidnapped."

"Kidnapped? How horrible!" Dessi replied, complete with a put-on shocked expression. "And you believe Jeremy had something to do with it?"

"It's a thought."

"Miss Malone, that betting parlor isn't in the best of neighborhoods. It takes a certain kind of person to run a shop with that clientele. He takes bets and does some very simple bookkeeping for me. But I would hardly say Jeremy was the kidnapping-and-plotting sort."

"Be that as it may, Mr. Dessi. I have to follow every lead I can," I replied, my mouth in a thin line. "I *will* find out what happened to Suzy."

"Oh, I do hope so," Dessi replied, meeting my look with one of cold calculation. "Please let me know if there's anything I can do to help."

"I'll be in touch."

Whatever was going on with Suzy, it had to do with Dessi. I was sure of it.

"I'm looking forward to it," he returned with a slow predatory smile.

Turning to leave, I had to reign in my temper. I really wanted to knock that smile off his face.

It looked like I was going to be making a late-night visit to the betting shop. But first, I had to get back to North Center, change, and make it to Mantovani's by 4:30 p.m.

I made it. Just in time. But I really should have eaten something before I left the house. The smell of Italian herbs and freshly baked dough sent my stomach rumbling and my mouth watering.

Petite Pete got an apron for me and showed me the menu. It was fairly simple. They offered a few Italian dishes, but mostly, it was a pizza joint with a salad bar. A salad bar that looked *really* good, not to mention those breadsticks. Ugh, I was hungry.

I met the rest of the wait staff. There was Marion and Carl, two young college kids, and Phil, a feminine middle-aged drama queen. Lou and Tom worked in the kitchen, and Sally worked behind the bar. Marco was currently filling in with Lou and Tom, prepping pizzas, but Peter said he'd move out to the floor at 6 p.m. for the dinner rush.

And then there was Shelly. I wasn't sure what she had going on with her hair, but it looked like it might be housing several woodland animals. It was a dark-blonde color, puffed up several inches high, with a fan of bangs covering her eyebrows and cheeks. The back was pinned halfway up, likely to keep the critters in. The remaining hair was curled and teased within an inch of its life, then sprayed to shiny shellac that looked to be able to withstand category-four winds. Shelly Mantovani was Peter's wife and Domenico Poggiali's sister. I guess when you're Dom's sister, you can wear your hair however you like and no one says anything.

Busy flitting about in the back, Shelly gave helpful tips to the servers in her painted-on jeans, stilettos, and tight hot-pink tank top. She pointed out that the cooks were adding too much cheese or sausage with her dark-teal nails and then teetered back into the office in the back.

After she left, the employees rolled their eyes and went back to what they were doing. They seemed to respect Petite Pete but listened to Shelly only while she was watching. Peter seemed oblivious to the whole situation.

A few orders and filled drinks later, I finally had a few minutes to mosey into the kitchen. Marco was still prepping ingredients and starting on some of the new pizza orders while Lou and Tom were finishing pans of lasagna and chicken Parmesan and sliding them into the warming drawers. It smelled good back here but was hotter than Hades near the wood-fired pizza oven. Shifting further from the heat, I poked around a bit.

"So, Shelly sure is a character, huh?" I prodded, knowing that she was Marco's aunt, but a new waitress wouldn't.

Tom and Lou slid glances toward Marco, and Tom replied, "She's all right. A little odd, but nice enough."

Marco laughed. "It's okay, guys." He turned to me. "Shelly's my aunt. She's a little on the eccentric side and tends to micromanage, but she doesn't typically hang around for long. She just wants to be helpful."

"Oh, sorry! I didn't know you were related." I pretended to be surprised.

"It's all right. Aunt Shelly takes a little getting used to. But like I said, she'll get bored and head out pretty soon." Marco pointed. "Look. There she goes."

Down the hallway, I could see the garish rail-thin Shelly heading out the back door, Coach bag in hand. Marco seemed pretty normal and easygoing. No red flags yet, but because he helped off and on in the kitchen, no one was used to seeing him regularly. It was easier for him to be missing for any length of time than the other employees.

Now that Shelly was out of the office, I had a chance to snoop in there. I lingered, chatting for a few more minutes, then headed back to the floor to check on my tables and deliver pizzas.

Sally had a pitcher of beer waiting for one of my tables and told me to watch my ass. At my questioning look, she nodded to the table behind me. It was full of college-aged guys staring at my butt. I nodded a thanks and delivered the beer.

Sally certainly was a woman of few words, but she had sass. She had short, straight dark hair and didn't take shit from anyone. She wore her red Mantovani's pizza T-shirt tight, with the sleeves cut off at the seam. I liked her immediately.

When I had the chance, I slipped into the back office. Peter was busy in the back with the cooks, and it was easier without him hovering, telling me what was important and what wasn't.

Checking to ensure I wasn't visible from the kitchen, I surveyed the room. It seemed Shelly and Peter both had desks. One was larger and was covered in a lot of busy things. Framed photos of Shelly and Peter, a rhinestone-covered stapler, a personalized stationary, and other superfluous knickknacks took up the majority of the space. The other was modest and organized, with a small stack of file folders on top and a couple of file cabinets below. It wasn't hard to guess which desk belonged to whom.

I quickly flipped through some of the files and dug through the drawers a bit but couldn't stay long. My presence would be missed if I didn't get back out on the floor. I did, however, find a bank ledger—filled out by hand, oddly enough—and took a few minutes to scan and take photos of the typical expenses and deposits in comparison to the nights Marco worked, looking for connections, less nightly income, higher expenses, anything.

At the back of the room was the safe Peter had told me about. It was locked and seemed pretty secure. He had told me the night's cash-deposit bags went there at the end of the shift. Every two to three days, someone, typically Pete, took it to the bank.

Being Friday night, the place started to get busy, and no one noticed me slip back out of the office to grab my pizzas, which were on the counter. Thankfully, they were still hot.

"Where'd you run off to?" Phil asked as he walked by.

"I had to use the john. Girl issues," I replied, raising my eyebrows.

"Well, I got drinks for the two-top by the door for you. They're ready to order." He gave me an eye.

Oops. I made a mental note to keep an eye out for his charges to even the score.

I strode over to my new customers, remembering that two-top referred to a two-person table. "Are you ready to order?" I asked. They looked to be a father and his daughter, who was middle-school age, if I had to guess.

"Yes, we'd like a large supreme pizza," the dad supplied.

"Don't forget the pineapple!" the blonde girl piped up.

"Oh, how could I forget." The dad rolled his eyes and then smiled at the girl. "Can you add pineapple to half of the pizza?"

"Sure thing," I replied, jotting down the order.

"Pineapple's my favorite!" the girl said, eyes shining.

I grinned back at her when I heard a scraping on the floor behind me as a customer lunged from his chair to grab Marion's arm.

"Hey, I told you I wanted extra onions! Does this look like extra onions to you?" The customer, a tall man who'd obviously had too much to drink, had his hand wrapped around Marion's bicep. Her eyes went wide as she leaned away from him.

Stepping between them, I put a hand to his chest, pressing him back to fall into his seat. He grabbed the arms of the chair to get back up, but I already had my hands on his forearms, holding him down, my face close to his.

"If you'd like extra onions, I would be more than happy to get them for you. All you have to do is ask." I ground out the words between gritted teeth. "Are you asking?"

I had startled him and noticed him trying to decide if he should get angry. A look around the room showed the other staring patrons and made him pause as he stuttered, "Um, yeah. I want extra onions."

"Great," I said, nodding. "I'll be right back." I gave him a pointed look and guided Marion into the kitchen, meeting Sally's silent high five as I walked by the bar. I had wanted to dump the pizza on the man's lap but didn't think Peter would appreciate that.

"Oh my goodness! Thank you for handling that jerk!" Marion exclaimed. "I'm so sorry. I didn't know what to do."

"It's not your fault he's an ass." I put a hand on her shoulder. "It's fine. I've got his onions, and I'll take his table for the rest of the night, in case he forgets his manners again." I winked at her and walked back out to take the man some extra sautéed onions with a side of hairy eyeball.

The shift at Mantovani's ended at 11:30 p.m., but I had to stick around to help clean up and restock for the next day. I saw Peter alone in the hallway but told him I'd give him a call tomorrow. By the time I got out of there, it was closer to 1:00 a.m.

My stomach was full-on growling, and a few times while clearing tables, I was seriously tempted by untouched pizza left in the pan. Heading out to the parking lot, I focused on the leftover pork chops in my fridge. It wasn't until I got to my Jeep that I remembered I had one more stop to make before I could go home and finally get something to eat.

Driving back to the betting shop in Humboldt Park, I parked across the street. Jeremy's yellow car wasn't here, and at this late hour, the shop looked closed. I got out and crossed the street, keeping an eye on the building. No lights and no movement behind the curtains. It was a good sign. There were glass windows in the front, but I couldn't see much around the dingy curtains. What I could see looked like a lobby with an interior door, possibly to a back office.

I crept around to the back door and tried the handle. Unsurprisingly, it was locked tight. I didn't see anyone nearby, and it was a dark alley, fairly well hidden by the shadow of the building. I scanned the wooden door, but there were no obvious cameras or alarm systems, so I pulled out my lock-pick set and went to work. I was able to get the door opened fairly quickly, the lock being small and cheap.

Easing the door ajar, I stepped into a dark room. In the faint moonlight, I could see trash and boxes lined against the wall of a small storage room. Keeping my phone tight to my leg, I turned it on for light, slowly easing it away to control the brightness in the room. There was a second door, leading into the main building. This room seemed too small to be the door I saw from the lobby windows, confirming that there was an office or something between the two. This door was metal, and the keyed bolt lock was heavier duty than the one I had just picked. *This is curious.* It would take more work to open. But while scanning the door, I noticed wires along the top edge. It appeared to be connected to an alarm.

I backed up in surprise. It made sense to have a system on a betting shop, but the way this one was hidden, behind the *second* door, seemed a bit much. I suspected there was more going on in the building than gambling. Sifting through the boxes, I found mostly junk; trash, Vienna Beef takeout bags, old office supplies, but no paperwork or ledgers that I could see. The valuable stuff was likely behind the door.

I heard a foot scuff and froze. Holding my breath, I waited a few seconds but didn't hear anything else. I was sure there was someone in the second room, but I had no idea who it could be. Easing out the door and quietly pulling it behind me, I slid my lock pick back in to reset the tumbler. I was back at the Jeep and around the corner before I let out a deep breath. That was a close call.

Chapter 6

The next morning, I skipped my run to drag myself into the office by 9:00 a.m. I was still tired from the late night and was chugging coffee like it was life support. So, really, nothing new.

Plunking down at my desk, I turned on my laptop to do some research. I scooped my hair up into a short, wild ponytail while I waited for the search engine to run a finance report on Petite Pete. He had separate checking accounts set up for himself and Shelly, plus Mantovani's Pizza account.

He owned the building outright, so he had either been in business for a long time or was doing good for himself. He could have been fronted money from his brother-in-law, but it seemed he had a decent revenue stream. If the pizza tasted anywhere as good as it smelled, there was no surprise as to why. I made a mental note to stop in as a customer when all this was over.

After sifting through Peter's finances and checking my email, I pulled up the Insideonline website. The Tribune was a fine paper, but Inside-Booster was a community paper featuring North Center coverage of the nearby suburbs, like Roscoe Village. With what I did for a living, it paid to be up on local news.

There had been another fire, in Bricktown this time, not far from here. That was Rhodes' fire district. I hoped he was okay. The fire had taken down a community center. What a waste. Neighborhoods needed their community centers. I clicked on the link for the fire and police reports to find there had been a rash of incidents in the last few weeks. The one three days ago was at a nonprofit organization that provided housing programs. A few days before it, a new preschool in Ravenswood had caught on fire.

The flames happened at night, and no one was hurt, but the building was burnt badly enough that they would have to rebuild. Because the program was city-funded, a new committee was being formed to support the rebuilding. The preschool had only been open for a few months, but they'd luckily found a local church to house them in the meantime.

I scratched my head. Something about the fires bugged me. It seemed awfully strange that they were all community programs. Why would anyone target them? They were for the good of the people and didn't profit any one individual.

Before I could continue down the rabbit hole of research, Sam Mennon barged in the front door, looking more ragged than usual, his eyes wild.

"Did you find anything out about that Jeremy Jones? I ran a background check on him, and he's a first-rate scumbag! He was in and out of juvie as a kid and has been brought in on all sorts of charges from drunk and disorderly to public intoxication," Sam shouted excitedly, waving his arms for emphasis.

"You ran a background check on Jeremy? How?"

"I run PhishNett. I have access to all sorts of databases," Sam replied, waving me off. "Did you know about Jeremy?"

"Yes, I ran a full report on him as well. I know his history, but that doesn't necessarily mean he had any motive to harm Suzy. There's been no ransom."

"Well, what's your next step?" he pressed. "We have to find her!"

"I know, Sam. I haven't given up," I said, standing up. "I've been following Jeremy, trying to figure out what he's up to. So far, he's only been going between his place and the betting shop. The times I've caught him out and about, he's out grabbing food at Al's Beef, Yolks, or HERO's, not meeting up with Dessi or anyone else significant. The only people coming and going from the betting shop looked like regulars, not high rollers, and definitely no women."

I felt bad that I didn't have anything else to give Sam. I shared in his frustration. "I stopped by the betting shop last night to poke around. The back door was open," I fudged. "So I poked around a bit. But it was only open to a storage room with trash and food wrappers. The inner door was locked and armed with an alarm, so I couldn't go any farther."

"What kind of food wrappers?" Sam asked slowly, face draining of color.

"What?"

"You said there were food wrappers. What kind?" Sam grabbed my arm, eyes wide.

"Uh, Vienna Beef," I answered, pulling back and giving him a look of warning. Sam was losing it. The stress of Suzy's disappearance was taking its toll on him. "Nothing special; just that Chicago dog place off Damen Ave."

"Holy shit!" exclaimed Sam, grabbing my arm again. "It's Suzy!"

"What do you mean, Sam?" I glanced at my arm, frowning. "Calm down and explain."

"It's Suzy! I knew it! She's leaving a trail for us! Those are our favorite date-night restaurants."

I looked at him incredulously, eyebrow raised. "*Those* are your favorite date-night restaurants?"

"Well, they're nothing fancy, but when Suzy and I first got married, we didn't have a lot." Sam's hands fluttered as he explained. "She had never gone to school and was working as a receptionist. I had, but I was underwater in college loans and hadn't been able to find a job. We had to scrimp and save every penny to take the chance on PhishNett. It was a huge risk and a lot of money, but it paid off. In the meantime, we couldn't afford to go out to eat much, so once a month, we'd have a date night and grab the cheapest places we could find. Eventually, we found some that had really good food, and those were our favorites. We still visit them to remember when that's all we could afford."

Sam's eyes grew wide. "That's it, isn't it?" he asked. "Doesn't that mean Jeremy has her locked up in the betting shop?"

"Maybe," I hedged. "But I doubt it's enough to get a search warrant." It was a great story, but I still wasn't convinced.

I had Sam write down the rest of the restaurants Suzy and he visited and tried to calm him down a little. It sounded like a great lead, but I didn't want Sam to be let down if it didn't turn out to be Suzy leaving breadcrumbs.

I told him I'd follow up on the lead and call him by dinnertime, but I couldn't convince him to go home to rest. He wanted to ride along to find out firsthand. After making Sam promise to keep calm and let me ask the questions, we took off in my Jeep for Al's Beef, the first place I saw Jeremy getting food.

The guy behind the counter at Al's looked high as a kite and stared at my photo of Jeremy for nearly ten seconds until I had to ask him again if he recognized the man. I glanced at the cooks, and they just rolled their eyes and filled orders.

"Uh, I think so," he replied, blinking to focus.

"He came in here a few days ago. Do you remember what he ordered? Did he say who he was getting food for?" I asked.

"Uh, I don't think so," he replied after several more seconds.

I glanced over at Sam. "This is one of your favorite date-night locations? Really?"

He shrugged. "The Italian beef is really out of this world. The counter guy's a little iffy, but the cooks are great."

We stopped at Vienna Beef next, as it was the closest and I wanted a Chicago dog. We didn't have better luck there. They didn't even remember seeing Jeremy, and I wasn't sure when or even *if* he had been there. I had only seen the bag in the storage room; it could have been left a long time ago.

We walked back to the car, and I edged into traffic to drive to Lakeview for Yolks.

"HERO's is closer, but I ran into Jeremy there, so I doubt they'll want to give me a lot of information," I explained to Sam.

"You ran into Jeremy there?" he asked. "You mean you talked to him in person?"

"Yeah, I harassed him a bit. I was trying to get a reaction from him."

"And?"

"And he definitely knows Suzy, at least more than just bumping into her at the gas station," I supplied. He deserved to know what I knew. He was paying me, after all. My only concern was keeping him from jumping to conclusions due to his heightened emotions. "That's why I've been looking into the betting shop and Dessi."

Yolks was pretty busy when we got there, as it was nearing the lunch hour. I waited patiently for the host, trying to keep Sam calm. She would likely share less if she got a bad vibe from us.

"Hi, Starla," I said, reading her name from her apron. "I know you're busy today, but could you answer just a couple of questions?"

"Sure," Starla replied, already starting to look at us strangely. Sam was vibrating.

"I'm looking for my friend. He came in here a couple of days ago. Did you see him?" I showed her the picture on my phone.

"He does look familiar," she said, squinting at the photo. "I think he was picking up something to-go."

Bingo. "Do you remember what he ordered?" I asked. "Or anything unusual?"

"Unusual? Uh, not really," she answered, frowning now. "I think he got two orders. Maybe?"

I could tell she was uncomfortable with our questioning and the growing line of people behind us. "It would really help us out. We're having him for dinner next weekend and don't know what he likes to eat. My husband's afraid he might have some sort of allergy or something."

"Oh! Well, I don't remember anything about any allergies," Starla offered, suddenly more comfortable with sharing. "I think he got crepes—the Bananas Foster. I think he got two orders of the same."

I had to put my hand on Sam's shoulder as he rocked to the balls of his feet excitedly.

"That's so great, Starla! Thanks for the help," I exclaimed. "We could definitely make something with bananas for him!" I edged Sam back out the door.

"Bananas Foster! I knew it!" he said. "That's what she always gets!"

"Sam, what do you normally get from HERO's?" I asked, still trying to contain his excitement, but I had to admit a kernel of hope was growing in me.

"HERO's? Donuts and coffee, always. But Suzy's favorite is the maple-bacon long johns."

It was my turn to freeze. "Maple bacon? You're sure?"

"Definitely. Anytime they had it, that's what she'd get," Sam explained. "If they were out, she just got the plain maple long john. Always a long john. Did you see what he got at HERO's?"

"Yes. Maple-bacon long john," I replied in disbelief. The kernel bloomed into full-blown popcorn in my chest. It seemed too good to be true, but there it was.

"Holy shit," I said, finally agreeing with his earlier exclamation. It also meant the noise I heard behind that steel door had likely been Suzy. A few paces away and I never knew. I still couldn't figure out what in the world Jeremy was doing with her all this time, though. And why was he buying food she liked? I doubted she'd have left Sam for him. Was he a stalker with a sick crush? Was he abusing her?

I was so *taking him down.*

After dropping Sam off at my office to get his car, I headed over to Mariano's deli for a late lunch. We had decided—mostly me arguing—that it was better to wait until tonight to break Suzy out.

It took all my convincing, as Sam had wanted to barge right over to the betting shop to get Suzy out. I wanted to, too, but really, we'd never get past Jeremy and Dessi's goons on our own. We still didn't have enough to get a warrant for police help. Sam's story about the restaurants sounded made up, even to me. The cops would just question Jeremy, and it would likely lead to Dessi moving or hurting Suzy.

I had a plan, a backup plan, and even an "if it all goes to shit" plan, but I kept that in the back seat and hoped it wouldn't be needed.

Sam would make things more complicated. I would need to bend the rules to get Suzy out safely, and I didn't want him in on it. I was a licensed PI and had relationships with the local cops and lawyers. Knowing my rights, I could bullshit my way through a bad situation better on my own.

The only way I could convince Sam of not calling the cops or busting in on the betting shop on his own was to promise to take him with me. It would be easy to go on without him, and safer for him, but I never broke my promises. Sometimes I broke rules, but I never broke promises.

I ran through the salad bar at Mariano's and took it to Hamlin Park to eat. Sitting on a park bench, I called Petite Pete about tonight's shift.

"Hey, Pete," I said when he picked up the phone. "Is the schedule free for me to come in tonight?"

"Yeah, we have some wiggle room with servers. We could use you," Pete replied. "Did you find out anything last night?"

"Nothing concrete. I have a few things to follow up on tonight, though. And I want to see if I can get anything else out of the other employees."

"Sounds good. See you at the same time?"

"Yep," I confirmed. "See you later."

I sat for a few more minutes to enjoy the early afternoon. The days were getting warmer, but there was still a nice breeze in the air. Leaning back, I took a few minutes to soak in the warm sunlight.

I had a few hours to kill before my shift at Mantovani's Pizza. As I wandered around the park a bit, I realized I was only a few blocks from Fire Station 56, so I crossed the street to see what Rhodes knew about the local fires.

When I walked up, one of the firemen was outside, washing the fire truck. Approaching him, I asked if Captain Rhodes was on duty today. He gave me a once-over and told me to hold on while he went to get him.

Rhodes quickly came out of the office with a frown.

"Everything okay?" He stalked right up to me.

"Yes, of course," I said. "I just stopped by to chat."

"Oh, okay," Rhodes said, his body physically relaxing. "Are you out for a walk?"

"Yes. Well, sort of," I answered. "I was having lunch over at the park and decided to walk over."

The other firemen were standing around us, grinning at the exchange. I had a feeling Rhodes was going to get a good ribbing after I left.

He motioned me over toward one of the benches in front of the fire station, farther from the crew. He shot a look at the other firemen but didn't sit. I wasn't in the mood to sit either, so we both stood there, shifting back and forth in front of the bench for a while.

A slow smile spread across Rhodes's face, probably at our shared discomfort. I didn't want him to get the idea I came over to get another date invitation, so I spoke first.

"How's the fireman who got hurt the other day?" I asked.

"He's doing fine. Thanks for asking," Rhodes responded with a small smile. "It was a minor burn, and he should be back on shift next week."

"That's great," I said, sincerely glad to hear it. "I noticed there was another fire. A community center? In your neighborhood, I believe."

"That's right. It was last night. Right here in Bricktown. I wasn't on shift for that one, but it was a good one," Rhodes replied, raising his eyebrows. "Thankfully, no one was hurt."

"Good news," I replied. "I did a little research. Looks like there have been quite a few incidents in this area recently. They've all been city-funded programs and in a short window of time. That's a little odd, isn't it?"

"Yes, I suppose so," Rhodes answered with a small frown. "Are you investigating a case?"

"Uh, no. Not really," I replied, running a hand through my wavy hair. "It's more like curiosity."

"I know the cops are looking into it, but I don't really know much about them. They call in a fire; we respond."

"Was there anything abnormal about them?"

"Mal. You know I can't tell you anything," Rhodes said, crossing his arms across his wide chest. He stood wide-legged in his navy button-up uniform shirt and pants.

"But," I urged. "Something's obviously going on here, right?"

"Well, yeah. It looks like it. It's not common to have this many fires in one area, this close together."

"I may be able to help figure out what's going on. Fresh eyes and all that. You could tell me random fire-related information. Let me figure out the rest myself. I don't know many facts about them. I don't even know if it's normal for a burning building to have that much smoke. It was really dark. I was expecting bright flames."

Rhodes' eyes twinkled at my comment. "Fires are rarely bright. Most of the time you can't see your hand in front of your face."

"Really?" I said, surprised.

"Actually, it's a common mistake. I hear it all the time. Movies..." Rhodes shrugged by way of explaining.

"Well, see. You have a wealth of information," I said, gesturing to him, glad he had proved my point.

"This isn't an official investigation; just your own personal curiosity? No financial influence behind it?"

"Right."

"Hmm," Rhodes replied, raising a dark eyebrow. "How about we discuss this further over coffee?"

"Coffee?" Oops, I hadn't intended this to be a date.

"Well, I *am* on shift right now. Since this is a *personal* discussion and not *professional*, I would have more time to chat over coffee," Rhodes said with a twinkle in his. He was obviously enjoying my discomfort.

"Well. Okay," I replied, not backing down. "Are you free tomorrow afternoon?"

"As a matter of fact, I am," Rhodes accepted with a wink that made me wonder what I was getting myself into.

We made plans to meet the following day at HERO's Coffee Bar. I still wanted to try their coffee, and I wasn't sure I wanted to introduce Rhodes to Mo just yet. As I walked away, I could feel his eyes follow me down the street. That man did make me uncomfortable.

Chapter 7

Back at home, I was still making a list of what I needed for later that night as I changed for work at Mantovani's. There was nothing else I could really do before then, so I decided to keep my shift.

It would allow me to keep a closer eye on Marco and chat up Lou and Tom more. They were easy to talk to and worked pretty closely with Marco most nights. Maybe I could try with Sally, too, but I'd had little luck getting much out of her the night before.

I made it into the restaurant at a quarter to 5:00 p.m. Even though I had eaten before I left the house, the smell of pizza hit me once again. And again, I vowed to make it back here unofficially in the coming weeks. I hoped I'd be done with Pete's case by then.

Since I'd been here once before, I knew where to sign in and didn't have to find Pete. On my way to the server's station to see which tables were mine for the night, I was caught up short when someone grabbed my arm.

"Mallory, right?" Shelly asked, looking me over.

"No, just Mal," I replied, eyeing her hand and giving her a hard look.

"I don't remember hiring you," Shelly said, letting go of my arm.

"Pete, uh, Peter hired me the other day. I'm just filling in on a few nights here and there. It's a temporary job." I nodded casually.

"Huh. Normally, all hires go through me as well, as we are *both* managers here." Shelly patted her hair, likely to make sure none of the inhabitants had escaped. "Where have you waitressed before?"

"Well, I worked for a few years at Malnati's in the Loop. I can get you my resume if you'd like to go over it," I bluffed, hoping Shelly didn't care about paperwork. I didn't even have any new-hire forms since I was getting paid from an alternate contract.

"Ugh. Well, I guess that'll do," Shelly said, waving me off. Giving me the stink eye, she sauntered back to the kitchen.

"One down," Sally said as she walked by, her short dark hair fluttering around her chin.

"Excuse me?" I asked.

"Shelly. She'll come out one more time. Always two visits. Then she leaves," she said, washing glasses at the bar sink.

"Thanks for the warning," I said, leaning forward in an attempt to make friends.

Sally nodded in response but said nothing else, so I left for the server line in the back.

Earlier, Pete had told me that Phil and Marion would work a couple of early dinner tables each. Phil always covered the afternoon and early dinner shift, with either Marion or Carl. Carl had just come in for the dinner rush. He and Marion were laughing at something Phil said. As I wandered in, I watched their body language.

"She tried to set you up with her girlfriend's manicurist?" Carl said incredulously.

"Yes! Seriously," Phil exclaimed, throwing his hands up in the air. "She thought I would take her out for a nice dinner somewhere. She told me I'd like her because, as she put it, '*She's older and hasn't found love. Just like you! It's a perfect match!*' So, not only does she think I'm straight, but she thinks I'm old and desperate. I really don't know whether to laugh or get angry! And I'm certainly not going to cry," he added with a hand on his hip, head cocked.

"Wow, I can't believe her nerve. But, you know, that's just Shelly for you. Last week, she told me I should consider getting a nose job!" Carl said. "You can't take her seriously."

They quieted down when they saw me approach but continued their discussion, albeit a little less enthusiastically.

"Looks like a few more people are making their way in," I said, letting them know customers were being seated.

Marion quickly gulped down the last of her soda and walked out to see whose table was being set. Her long dark hair swayed back and forth as she walked.

"That had better be her last soda of the night! That girl has a bladder the size of a walnut," Phil exclaimed, rolling his eyes at Marion's back. "I swear she's always in the bathroom."

"Give her a break, Phil," Carl said. "She's working 4 nights a week and is taking a full load of courses at U of C. She's probably just enjoying a few minutes of alone time."

"Whatever," Phil said unapologetically. "I wouldn't care, except when I have to fill drinks for her tables."

I made a mental note to fill drinks before snooping around tonight. Getting Phil on my case could draw attention. Glancing back out to the floor to make sure I didn't have any tables yet, I walked back to the kitchen to poke around.

Lou and Tom were prepping pizza dough when I walked in.

"Hey, Mal. Good to see you back again," Lou said, looking up.

"Hey, Lou. Tom. How's it going?" I nodded to each of them.

Tom nodded back.

"Not bad," Lou answered. "Ready for the weekend to be over. The wife and I are headed out of town for a few days."

"Aunt Shelly gave you time off?" Marco asked, walking into the kitchen and tying on his apron.

"Uh, not at first. I had to talk to Peter about it. He helped to get it signed off," Lou explained with an eye roll. "Sorry, kid."

"That's ok. I was just hoping she was being agreeable. I wanted to request off a few weekend days next month," Marco said as he began to chop up the vegetables for pizza toppings. "Probably a good idea to talk to Uncle Peter about it first."

"Who knows. She may be more agreeable to you, being her nephew and all," Lou said hopefully.

"Somehow, I doubt it," Marco said with a grimace. "She's always been fond of Dad. But me? Not so much."

Marco continued to prep the pizza toppings as Shelly made her way back out to the kitchen.

"Marco! How many times do I have to tell you? That pepper is diced way too large. Small squares! And

Lou, those dough balls are too large! Make them smaller."

Lou stared at the dough balls. "If I make them any smaller, they won't fit the pan."

"Then, stretch them thinner. Unless you can't?" Shelly replied with a sneer.

"I can do it," Lou sighed.

"Honestly! You would think I didn't remind you guys every night!" Shelly waved her hands in the air. She waited to see them correct their actions and then turned to me. "What are you doing back here?"

"I was just saying hi," I explained. "No tables yet."

"I'm sure you can find something to do," Shelly said, ushering me out. "You were probably distracting them."

We walked back out to the floor to see my first table getting sat. Shelly eyed me as if to say, *"I told you so."*

I struggled to not roll my eyes until I had turned away from her and walked to my table. I was so glad I didn't have to do this every night.

Saturday seemed busier than Friday, and it took me a while to make it back to the kitchen. Marco wasn't there, and the cooks were busy, so I took a short restroom break. I checked the stock room on my way back, but didn't see any sign of Marco there either. He should have been moved to the floor by now, but I hadn't seen him transfer yet.

I didn't have time to wander around much, so I went back to the floor to check my tables and bumped into Phil.

"I swear! Did you see Marion back there? She needs to get her tail to the floor. Her tables are asking me for refills. I'm busy enough with my *own* tables!" Phil said dramatically.

"I didn't see her, but I can help," I said. "What do they need?"

Phil rolled his eyes and pointed. "Pitcher of Coors Light. Whiskey on the rocks. I'll get table four's soda refills."

I went up to the bar to ask Sally for the drinks.

"Hey, Sally. I need a pitcher of Coors Light and a whiskey on the rocks."

"Sure thing," Sally replied, grabbing a pitcher.

"You were right about Shelly," I said. "She left after her second round."

"Every day," she replied with a wink.

"She's not the easiest woman to work with, eh?"

Sally shrugged.

"Seems like she and Marco don't get along all that great. Kinda surprising, with her being his aunt and all," I tried one more time.

She didn't look up from the whiskey she was pouring, "She's the boss's wife." As if that explained everything.

Well, this is going nowhere. I wondered what the issue was between Shelly and Marco. I also wondered where Marco had gone off to.

Delivering the drinks, I spied him finally making his way to the floor. He had already updated the table assignments, but we were waiting for him to arrive to shift tables. It was a relief to give up one of mine with the rush we were having. I nodded to him as I passed, noticing a flushed look on his face. He looked a little worked up but was attempting to shake it off with an obligatory smile as he waited on his first customer of the night.

Full of suspicion, I finished checking on my tables and refilling drink orders, then made a second trip to the back to snoop around.

Meanwhile, back in a dirty betting parlor,

"Omigod, omigod, omigod!" chanted Suzy as she paced inside the small back offices of the betting shop. She had known she was living on borrowed time, delaying Jeremy as long as possible, but the situation was getting more dire. He had run into that private investigator, presumably hired by Sam, and had gone ballistic! It took all the tricks she had to cool him down. She held her head in her hands, depressed, a soggy, crying mess. She had to get herself together and think of a way out.

Her hair was once again back in a rubber band, and her clothes were starting to get a little worse for wear, even with the nightly rinsing of her shirt and underwear. She had to put the clothes back on wet, as she didn't want to sit naked in the bathroom all night. Bathing in the sink was a little difficult with only paper towels and hand soap, but she did what she could. She shivered a little in the wet clothes and the chilly shop.

If only I could get a message to the detective, she thought. She had left breadcrumbs of their favorite restaurants and could only hope that the private investigator Sam had hired was putting it together. After Jeremy had told her about the detective calling, she had added a couple of food breadcrumbs to increase the clues. But she didn't even know if the PI was following Jeremy or how seriously she'd been looking into him until today. It was obvious the PI was pursuing him now, but she prayed she survived long enough to be found.

Suzy stopped walking and surveyed the room again. A determined look came over her face. She couldn't wait on the PI. She had to act fast, act now. If she didn't figure something out, she'd be getting a new pair of shoes. The concrete kind.

Chapter 8

As I made my way to the back, I almost immediately ran into Marion. She was coming around the corner at full speed.

"Oh, my goodness," Marion exclaimed, grabbing me to right herself. "I'm so sorry!"

"That's okay, Marion," I replied. "Everything okay?"

She nodded her head, still flustered. "Yes, I was just in a hurry and wasn't paying attention."

"Phil and I got refills for your table," I reassured her. "We added the drinks to their bill for you."

She looked stressed at that. "Oh, sorry! I was trying to hurry but haven't been feeling so good."

"No big deal," I told her. "Although, I would thank Phil if I were you. He can be a little cranky."

She glanced towards the floor, nodding. "Yeah, I'll do that. Thanks!"

I watched her hurry back onto the floor. I had been in the restrooms and hadn't seen her. *What in the world was she up to?*

I poked around the back rooms, quickly taking note of the surroundings and looking for any changes since Shelly left. I noticed her drawer was cracked and nudged it open. The same folders from the night before were there. Nothing was obviously different. Files with local menus, personal information and contacts for her manicurist, florist, and hair salon were still in place.

Checking the safe, I found it still locked tight. I rattled the handle and gave it a good shove to be sure it was secure. It was a mini refrigerator-sized floor unit with an old-fashioned combination lock. Considering it, I spun the dial and tried again.

Peter said Marco didn't have the combination to the safe, so if he or anyone else was pilfering cash, it was more likely to be from the cash register. The one at the end of the bar, not in Sally's direct line of sight, but close enough that she likely knew who was coming and going. Of course, that wouldn't explain the times money went missing from the safe.

It was really too bad I couldn't get a read on Sally. *That would make this whole investigation so much easier.* Unless she was in on it.

Back on the floor, I checked on my tables and went to the bar for a pitcher refill and to run a credit-card payment for one of my tables. I nodded to Sally as I walked by.

"I need a refill on the Miller Lite, please," I said, handing her the pitcher.

Sally took it and wordlessly filled it for me.

Pulling up the other table's bill on the computer, I swiped the card. "You know, it's surprising they don't keep more cash in the drawer. I guess most people pay with plastic nowadays."

Sally gave me a sideways glance and shrugged her shoulders. "Guess so," she replied.

Huh. Well, that was informative. I found Sally exasperating, but honestly, *I* wouldn't be dishing out information to a newbie, either. I was filled with frustrating respect for the sassy brunette.

Meanwhile, back in a disgustingly scummy betting parlor,

Furiously banging on the door, Suzy cried for help. She had been tearing through the building, trying to find another way out. Crushing desperation filled her, thinking on repeat of her first night in the place, thirteen long days ago. Unfortunately, she wasn't having any more luck than she had then.

Suzy slid down to the floor, tearing up, her forehead in her hands. She banged her head against the door, looking up, searching for answers. The ceiling was plaster, not a hung one, so there weren't any access panels she could use to escape. Of course, she already knew that. But, for the first time, she noticed a new detail.

There were smoke alarms.

It was officially one o'clock. I finished my cleanup at Mantovani's and hung up my apron in the back. It had been a long shift, and I had made it into the back two more times to poke around. Marco and Tom were pretty chatty, and I felt I had a better lay of the land. Not a total waste of a night.

I knew Sam would already be at my office, waiting for me even though I told him not to meet me there until 2:00 a.m. I didn't want to get to the betting shop until I was sure there wouldn't be anyone there. Being Saturday, three o'clock would probably be better, but Sam was bouncing all over the place to break Suzy out. I planned to stall a bit while we went over the plan but knew I couldn't drag it out much. I just really needed him to behave himself while we were there. He would need to stay in the Jeep.

Stopping by my place, I changed out of my oregano-infused red Mantovani's shirt and into a dark-blue V-neck tee and my black skinny jeans. I wanted to blend in with the background as much as possible. In the dark, my hair wouldn't be too noticeably red, and a black cap would attract more attention in the warmer weather.

By the time I packed a bag of things I would need and made it to my office, I noticed that, sure enough, Sam's black Audi was parked on the side of the road. I pulled up behind him as he jumped out and ran to the Jeep. He was dressed all in black, complete with a stocking cap and black gloves. It looked like he was preparing to rob a bank *or break into a building*. It was just a little obvious.

"I'm ready!" he exclaimed, bouncing on his feet at my passenger door.

It was then that I noticed the utility belt. It had a Batman symbol on it that looked to have been blacked out with a black magic marker. I unlocked the door and lifted an eyebrow.

"You *do* know you are staying in the Jeep, right?" I asked as he got in.

"But I can help you out!" Sam complained.

"Sam. We've been over this! You're safer in the Jeep. I am not going to wiggle on this one." I held up my hand. "I *will* leave you here."

He looked like I kicked his puppy. Then he started to tear up. *Damn.*

"I just don't know what to do without Suzy, Mal. I've been going crazy over the past two weeks," he gripped my dash. "I *have* got to get her back."

"I know, Sam. Don't worry. We'll get her." I would do everything in my power to uphold that promise.

I went back over the rules. He would stay in the Jeep at all times, no matter what happened. If cops got involved, he was just tagging along on an investigation. He stays in the Jeep. He doesn't know anything. He stays in the Jeep. I may have reminded him about that last one a few times.

By the time we finished going over the rules, it was 2:15 a.m. Close enough. I started the Jeep and headed toward Humboldt Park.

I really hoped he would stay in the vehicle.

Meanwhile, in a grungy betting shop,

For the last hour, Suzy had been trying to find something to light a fire. There was plenty of paper around, but nothing to cause a spark. There was a small kitchen with a sink, a fridge, and a microwave, but no stove or toaster oven. She tried to microwave towels, but that didn't work. She tried dried and wet towels, but only a little steam came off the wet ones.

Getting frantic, she began microwaving everything she could think of. In a desperate frenzy, Suzy finally remembered there were a few metal utensils. She let out a yip, tossed a metal fork into the microwave, and let it rip. It sparked a bit, but then nothing happened. She was so shocked, having always believed metal would catch on fire in a microwave. Wasn't that what happened in the movies? She left it on for a full five minutes, and still, nothing happened.

Feeling out of luck, she lumbered back to the bathroom to yet again dry her eyes. She was starting to feel hopeless again. Leaning against the sink, she looked at the faucet.

Suzy remembered a time, not long after she and Sam had first married, when she took a really long, really hot shower. After opening the door, the steam had made its way to the smoke detector directly outside.

She had spent the next ten minutes waving her towel at the small, shrieking mechanism until it finally cleared out. It wasn't until she turned to get dressed that she realized Sam was behind her the whole time, leaning up against the hallway wall, watching the entire show with a grin on his face.

Smiling at the memory, she twisted the hot-water faucet to full blast. This would work. She was determined to get out and see Sam again. She closed the door to let the steam built up and prayed it was enough to overwhelm the smoke detector.

When we got to the street with the betting shop, we took a slow drive by the building, checking for lights or any sign that the place was open. Luckily, it looked like it was already closed up for the night, and I didn't see Jeremy's yellow car out front. *So far, so good.*

I parked a couple of buildings down and told Sam I would be back. I gave him a stern look and told him to stay put. He promised he would, but I had my doubts. If I could do this quickly and quietly, maybe I could get in and out before his patience ran out.

Grabbing my duffle bag from the trunk, I said a small prayer. I walked up the sidewalk and rounded back to the rear entrance like I had the time before and once again picked the lock.

Meanwhile, in a dirty yet steamy betting shop,

Suzy swung open the bathroom door to let the steam escape, but only a small whoosh floated out. Standing at the door, she beat at the smoke, hoping it would make it in the detector's path. The steam rose and drifted upward but started dissipating before it got there.

She cried, "No, no, no! I'm getting outta here!"

Running all the way into the room, she waved the towel furiously up and down. More steam escaped the room and then she ran back out and beat it directly towards the smoke detector. *Almost, almost!*

The storeroom looked the same as it had the other night: messy and filled with boxes. I crept forward, using my penlight to light my way. The wire was still attached to the top of the door. I figured it was connected to a personal alarm system, not a commercial alarm company.

As soon as the wire tripped, I wouldn't have much time. I figured less than ten minutes, but maybe closer to five. It was a good guess that it went straight to Jeremy, but it could go to an internal security team owned by Dessi. I was praying it was just Jeremy.

I wasn't sure what condition Suzy would be in, if she had been abused, or if she was shackled, so I had bolt cutters and a small first-aid kit in my bag, as well as my taser strapped to my leg. I wasn't carrying my Glock. If something went wrong, it showed intent, and the taser should suffice for one person. I hoped it was enough.

I scanned the door but wasn't sure I could pick the lock, and the hinges would take too much time to cut through, so my best bet was to take out the doorknob. It looked to be the weakest spot. I picked a car jack from the supplies in my bag and placed it on the floor, ratcheting it up to the doorknob. The alarm was likely to sound as soon as the connection between the door and the frame was lost.

Once the doorknob was broken, I would use a screwdriver to release the latch, and I had a crowbar ready in case the door bent at all and stuck. I readied myself and started ratcheting the car jack against the door handle. Just as I was getting purchase against the handle, an alarm went off inside the shop. I jerked back, shocked. That was a fire alarm, not a security alarm. After a moment of fear that Suzy was stuck inside with a real fire, it struck me that she had probably found a way to trip the fire alarm. *Yeah, Suzy!*

If she had set off the alarm, she likely wasn't tied up. So I made a quick decision to let it play out. Pulling the car jack, I let out the tension, dropped all my tools in the bag, and made my exit back the way I came. I ran right into Sam.

"Didn't I tell you to stay in the Jeep?" I scowled. I knew he wasn't going to stay put. "Change of plans. Suzy set off the fire alarm." I tossed him my bag and told him to put it back in the trunk.

Dialing 911, I went around to the front door, watching Sam scurry off to follow my orders. I reported the fire, kicking the front door open. It was now an emergency situation, and I had the opportunity to break in legally.

There was a fire department on North Kedzie Avenue, only a few blocks away, so I knew it shouldn't take long for the crew to respond. I was betting on less than two minutes, plenty of time before Jeremy or Dessi's security could arrive. Once the fire department got here, we'd have all the muscle we needed to keep them at bay.

The interior door through the lobby was made of metal, with no windows and alarm wires around the frame. I tried kicking it down, but it was sturdy and not budging. I knew it was a gamble to wait for the fire department instead of entering the way I had originally planned, but I thought the odds were in my favor. *Finally.*

"Suzy!" I yelled through the door. I wasn't sure if she could hear me over the alarm, but I was going to try. "This is Detective Malone. The fire department is on its way. I'm here to take you home!"

I heard a female voice, but I couldn't make out any words.

Please don't be a real fire.

"Just hang in there another minute! They will be here soon!" I yelled again, watching Sam run up the walkway, frantically wringing his hands.

A light flipped on in several nearby residences to see what was going on with the alarm. A few of them stuck their heads out the door or stepped out in robes, eager to be in on the middle-of-the-night drama. Finally, the welcome sound of the responders pierced through the night.

The fire trucks pulled up right in front of the shop, lights whirling. The men poured out of the vehicle with axes, and my own anxiety dropped substantially, just seeing them arrive.

I pulled Sam to the side and out of the way as the firefighters headed up the front stairs. When I called it in, I warned them there was a metal door, and they had a wedge with them already in hand. They systematically inserted it into the latch and hammered until the door sprung free. The wailing of the still-sounding alarm barely covered up the cry of Sam's name as it was shouted from the pretty brunette inside.

I had never found the sight of a woman so desirable, greasy hair and rumpled clothes included. Weeks of frustration and doubt slid off me as Suzy shakily stepped over the threshold. She practically fell into Sam's arms, probably from adrenaline.

A couple of the firefighters gently led the couple to the truck to assess her health. The rest of the firefighters went into the building to clear the scene. Outside, the crowd had grown, and I spotted Jeremy at the edge of it with a buddy in tow. The look they gave me would have melted me on the spot if I were worried about them in the least. Good for me I wasn't.

They didn't stick around long. I pointed them out to the cops who had finally shown up, but there were too many people and they took off before the officers could get to them. I welcomed the opportunity to let Jeremy know what I thought of him, but that wasn't my priority tonight. He would get his due.

Suzy detailed out the whole story to the cops and firefighters. She was surrounded by concerned faces, covered in blankets, and given warm coffee and a cookie. I wasn't sure where the coffee and cookies had come from but was glad to see the small smile on her face as she relaxed for what was likely the first time in weeks. Through her exhaustion, the look shared between her and Sam was a beautiful thing. He lightly rubbed her back or tucked a stray hair behind her ear as she rehashed her tale.

It was nice to finally see her in person for the first time. I was impressed to hear how she had been able to maintain her wits while manipulating Jeremy as she had. When she told the story about setting off the smoke detector, we all laughed along with her, even though I could see tears in Sam's and her eyes as well.

After what seemed like forever, they decided she was fit enough to be released. I promised the cops I would see the Mennons home safe and bring them downtown sometime before noon the next morning. Sam had already hired security to monitor their house overnight.

We all needed some rest before we wrapped this thing up. Suzy went back into the building briefly to hand over accounting ledgers to the cops. They had already called out an APB for Jeremy and Dessi for questioning. I planned to bring in all the intel I had gathered on them the next day. With her statement, it should be enough to put them behind bars.

As I drove back to my office to get Sam's car, he and Suzy snuggled in the back seat, wrapped tight around one another. I gave Suzy my card so she could call if she needed anything. Following them home the rest of the way, I made sure they made it inside safe and sound, waiting for the security van at the curb next to the house. I wasn't taking any chances with these two tonight. Sam had a state-of-the-art security system, so I wasn't worried about them inside.

Driving home, I felt a real sense of accomplishment and peace. It was the reason I did this job. But I prayed I wouldn't have another one like it for some time.

I felt a deep need to help people out, especially those who had been taken advantage of. It was with complete satisfaction that I went to bed and rested like I hadn't in weeks.

I could only hope we had enough evidence to put this case to bed.

Chapter 9

When the sun came in through the window the next morning, my good mood had partially evaporated. The work to wrap up the case loomed over me. I had to take Sam and Suzy downtown to file their official statement, formally pressing charges against Jeremy Jones and Fabian Dessi. Dessi was slippery, but the evidence was solid.

I was still exhausted from the night before but reluctantly dragged myself into the shower, stopping only to brew a fresh pot of life essence. After a quick scrub and a couple of cups of coffee downed while dressing, I was out the door to get the Mennons.

Sam and Suzy were ready when I showed up. He was grinning like a fool, and Suzy still looked exhausted but clean and happy, the stress lines gone from her eyes. It was a marked improvement from the night before.

"Morning, Mal!" an over-exuberant Sam exclaimed, hand wrapped around Suzy's.

"Morning, Sam," I said. The perkiness was an improvement over the last few weeks of depression. I'd take it. "Looking good, Suzy."

"Good morning," she said, walking over to me, looking fresh and composed. "I never properly thanked you last night. All the work you went through to find me. I appreciate it. Also, thanks for never giving up on me."

She surprised me by hugging me. I wasn't much for physical affection, but I patted her awkwardly on the back, her mahogany hair brushing my arm.

Stepping away, I said, "Well, you ended up having the situation well under control. You were the one who set off that alarm."

"Sure." She grinned in response. "But you called it in. Who knows who would have gotten there first if you hadn't?"

"Well, it all worked out in the end," I replied, climbing in the Jeep. "Now, we just have to put a nail in the bad guys' coffins. I only have one really important question to ask you."

Suzy looked at me with a quizzical expression. "Sure."

"How good did that shower feel last night?" I asked, smiling at her in the rearview mirror.

"Ah, that was heaven!" Suzy replied, eyes rolling back in her head at the memory. "It felt so good to wash my hair and put on clean clothes. I took a shower to get rid of the grim, but then I took an hour-long bath, shaved my legs, and scrubbed every last inch! Sam sat with me the whole time. He was afraid to leave my side."

Sam stole a glance at Suzy, a special smile spreading across his face. I could imagine they had a nice reunion. He reached his arm across Suzy's shoulders and pulled her in for a hug. I softened a bit, smiling inside.

I kept an eye out for Dessi's guys on the way to the police station and in the station's parking lot. I wouldn't put it past him to try to intercept us from filing our statement.

Ushering the Mennons into the building, I covered them from behind, not seeing anyone unusual. The police station was already buzzing with activity, as it should be this close to noon.

"We're here to see Officer Murphy about last night's kidnapping case," I told the fresh-faced police officer at the front desk.

"Officer Murphy's off; the case has been given to Detective Rodriguez. He's waiting to hear from you," the young rookie replied.

"That's just wonderful," I ground out. Rodriguez. Of course, the cheating, good-for-nothing asshat.

"I can show you to his office," he said.

"That's okay," I replied. "I know where it is." I turned and led the way, hoping we didn't catch a disease from his chairs.

"Rodriguez," I said, standing at his office door. "I guess congratulations are in order. I didn't know you made detective."

"Malone," he said, moving to shake my hand. "Thanks. I heard you were the PI on the Mennon case. I just got filled in on the details this morning. It's good to see you."

Rodriguez was dressed in slacks and a button-up shirt. As a detective, he could wear plain clothes.

He'd always looked good in his uniform, but he filled out a dress shirt even better. His dark hair was trimmed cleanly, and the light-blue of the dress shirt contrasted nicely with his slightly tan skin, thanks to his Mexican-American heritage. He was pretty young to make detective, being only thirty-one. I wondered what he had done to pull that off.

"I'll bet," I murmured, wiping my hand on my jeans before gesturing the Mennons in. "This is Suzy and Sam Mennon. We're here to file official charges against Jeremy Jones and Fabian Dessi for kidnapping. Suzy has evidence and is willing to testify against him."

"Great," replied Rodriguez, coming around his desk to shake the Mennons' hands. "Thanks for bringing them in, Malone." He gestured for us to sit.

"We put out an APB on Jeremy after last night's rescue, but no word yet," Rodriguez continued. "I'm sure we'll hear something soon, though. The VW is fairly easy to ID. Mrs. Mennon, can you please start at the beginning?"

"And Dessi?"

"We've already called him to come in, but he's a much bigger fish. We'll need to be careful we have enough evidence before we try to press charges."

I listened as Suzy rehashed the events of the past fourteen days, amazed again at how well she had kept her cool. She nervously played with the ends of her long, straight hair as she told the story.

Rodriguez sat back and listened attentively, intelligent eyes taking in all the details, only stopping her once or twice to ask for additional information. It was a real shame he was such a dick. Glancing at the armrests of the chairs, I pulled my elbows off and kept my hands in my lap. Who knew what he did with them in private?

Rodriguez already had the books from the betting parlor. Suzy pointed out the two different sets, one kept for the legal tax records and the other which held the true, fully detailed numbers. She explained how she'd coached Jeremy on the books and about the notes.

"Dessi will be coming in later today," Rodriguez explained. "But unless we have anything solid on him, he's going to claim he had no idea this was going on. Did you ever overhear Dessi himself on the phone, giving orders to Jeremy, or did you see any notes written from him?"

"Well, no," Suzy replied. "Jeremy was on the phone with him a few times, but I never heard the other side of the conversation. He said he met with Dessi when he handed over the income and went over the books with him, but I never actually saw the exchange. I was supposed to have already been out of the picture, per Dessi's orders."

"Yes, but unless you actually heard his voice, we don't have anything to charge Dessi with," Rodriguez explained.

"But Jeremy was on the phone with him!" I argued. "He told Suzy that's who was on the phone. Suzy will testify to it. The evidence is solid."

"He can claim Jeremy was passing off the blame to someone else. The evidence is solid, but not for Dessi. Come on, Mal. You know how this goes. He's got ties everywhere. It's going to be harder to get him."

I did know that; it was exactly what I had been afraid of. Hopefully, we could find a way to nail him for his part in Suzy's kidnapping.

"Back to the bank deposit box at Heward Bank," the detective reflected. "Tell me more about that. Are you sure it was Pietro Marchi?"

"Not exactly," Suzy answered. "Jeremy told me Dessi wanted him to take care of me because I had seen the 'Big Boss,' as he called him, with compromising information."

"Well, we can take care of the identification part pretty easily." Rodriguez swiveled his computer monitor toward the room so we could see as he pulled up pictures. I recognized Pietro Marchi from the news and Fabian Dessi's photo along with others I assumed worked with Marchi.

"Do you recognize any of these people?" Rodriguez asked.

"Yes," Suzy replied, pointing at the pictures. "That's the two guys who came into the bank. He's Mr. Waters, Frank Waters. I don't know the other guy with him, but he's the one who was going through the box."

"I'm not sure who Frank Waters is, but *that* man is Andreas Marchi, and the other one is Pietro Marchi." Rodriguez pointed at the pictures as Suzy had. He glanced at me. "Supposedly, Andreas has nothing to do with the family business. He gets together with Pietro and the other family members a few times a year but, otherwise, does his own thing. He's a lawyer but specializes in patent law. I have no idea what he'd be doing with Pietro at the bank or why he's going under the alias of Frank Waters."

"But Frank Waters has been coming to the bank for years," Suzy offered. "He's a long-standing client."

"That may be, Andreas likely used false identification with this alias. We've never looked into

Andreas much, as he didn't really have any ties with the family business. Or so we thought." Rodriguez seemed to consider this for a moment.

"George," Rodriguez called out his door. "Get ahold of Heward Bank. We need access to Frank Waters' safety deposit box. I'll work on getting a warrant." He looked back at us. "If he hasn't pulled out of Heward Bank yet, we may be able to nail Andreas and Pietro Marchi with this. Suzy, we should get you to a safe house in the meantime."

I studied the scumbag across from me. Yes, I wanted Dessi and the Marchis to go down as badly as he did, but I knew Rodriguez was thinking how good this would look for his career.

"Actually," Sam spoke up for the first time since we sat down. "My house is outfitted with the best security system available. It's pretty much impervious to anything next to a grenade launcher. I've already got physical security on standby. I can have them ready to pick us up when we're done here."

"And how do you know it's the best?" Rodriguez asked.

"Well, because I created tech for the system." Sam had the grace to look humble. "I also tested it myself. From a technical standpoint, I can't get in. Physically, the house has been reinforced with steel plates. It'll stand."

I looked over at Sam with growing respect. I could tell Rodriguez wasn't thrilled by not being in charge of Suzy's security, but he couldn't force her to go into hiding. It made me like Sam a little more, solely because of that.

"Suzy?" he asked her, still trying to gain the upper hand. "It's *your* safety and *your* call."

I wasn't surprised when Suzy slid her hand into Sam's and said she would be safe with him. I didn't even bother to hide my grin. "Well, that settles it, then," I said. "Detective, did you have any other questions, or can we get these two home now?"

Rodriguez had Suzy sign the statement she had given, documenting the last couple of weeks. Sam and I signed one for our accounts. Finally, we were free to go. Sam said the security team was waiting for them outside to take them home, so I waved goodbye to them and told them to be careful.

As I was walking out of his office, Rodriguez stopped me short.

"I meant what I said. It's good to see you."

He actually said it straight to my face. I was impressed.

"Ri-ight," I said, stepping around him.

"Seriously, Mal," he said, frustrated. "Do you really hate me so much? Still?"

"No. I don't hate you, Alex," I said grudgingly. "But I can't say I like you."

"Fair enough," he accepted. "You did a good job on the case. It would have been a cold one had you not picked it up."

"Don't look so surprised. Just because I'm not on the force, doesn't mean I'm not a good investigator."

"You always were," he said, leaning in. "You should have stayed at the academy. You would have been an asset to our team."

"Please. As if I would want to answer to someone else," I replied, frowning. "I'm quite happy where I'm at. I get to call the shots. I only work the cases I want. No one looks over my shoulder. Why on earth would I give that up?"

"Stability," Rodriguez answered, eyebrow raised.

"Definitely not from you," I tossed back, stalking out the door. I was done here.

When I stepped out the precinct door, I saw the unmarked black van pulling away with the Mennons. I waved and walked out to my Jeep, heading back to the office. I had a one o'clock meeting with Petite Pete to go over his case, and I was hungry.

I was going to have a little more free time soon. The Mennon case was wrapping up, and I had seen enough at Mantovani's. I just needed to walk through it with Peter.

Even though my contract with the Mennons was technically closing, I would follow through with it and help gather any evidence I could to put those responsible behind bars. Suzy would not end up as a statistic if I had anything to do with it.

I wasn't too worried about the lack of work coming up, though. Something always ended up on my desk. And if not, I would take advantage of the time and get up to date on my bookkeeping. *Oh, joy.*

It had taken longer than anticipated at the precinct, so I swung through a drive-through for lunch. The mocha latte did a lot to soothe my *Detective-Rodriguez*-frayed nerves.

Chapter 10

I didn't have to wait long. I heard Pete coming in the lobby door and rose to greet him. Right on time. He must have been curious about my request to follow up in person.

"Do you have news for me?" Pete jumped right to it.

"I believe so," I replied, gesturing for him to sit.

"So you caught him? Do you have proof?" Pete asked, leaning in.

"Well, you were right. Someone *is* taking money."

"Oh, no!" He sat down in the chair and put his head in his hands. "I really wanted to be wrong. I really like the kid!"

"Hold on there, Pete," I said, lifting my hands up. "I said you were right that someone was taking money. I didn't say it was Marco."

Peter stilled, then lifted his head. "It's not?" He looked confused. "Oh, well, that changes things. Is it Marion or Carl?"

"No," I replied. "Not them either."

He stood up. "Well, dammit, *tell me*! Who's stealing from me?"

I cocked my head. "Not really sure it can be called stealing when it's the owner."

"*I'm* not stealing from me," Pete exclaimed, throwing his hands up.

"I didn't say you were." I looked pointedly at him.

"*Oh!*" Then, "Oh…" Realization dawned on him. He slowly sat back down, a dazed look coming over him.

"Are you sure?" He asked, looking sad.

"I'm pretty sure," I said, nodding. "I've been paying attention to the pattern. It finally became clear. Shelly runs the deposit most days. She's the only other person with access to the safe. I made a timeline of when you run the deposit. Those days coincide with when the register came up short. Marion and Phil confirmed them because they were worried they would be blamed and the money deducted from their pay."

I was pretty sure Sally had seen her take money from the cash register but wasn't about to rat her out. Sally wasn't the type to speak ill of the owners.

"Last night was the nail in the proverbial coffin. Shelly was leaving to get her nails done but came back to get the deposit. Normally, it's made every two to three days. According to your records, however, you took it on Friday," I explained. "That's only one night's worth of cash. But you can confirm it yourself. Call the bank and compare it to last night's income."

Pete just sat in his chair, shaking his head. "Why would she do this?" he asked.

"It's hard to say," I replied, feeling sorry for the guy. "She may not realize how much money she's taken over time. I don't get the indication that your business has been suffering lately. Have you been bringing home less income recently or changed your capital withdrawals?"

"No," Pete said. "I take a modest management salary for each pay period. Shelly has a smaller one. She wanted a small allowance of her own. She did ask me about increasing it, but she doesn't do that much with the business. I told her we couldn't afford an increase unless we expand. We do good business, but we have a small building. There's only so much room for tables."

"Well, that explains her attitude toward Lou and Tom." I rolled my eyes. "Shelly yells at them every day to use less ingredients."

"Really?" Pete said, surprised. "I didn't know about that. But it explains some of the tension in the restaurant while she's there."

"So, what about Marco?" Pete asked after he let the information sink in a bit. "He has been acting strange."

"Well, Marco threw me off," I replied, nodding my head. "He was acting suspicious and sneaking around." I grinned. "That's because he's getting busy with Marion in the back room."

"Really?" Pete said, surprised. "Marion?"

"Yep."

"That's why she's been taking long bathroom breaks," he said, the light clicking.

"Yep."

"Oh, man. Marco probably didn't want his dad to find out about it." He rolled his eyes. "Wow, Phil is gonna have a heyday with that one!"

"Are you going to expose him?" I asked. It was out of my hands now.

"No, but I will talk to Marco." A serious look took over his face. "He can't keep doing that at work, on work hours. I won't tell on him, but it's likely going to come out sooner or later. These things typically do."

I agreed. "So, what are you going to do now?" I asked.

"Well, I guess I'm going to go home and have a talk with Shelly." He looked me in the eye. "You really don't know how much I appreciate this."

"I just told you your wife is skimming from the family business," I replied with a surprised look on my face. "And you're appreciative? That's new."

"Oh, it's not good news, for sure," Pete leveled. "But it's better than dealing with Dom about Marco skimming from me. I'm not sure how I would have handled that one. That sort of thing would have been bad for Marco's future and for Dom's reputation. Not to mention bad for my health if Dom didn't believe me."

"Well, then. You're welcome," I said, smiling. "Always glad to have a happy customer."

I handed him the final billing on the case. He only owed me a bit more than the original deposit. Petite Pete settled up and headed out to deal with Shelly.

Alone, I swiveled in my chair, thinking about the case. It always felt good to close out another one. The embezzlement case ended up being simpler than originally anticipated, but that was why going undercover was so helpful. I was able to find out more about Shelly's habits and the information on Marco as well, just to close the loop. Making my usual wrap-up comments, I packed up all of my notes on the case and filed it away.

Grabbing my coat and keys to lock up, I headed over to Grounds for a celebratory cup of coffee. I left my jacket unzipped to enjoy the breeze.

"Mo! How about a mocha cappuccino, extra foam?" I called out when I walked into shop.

"Good to see you, Mal!" Maurice replied. "I had begun to think you broke up with me and started a love affair with another coffee shop. My heart was broken." Maurice put a hand to his chest dramatically.

"Never," I replied, crossing my heart and smiling. "I've been busy wrapping up some cases. Two at the same time."

"Ah, that explains it." He smiled. "Two, huh? Did they end well?"

"Well, one, definitely. The other one, sorta? It ended up good, but my client still has a few things to work out. Trouble with family. I'm glad that's not part of my job. Mine ends when I figure out what's going on. I don't have to sort out the mess."

"Do you have another case already?" Maurice asked, tamping the espresso grounds. "You still look like you're trying to figure something out."

"Well, not really," I replied, toying with the sugar packets. "I still have a few issues to clear out on the happy-ending case. I'm also working through a few other unrelated things."

"A personal-interest case?"

"Sort of. Have you heard what started the fire a couple of days ago?"

"Well, I did hear it wasn't an accident. Some of the employees came in here yesterday and were talking about it," Maurice replied. "I guess it looks like someone used an accelerant. Do you know someone who worked there?"

"Not exactly. No relation, no client, no official case. I guess I'm just curious. There's a lot of strange coincidences related to the fires," I replied. "Let me know if you hear anything."

"Sure." Maurice nodded, then chuckled. "Always curious."

I shrugged as he slid my cappuccino across the counter.

"Enjoy!"

"I always do." I smiled, taking a sip. Closing my eyes, I savored the taste and practically melted. "Oh, Mo! Delicious! See? I could never leave you."

"Remember that when you're out on the town and looking at other coffee shops," he playfully warned. "I have spies everywhere. I know what goes on."

I winked at Mo as I walked out. He did always seem to have the scoop around town. I guess being a barista was akin to being a bartender. People talked.

Wandering a bit, I sipped the rich and slightly sweet concoction. But my phone interrupted my reverie.

"Malone," I answered.

"It's Alex," Rodriguez's voice replied. "They picked up Jeremy Jones' VW on the side of the highway. It's empty. There're no signs of Jones himself."

"Ugh," I grunted, not terribly surprised. "Any word from the bank?"

"Yep, the box has been emptied, and Frank Waters' money has been moved, accounts closed out," Alex responded. "I can't say I'm surprised. I had hoped, with the belief that Suzy was gone, they would be lax and leave their cover in place."

"They didn't get to where they are by acting retroactively," I replied, crossing a street.

"True," Rodriguez admitted. "Dessi should be here soon. I'll let you know what happens."

"I can't wait," I replied dryly, clicking off the phone as I stepped into HERO's Coffee Bar. I tossed my empty coffee cup in the trash can, eyeing Rhodes' by the donut case.

"Did you already get a coffee?" he asked, having seen me dump the evidence.

"That? That was just to warm me up for the main event." I smiled, rubbing my hands together. "I definitely still want a cup."

"Do you want a donut or a sandwich?" Rhodes asked, pointing at the case.

"I hear the maple bacon is to die for." I grinned. "Nah, I'm good. Just coffee for me."

"Me too." He nodded, considering. "I'd rather have bacon-flavored bacon."

I ordered an Ethiopian pour-over, and Rhodes ordered a small brew, black. After I added some half-and-half to mine, we picked a table near the windows. The blackboard behind Rhodes read, *"Don't hate, caffeinate!"* I grinned.

"Ethiopia sure grows some good coffee beans," I considered, sipping my cup of joe.

"Glad you like it. Cute shop." He settled into his chair and looked around the place.

"Thanks for the coffee," I said, settling in. "Did you have a busy night last night?"

"Nah. A few BLS calls. Nothing exciting." At my raised eyebrow, he added, "Basic Life Support."

"It must be hard to be woken up all night long. Like having a baby who never learns to sleep through the night."

"You get used to it," he replied with a shrug. "Although, working with the guys...is sometimes like having little kids around."

I smiled at his answer. It was obvious he cared for his crew.

"So, Mal... Is that short for Mallory?" Rhodes asked.

"Definitely not. My dad wasn't *quite* so cruel as to name me Mallory Malone," I said, shaking my head. "But no, it's just Mal."

"Oh-kay," Rhodes replied, noticing my definitive tone and deciding not to push it. "We'll stick with Mal, then."

"So, what do you know about this rash of fires?" I said, changing the conversation. "Isn't it strange that the community center was just the most recent of several city-funded programs that have caught on fire?"

"Well, there have definitely been a few," Rhodes answered, letting the topic lie. He took the lid off his cup and sipped the beautiful brew.

"They've all been funded in the last year or so. Seems like someone doesn't want them to succeed," I said, pushing my hair behind my ear. "Who would want to sabotage the programs?"

"I'm not sure, but it's a shame, really," Rhodes replied. "The community center was getting good participation. I was hoping it would reduce some of the violence we've seen in my district lately. It's easy for kids to get into trouble when they're bored and trying to find things to do. Besides, they had some good programs where they could get tutoring help or join basketball teams."

"Doesn't make sense." I shook my head. "I can't think of anyone, short of city gangs, who wouldn't want that."

"Right?" Rhodes agreed, leaning back in his chair. "No one was more upset about it than Sully. He's one of our assistant chiefs and one of the key people who helped get the center off and running. He's very involved with community service and has supported several programs around town. In fact, a few are the same ones that had fires. No one would like to get to the bottom of this more than him."

"Have all of the fires been ruled as arson?" I asked, cupping my warm cup and letting the heat creep into my hands.

"Well, I'm not sure if it's been made public yet, but I can tell you, you're on the right track," Rhodes said, giving me my answer. "But I have to ask, why are you interested in the fires if you aren't on a case?"

"Well, it's a problem of mine." I shrugged. "Curiosity. Once I get a whiff of something suspicious, I have to keep digging at it. Not the best trait in the world, I suppose."

"I've seen worse," Rhodes said. "Have you always been like that?"

"Yes, since I was little," I answered, nodding. "My dad was a police officer. I wanted to be like him. Didn't make it through the academy, though. Decided I'd rather be my own boss. So, I got my detective license instead." I gestured towards him. "What about you? Did you always want to be a firefighter?"

"I had an uncle who was a firefighter." Rhodes smiled softly, running a hand over his shaved head. "I spent a lot of time at the station with him after school. Kept me off the streets. It felt natural for me to test for it after high school. I went to college after I finished at the fire academy. I wanted to finish my fire science degree."

"It wasn't a requirement for the job?" I asked, tilting my head.

"No, but some of us do. If you want to become chief or teach, it helps."

"So, what was your motivation?"

"I always dreamed of teaching fire science one day. A few years ago, I finished my certification for Fire Instructor. Maybe when I retire." He gestured with his cup. "Fire suppression is a young man's job. Can't do it forever."

"No dreams of Fire Chief," I asked?

"Nah." Rhodes shook his head. "I'm not a white shirt. I'm happy being the captain. Just earned that last year. Doubt I'll go any higher up. Too much politics."

I definitely understood that. I couldn't do that, either. It was one of the things I liked best about working for myself. I never had to bargain or worry about other people's needs. I made all my own decisions.

"So, what does Sully think about all these fires?" I asked. "Doesn't he think they are suspicious?"

"I haven't talked to him about it personally," Rhodes replied, shrugging. "I heard through the grapevine that he was upset about it. Makes sense, considering the work he put into them."

"Would he be open to discussing it with me?" I asked with a note of hope in my voice. "I could ask him what he knows."

"He'd talk to you about the different community projects, but I doubt he'd give you any information about the fires themselves."

I shrugged. I had other avenues to get that info. "So, is it easy to tell if it's arson?"

"No, not necessarily."

"I thought you said you could tell if an accelerant had been used."

"You can, but that doesn't mean it was arson. The accelerant could be coincidental. It may have been an accidental spill, or the fire could have spread into an area that had a kerosene lamp or into a garage with gasoline."

"Okay, so how do you know if arson is involved? What do you look for?"

"Often, it's the things that *aren't* there," Rhodes explained. "If you have a house fire and family pictures are on the wall, it's less likely it was arson, or the fire was done by someone else. If you notice important family possessions have been removed, then there's more chance of arson. Look for valuables, things that someone wouldn't likely let burn."

I nodded my head. It made a lot of sense. It was one of the most important things I'd learned as a PI: looking around a scene for things that should be there or things that were missing. The intellectual conversation with someone in a similar profession was unusual but in a good way.

"It's pretty common for kitchen fires to have been started by towels too close to the stove, especially with gas stoves," Rhodes continued.

"Or a grease fire while cooking?" I asked.

"Right. Two big problems with grease fires. First, oil rides on water. Water will not put the fire out;

it just splashes it everywhere, spreading it very effectively. The other, if you get a big breath of grease-fire smoke, you can't breathe. A good lungful of grease smoke, and you're on your knees. It's wicked." Rhodes shook his head, smiling slightly.

"You love it, don't you?"

"More than I'd like to admit," Rhodes said, leaning in toward me privately. "It's one thing you have to keep in mind. A good day for a firefighter is a bad day for someone else. You come out of that fire all charged and then are expected to look somber for the family outside and sometimes a television crew."

"I really appreciate you sharing all this insight with me," I said, enjoying the camaraderie. "It's pretty interesting. Like what you said the other day about fires not being bright. It makes sense when you think about it, with the smoke and all. I just never really have."

"I enjoy talking about it. It's not like the movies make it out to be." Rhodes laughed. "You can't see your guys next to you. That's why you have the speakers in your mask. Can't hear very well, either. It's kind of muffled, like you're underwater. Unless the fire is free burning; then, it's extremely loud and crackling. You come out of it smelling terrible, snot running out of your nose. Definitely not like the movies. The guys aren't movie-star gorgeous, either."

I liked the look of Rhodes laughing, leaning forward in his chair, conspiratorially. He had such an easy way about him. Comfortable and affable. However, I disagreed with him; I'd seen those guys at the station. They might not be movie-star gorgeous, but they had a rugged look that was certainly attractive. Especially Rhodes. I leaned back in my chair to look at him better.

"Don't sell yourself so short." I gave him a half grin.

He looked up at me with a slow smile, burning into me with his intense gaze.

Whoa.

"I sure did enjoy coffee with you. Next time, I'll cook you dinner, then maybe breakfast."

I barked out in laughter, eyes sparkling. "You certainly aren't a shy one." I liked that about him, though. Always knew where he stood.

"It doesn't pay to be shy in this world," Rhodes said, still smiling. "I like you. I'm attracted to you. It's that simple."

I respected and liked his honesty. I just wasn't sure I had room in my life for a relationship, but I was surprising myself by considering seeing where this went. It's not like it had to be very serious. "Well, let's talk about dinner and see where it goes."

My phone rang as we were talking about dinner plans next Tuesday.

"Mal," I answered, motioning to Rhodes that I'd only be a minute.

"Hey, Mal. it's Alex," came the voice on the other line. I frowned. "Dessi just left. He claims ignorance like I suspected."

"Shit," I replied, rubbing my forehead. "But not surprising."

"He says he didn't know about Suzy. That he's in charge, but he doesn't control Jeremy's actions. Even with the second set of books, we don't have enough to charge him. No signatures or notes of any sort to prove he had anything to do with them."

"Sounds about right, pinning it all on Jeremy," I said, my mouth in a thin line. "Like *he's* smart enough to set all of that up."

"Right. We don't have anything solid enough to pin on him."

"Yet. Give me time. I'll see what I can dig up," I said, hanging up. I looked over at Rhodes, who was frowning, taking in my part of the conversation.

I had to talk to Suzy and see what else we could get on Dessi. They would continue to look for Jeremy, but Suzy had to be careful, in case he or Dessi came for her.

"Everything okay?" Rhodes asked, concerned.

"Yes, just my last case. There're a few loose ends that need to be tied up," I replied, grabbing my jacket, already on my feet. "Sorry."

"No worries. Well, let me know if there's anything you need. I can be pretty helpful when I need to be," he said with a wink. He stood and put a hand on my arm. "We still good for dinner on Tuesday?"

"Yes, thanks. I'll be there." I smiled in return, reaching up to lightly touch his hand.

I headed out, already planning what to do next, wondering if I really had time for dinner next Tuesday. And maybe I was a little worried I had already started to get in over my head with Rhodes.

Chapter 11

Pulling into the Mennons' driveway about an hour later, I waved at the Sentinel Security team sitting in a black SUV. It was Wyatt Parker's guys. I had never collaborated with them on a job, but I knew who they were and had run into them while working.

Six months or so back, we'd been hired by separate partners on a corporate-espionage case. The company was breaking up, and the partners were all gathering intel on each other to use as leverage. Wyatt's team was providing security for a particularly concerned partner who was afraid for his well-being.

Wyatt and I had approached each other to set some ground rules after distantly observing each other's objectives. Luckily, we were able to work around our missions without incident, as the partner I was working for was simply gathering facts on overall business dealings. Neither had nefarious plans for the other, so we were able to share some nonconfidential information.

I grinned at the memory of a few late nights waiting in parking lots for the partners to leave the office for the day. Wyatt's team was fun. They had incredible focus on the job, but in between? They were a riot.

I walked over to the driver's side door to let them know I was there to see Sam and Suzy.

"We know who you are, Malone," said the burly guy sitting in the driver's seat. I didn't recognize him; he must be newer. "Sam and Suzy said you're on the safe list. You can go on in. I already notified Wyatt."

"Sounds good." I nodded, heading up the drive.

The front door opened, and a tall, lean man I knew as Wyatt Parker ushered me in. I wasn't surprised to see he was handling this case personally; Sam would have insisted on it.

I nodded a hello and glanced in for the Mennons.

They were sitting at the kitchen table, going over paperwork.

"Hi, Mal!" Suzy said, standing to hug me.

"Hey, Suzy, Sam," I said, helpless but to be wrapped up in Suzy's hug. She was such a warm, friendly soul. I was oddly fond of her and very glad her fate wasn't as Dessi had ordered. "Has Rodriguez called?"

"Yes, he filled us in on Dessi, the empty bank box, and Jeremy's abandoned car," Sam said. "Surely, they'll find Jeremy eventually. I mean, he can't hide forever."

I shrugged. "Hard to say. Criminals don't exactly run in the same circles as normal citizens."

Sam plunked back down in his chair, clearly frustrated Jeremy was still out there, a potential threat to Suzy.

Satisfied that the Mennons were safe, Wyatt moved back to the front room, where one of his team was looking over a screen showing a feed of various camera angles outside the house. I couldn't remember the man's name: Brian or Ben or something.

"What are we going to do, Mal?" Sam asked. "Can I hire you to find out evidence on Dessi? I won't feel like Suzy's safe until he and Jeremy are locked up for what they did."

"Sam, I don't think I could leave this case unresolved," I confided. "The cops are out, looking for Jeremy. I'm more worried about Dessi, and the problem is, I'm not sure if we'll be able to find dirt on him. But you can be sure I'll try." I sat down in the chair Suzy offered.

"Suzy, you're sure you never heard his voice on the phone?" I centered my gaze on her.

"Not really, Mal," she replied, frowning. "I saw his name come up on Jeremy's phone once or twice, but he'd leave the room to talk." She scrunched up her face to force a memory that wasn't there. "He'd come back in either mad or worried, going on and on about what Dessi said, but I never actually heard Dessi speak."

"Okay." I nodded, trying to think outside the box. "What about any information Dessi wouldn't want us to know? Any kind of criminal activity you might have heard about? Something we could look into for incriminating evidence, even unrelated to you?"

Suzy's eyes searched the table while her mind raced to find a shred of information. "Well...I remember Jeremy talking about Dessi fixing the horse races." Suzy paused, thinking. "Jeremy mentioned something about a horse Dessi was testing a new drug on, maybe? He was running some big bets for special clients on it."

I leaned in. "Suzy. That may work." I tried not to get too excited, but this was promising. "Any idea what the drug was, the name of the doctor he was getting it from, or the name of the horse? Any of that information could get us a solid lead."

"It might not have been a drug. It might have been some kind of procedure or something. I don't know. All I remember is that they said the horse was fixed up. But I do know the horse's name; it was 'Stand Up and Dance.' I remember because I was helping Jeremy with the accounting on that race, adding up bets, figuring odds, and tallying wins." She winked at me. "That part was kinda fun."

Suzy was a morbid woman. I shook my head, eyeing her incredulously. I had a real lead, though. Something I could look into. I just hoped it didn't fizzle up.

Meanwhile, in a small, cozy, and gaudily decorated apartment,

"What in the world are you talking about?" Shelly started to get loud. "You're *crazy*! *Marco* must be taking the money!"

Peter ran his hand through his hair and tried to calm down. "*Shelly*, I know it was you. Knock it off." He stood up from where he was sitting on the couch and walked to his wife. "Don't blame Marco for this! He's just a kid. I know you're taking money from Mantovani's Pizza."

She quit screeching when she realized Peter wasn't buying her story. "This is all your fault, you know. I really didn't have a choice. I don't have enough money for even the mere *basics*!"

"Basics?" Peter said, surprised. "What are you talking about? You get a decent paycheck, and I take care of groceries. I never argue when you go clothes shopping. It's true that we have a budget for expendables, but it's more than enough for new clothes and any other basics you need."

"*More* than *enough*? Are you *crazy*?" She was starting to screech again. "It's *barely* enough for clothes, not to mention any new jewelry or hair or nail maintenance. It wouldn't last *most* women a week!" She started pacing and shaking her hands around. "I'm practically living like a *nun*! Or, or *Mother Teresa*!"

"*What*?" Peter exclaimed. "We have a budget, and I've been trying to keep expenses down because you've been flying through it at the beginning of each month! You have groceries, a closet full of clothes, and a car to drive. Why do you need so much?"

"You really *are* insane, Peter! I need to keep up a certain *respectability*. Do you *know* who my brother happens to be? I'm expected to set a standard." She patted her blonde sprayed-hard helmet of hair. "You practically *forced* me to find another source of money."

"If you're so desperate for money, why don't you get a job?" Peter asked.

"I *do* have a job!" Shelly cried.

"What exactly do you do there?" Peter asked pointedly. "I *really* want to know."

"Well, I *never*." Shelly pouted. "I make sure the cooks aren't overusing ingredients and that the wait staff is, well, waiting on the customers!"

"We don't *want* the cooks to skimp on the food. We'll lose our customers!" Peter stalked over to her. "If you needed more money, you should have talked to me. We can come to some arrangement, but if you want to have a new wardrobe each season, I suggest you get a job. We don't need a second manager at Mantovani's. I only agreed to it because I thought you were really interested in the business. You can't just steal from it!"

"I don't care about pizza! I don't care about Mantovani's. I end up smelling like oregano when I'm there. I just want to shop!" Shelly screamed. "Maybe we should call my brother and ask him what *he* thinks!"

"Okay, Shelly." Peter slowed and picked up his cell phone. "If that's what you want to do, let's call your brother. We can tell him you've been skimming money from the register at Mantovani's. We can also tell him you told me to look into Marco as the thief."

"Wait, wait, wait. On the other hand," she said, reaching for his phone. "Dom's a busy guy."

Shelly and Peter stood in their living room, staring each other down.

"*Fine.*" She sighed dramatically, waving her toxic-green-tipped fingers in the air. "I'll quit taking money from the register. I'll *try* to keep to the measly budget and my minuscule paycheck."

"Well…Mantovani's isn't doing too bad. I can increase your allowance each month. It'll be yours to manage, but no more expendable budget. I'll manage the rest of the household expenses, including your car, insurance, and gas. But you have to leave Mantovani's alone. No more comanager, no more stealing." Pete leveled with her. "If you decide that's not enough money, you're going to have to find a job."

Shelly flopped down into a chair and rolled her eyes exasperatedly. "Okay, okay! I don't know *how* I'll make it work, but I'll find a way." She slid her eyes to her husband. "On one condition."

"What?" He eyed her suspiciously.

"You don't tell Dom about any of this."

"You want me to keep Dom out of it? Well, I have a condition as well," Peter added, leaning in.

"What is it?" Shelly asked, looking nervous.

"You have to apologize to the crew at Mantovani's."

"What for?" she gasped.

"For treating them badly, yelling at them all the time, and accusing them of theft!" Peter supplied.

"As if!"

The next morning, I pulled into Arlington Park and scanned the lot. They didn't hold horse races on Mondays, and the parking lot was fairly empty, but for a few cars near a side building. So I parked near them and slid out, coffee cup in hand and sunglasses on to block out the glare of the sun. I smoothed out my cream-colored slacks and straightened the red blouse I wore to look like I had money.

I had swiped on some red lipstick and wore pearl studs, but it was the nude shoes that bugged me the most. I really hated wearing heels. Typically, I stuck to flats whenever possible, but I thought the occasion warranted it. At least, I had found a pair with a slightly lower heel.

I slowed my pace as I got re-accustomed to the less stable shoe. It wouldn't do to look like I didn't know how to walk in them. It would blow the whole facade.

Although I knew only workers and support staff would be on the grounds on a Monday, I hoped there was enough business between the owners and vets that I would be able to be inconspicuous.

There were several buildings on the grounds, and I walked through to the stables. I saw a few people, but they seemed busy and on their own agenda, carrying supplies or feed. Walking into the nearest barn, I pushed my sunglasses back onto my head to see clearly. I scanned the name plaques on the wall: *Johnny B Great, Attila the Killa, Wakeful Tranquility.*

A short guy stepped out of a stall with an empty bucket and a lead rope over his shoulder. He locked the stall and nodded to me. I nodded back and walked on, heading out of that building and into another barn when I overheard a couple arguing near a stall marked *Black Magic Fever.* The woman lowered her voice and leaned in to deliver acidic remarks.

I couldn't make out what she said, but she was definitely upset. She gave him one last glare and strode out. He looked over at me sheepishly, obviously embarrassed with the display. I gave him a half smile and slight nod as I walked past, trying to read the name plaques without being obvious.

I passed a young-looking girl brushing down a gelding. A couple of people nearby were filling water and feed. Finally, I spotted *Stand Up and Dance* scripted on a plaque near the end of the barn. A man was in with the animal. He had a bag outside the door and was checking the horse over with a stethoscope. I stepped to the stall next to him—*Feed Me Seymour*—and stopped to take a pretend phone call.

"*Yes*, darling, I know. I won't be buying anything without your *explicit* approval. Why, you *know* that! I hardly know *anything* about horses." I laid it on thick and examined the animal in front of me while glancing at the vet from my peripheral vision. He was eyeing me. *Check.* "That was a onetime thing, sugarplum. I'm just *meeting* the guy. Oh, we're going to need a vet, too, won't we?" I smiled at the vet and wagged my fingers at him. "I mean, of course, *if* we decide to buy the horse. Oh, gotta go. I see him now. TTYL!"

I pressed a button on the phone to pretend ending the call and slid it in my pocket. "Hiya, sugar!" I fake drawled, sashaying over to the vet and fluffing my hair.

He smiled at me and held out his hand. "Hi." He looked a bit over fifty. His lightly graying and thinning hair was well-manicured, but he had a car-salesman smile. "I'm Dr. Edward Millwood. Did I hear you're looking for a vet?"

"Yes! Isn't this convenient?" I clapped my hands and smoothed my hair down, then leaned in. "My husband and I went to a horse race last weekend, and I just decided I *had* to have one! It's going to be so exciting," I exclaimed.

Dr. Millwood's eyes lit up with dollar signs. "Well, which horse are you looking at?"

"I'm not really sure, to be honest." I opened my eyes wide and played dumb. "I'm supposed to be meeting someone here, but I'm not really sure where I'm supposed to be. I just remember the name sounded funny."

The vet laughed a bit and said, "Well, I'm happy to keep you company while you wait. If you need some help looking the horse over, I'd be glad to assist. I specialize in racehorses, you see." He had a smarmy smile on his face and leaned in. "And if you happen to need a vet once you find the right horse, I am happy to offer my services. I have had a certain amount of luck getting them in the best condition to race."

He had bought the act and was ready to empty my bank account. He was the type to rob you blind and say "You're welcome" in the process.

I took his arm, gazing up at his eyes, the glassy stare of overcome awe still plastered on my face. "Oh, pumpkin, that just sounds wonderful! The minute I saw you, I thought to myself, 'now, *there's* a man who knows what he's doing!' The way you took care of that horse, running your hands over him and checking for injuries." I shook my head. "I can tell you're a gifted vet. So, how do you get a horse in condition?"

"Well, I have access to the highest quality vitamins. I assess the horse and create a very special mix based on their unique chemistry," he explained haughtily. Then he glanced at me and frowned slightly. "Of course, it all depends on how dedicated you are to get the horse's best performance. The highest quality vitamins and supplements can be expensive. It really depends on if you're looking to race for fun or if you're really serious about winning."

I could tell I was getting fed a load of shit, and I set a look on my face that said it tasted fantastic. "Oh, I am completely *committed* to winning!" My eyes got huge in my head, and I nodded enthusiastically, playing with the strand of pearls I wore. "I happen to be extremely competitive. I'm willing to invest *deeply* in this." I leaned in and toyed with his stethoscope. "However, I need to be off now and find that man! You have a card for me, Shug?"

Dr. McSleazy practically oozed all over the card he handed me, and I nearly twitched with the urge to wipe my hands on my pants after dropping it in my bag. I jotted my number and name— "Moll"—on his notebook and sauntered off, giving him a finger wave. Not the finger I wanted to give him, though.

As I was heading out, I spotted Dessi coming in from the other side of the barn. I quickly made my exit, hoping he didn't see me. I wasn't dressed as normal, but my red hair was kinda hard to hide.

I was planning on doing a little research to see what I could find out about Dr. Millwood when I got back to my office, but I needed to swing by for a coffee first. You know, just to wipe the taste of sleaze out of my mouth.

After a wasted hour of research on Dr. Millwood, I gave up. All I had found on Dr. McSleazy was an old directory, listing him at a downtown Chicago office. The office had long-since closed, and I couldn't find any reference to where he was now or what had happened to the business.

I pulled out his card again to look at it, but it was nondescript. It had a logo with a DNA chain and Dr. Edward A Millwood printed in block letters. No address, just a phone number.

I sighed; there was nothing I could glean from it. I flipped it between my fingers while I considered what else I could track down.

I googled the Chicago Tribune to find out what others were thinking about all of these fires. After another thirty wasted minutes, I frowned at my computer screen. There wasn't a single story about any of the incidents in the Tribune.

Pushing back from my computer, I crossed my arms and swiveled in my chair, thinking.

Leaning back to my desk, I looked up Insideonline again and found the original articles on the fires I had read before. *Huh,* we were in a small suburb in Chicago, but this many fires should be big news.

On my way to see Sully for more information, I realized I should stop for a bite to eat first. I hadn't eaten all day, getting caught up in research for much longer than I planned. Mariano's cobb salad sounded pretty good.

Meanwhile, in an Italian pizza joint dripping with tension,

"Good afternoon, everyone," Peter Mantovani said in the server area, where he had called the staff meeting. He shifted on his feet, worried about what she would say. "Shelly just had a few things to say before the dinner rush."

He gestured to his wife, who stood there, looking both angry and uncomfortable. She had her right hand at her hip, which was jutted out in a defiant attitude, fluorescent-pink nails curving into her skinny jeans.

"I just wanted to tell you all that this will be my last night here." She shifted to the other hip, lips pursed. "I have to wrap up a few things in the office. You know, paperwork, but then I'm packing up. I'm just way too busy to be able to come in all the time. Too much on my plate right now."

Shelly looked over at Peter, who cleared his throat.

"I know that, sometimes, I've been a little *demanding*, but that's really just because I wanted the business to succeed," she started.

Peter pulled out his cell phone and tipped it so Shelly could see the contact list was scrolled to Dom's information. He raised an eyebrow.

She jerked straight and blurted out, "I just wanted to say I'm sorry!"

Peter stifled a smile and looked at the crew. They all looked around at each other with eyebrows raised, a little in shock. Phil rolled his eyes to Marion, and Marco tilted his head with curiosity. Sally just stood there, taking it all in, face blank, gaze not focused on anyone in particular.

"I mean, like I said, I want the business to do well," Shelly clarified. "And I was just trying to do my *job*!"

"Okay, I think we're done here." Peter waved the crew back out to the floor. It was all they'd likely get from her. She had meant well—at least he thought so. He glanced back at his wife and frowned as she huffed and charged out, teetering on her bright-purple-heeled mules.

"The only other news I have to share is that Mal has taken another position, so she won't be filling in anymore," Peter explained. "It's a normal Monday night, so business as usual. I'll probably be looking for another person to fill in now and then, so if you know of anyone interested in a few hours a few nights a week, have them come fill out an application."

"Will do, boss," replied Sally, straight hair swinging as she turned to head out to the bar and began cleaning glasses from the afternoon crowd.

The rest of the crew filtered out to their areas and slowly got busy with work. They kept glancing back and forth between themselves, waiting for him to leave before discussing the news.

Chapter 12

I wandered into the front door of Fire Central, the administrative offices for North Side's fire department.

"Hi. I was hoping to see Assistant Chief Sullivan," I said to the secretary inside. "Is he around?"

"I can check," she replied and tilted her head. "Can I tell him who's asking?"

"Sure, I'm Detective Malone," I replied, reaching out to shake her hand. "I just had some questions I wanted to ask him."

"Nice to meet you, Detective. Are you on the force?"

"No, I'm a private investigator."

The secretary nodded and picked up the phone. "If you'd please take a seat, I'll see if he's available."

I walked over to a row of chairs on the far wall but stood instead.

"You're in luck, Detective," the secretary called after a moment. "Sully's on his way down."

"Thanks."

While I waited, I looked at the firefighter pictures lining the walls. It looked like yearbook photos, headshots of all the crew, captured every five years or so. I wandered until I found a picture of Marlon Rhodes, only the smile I was getting used to seeing wasn't on his face. I looked around and noticed none of the guys were smiling. The two women I found were, though. *Just like the police force.*

The door to my right opened up, and a tall man in his early fifties with graying temples came out. "Detective Malone?" he asked.

"Yes, sir." I stepped forward and took his offered hand. "Thanks so much for meeting with me. I just had a few questions I was hoping to ask you."

"Sure, we can go to my office." He turned and held the door open for me as he gestured down the hallway. Fire Central was a working fire station, and calls from other districts echoed in the overhead radio.

The assistant chief's office was a small bright room with a window overlooking the street. I sat in one of the two slightly worn chairs in front of a large, similarly worn desk.

"Chief Sullivan," I started.

"Oh, please," he interrupted me with a shake of his head. "Call me Sully."

"Sully it is." I smiled. "I just wanted to talk to you a bit about the fires that have been popping up all over town. I was in Roscoe Village a couple of days ago when the building caught on fire. It's my neighborhood, so I was concerned and did a little research. I was surprised to find there've been incidents all over, in different neighborhoods."

"Oh, yes. It's a real shame." Sully ran a hand through his hair and sighed. "I had high hopes for that place. It was a nonprofit that provided housing for those struggling to pay rent. I helped get that place up and running. It was a good program because part of it was working with facilitators to learn useful life skills. Anything from interviewing to computer classes and personal budgeting. They even had to provide general maintenance on their temporary residence. With help and guidance, of course, wherever it was needed."

"Sounds like a great program," I said appreciatively. "I heard a little about it when it kicked off, but nothing since. Will they be able to continue at a different location?"

"I'm not sure yet. They did lose a lot of equipment, but with insurance, they may be okay. We should know more after the next city meeting."

"I've heard you helped get the preschool in Ravenswood off the ground as well," I ventured. "Were all the fires associated with city-funded programs? Doesn't that seem suspicious?"

"Well," Sully started awkwardly, rubbing his face. "They had some funding from the city, but we also had fundraisers and donations from the neighborhoods, in particular, to put money into their own burgs. I'm not sure about suspicious, but it is a significant loss to the city."

"And you were backing all these foundations as well, right?"

"Well, yes. I'm involved in improving the Chicago suburbs. I donate a lot of my time, socializing these programs and getting donors to fund them. I spent too many years working fire suppression and seeing the problems in the neighborhoods. Anything I can do to tip the scale, I will." Sully looked pointedly at me. "Now, what are you getting at? Are you working a case in regard to the fires?"

"Uh, no." It was my turn to answer awkwardly. "This is actually mostly just general curiosity." I shrugged. "I didn't get to be a detective because I could leave a trail cold."

"I get that, but the police have been looking into these fires."

"So, they *were* arson?" I went ahead and asked. The worst he could do was not answer.

"I can't confirm that; the investigation is still ongoing," he replied unhelpfully. "There's not much I can tell you about that."

Well, that confirmed that.

"There's one other thing I thought was really strange." I frowned in confusion and watched his face carefully. "I didn't find any information in the Chicago Tribune about any of the fires. Isn't that odd?"

A flicker of something—anger maybe—crossed Sully's face.

"Humph. Well, that is odd. I hadn't noticed. But the Tribune isn't often as concerned about news that happen outside the downtown area. They have so much crime. I guess it's overshadowing the fires."

I didn't quite buy his story, but I let it lie.

"I'm sorry, but there's just not much else I can share." Sully shook his head and moved to get up.

I got his message loud and clear. Our meeting was over. That's fine; it was enough for now. I could always come back and bug him later if needed.

"I sure do appreciate your time." I shook his hand. "I just really want to see an end to these fires in our own backyard."

"Nobody wants that more than me, I can assure you," Sully replied soberly, ushering me out of his office and down the hall, where he escorted me out.

I nodded at the secretary. "Thanks," I said.

"No problem," she replied, bobbing her head. "Have a nice one."

Meanwhile, at the Mennons' house,

"Did you hear from Mal today?" Suzy asked, finding Sam in the kitchen.

"No, why?" he replied.

"It's just that I'm worried about her. She seems so stressed out and serious. I think she must work too hard."

"Well, we kinda want her to work hard right now." He shrugged.

"True, but she won't take payment to continue the case."

"I tried to pay her to continue working it. She said she didn't know what she could do yet, so we'd hold off."

"I know, honey, but she could use some help."

"What could *we* do to help her out?" Sam asked.

"I'm not sure." Suzy frowned. She hated the idea that Mal was out there working to keep her safe, alone. "But it feels like we should do *something*."

"Don't worry, sweetie." Sam wrapped his arms around his wife. "Mal will figure it out. She's really smart, you know. She found *you*."

"You *both* found me." Suzy grinned, running a hand up Sam's cheek and kissing him lightly. She was so glad to be back in his arms. "Have I thanked you for that yet?"

"Uh, yeah, but feel free to thank me again." He waggled his eyebrows and kissed her in return.

"Is this all you need?" Wyatt asked, clearing his throat as he walked in. He held up a slip of paper.

"Yep, that should do it," Suzy said. It was a list of grocery supplies she needed. Wyatt thought Amazon Fresh grocery delivery was too risky. He didn't want anyone unplanned coming to the house. He was sending one of his guys to get it instead.

"I noted which items need to be the brand name; otherwise, I don't care what brand they buy. Whatever's a good price," Suzy instructed.

Wyatt cracked a grin since they could obviously afford whatever she wanted from the store.

"Are you sure you want to cook, honey?" Sam asked, rubbing her back. "You haven't even been home for two days. You should take some time to relax and get back into the groove. There's no rush, like, ever, really. I could have food delivered, or we could hire someone to come in and cook. Just think about it, your own personal chef!"

"Oh, don't be silly." Suzy playfully swatted his arm and tilted her face to smile up at him. He would spoil her rotten if she let him. But she didn't need all of that; she had him. It was all she wanted. "I'm not injured and am perfectly capable of cooking. I sat around all day yesterday, and it about killed me. I can't just float around the house forever."

"It's been a day," Sam argued.

"Yes, and I can only handle so many hours of card games," Suzy replied, eyes huge.

"We could rewatch the Star Wars movies!" Sam countered, leaning forward excitedly.

"How about we watch one a night, Sam?" Suzy said, holding up a single finger. No way she could binge-watch them, but she could manage a couple of hours a night, especially when he used that schoolboy smile.

"Oh boy! Is popcorn on that list?" Sam asked.

"I'll add it," Wyatt replied as he walked out of the room, grinning and shaking his head.

I stalked back into my office with some takeout stir-fry from #1 Chop Suey. One of the biggest benefits of living in a city like Chicago was that there was international food everywhere. Pretty much anything I wanted, I could find. That, and good coffee.

I opened my laptop and sat down, pulling the Kung Pao chicken and chopsticks out of the bag. Leaning back in my chair, I crossed my ankles and propped my feet on the edge of my desk. Insideonline had several articles on the fires, and I figured the other local papers would too. I plunked through the websites, going back and forth between bites of chicken and peanuts.

My talk with Rhodes hinted that there had been several, but I only knew of three. I looked for any other incidents in the neighboring communities' electronic newspapers. I couldn't find anything on other building fires in the Inside-Booster, which was for Northside and the surrounding areas, like Lincoln Park, but there was a dumpster fire outside a food pantry. It didn't quite fit the MO, but I wrote it down on a pad of paper anyway.

I checked the News-Star and Skyline, the other neighborhood papers available on the website. I only found one other fire that had happened in Uptown, fairly close to Ravenswood. It was a continuing-education facility for adults, to learn basic computer skills and home finance.

I wondered if that was where the housing-program recipients had been getting their education. When Sully brought it up, he didn't mention the education facility had been burned down as well. I wasn't sure if that was an accident or not. *Maybe he figured I knew. Or maybe he was fishing to see how* much *I knew.*

I made a timeline of the dates and locations of the fires I had information about:

-April 17th, dumpster fire outside of the food pantry, Edgewater (may be unrelated)

-May 3rd, continuing education facility, Uptown

-May 7th, preschool, Ravenswood

-May 10th, housing program, Roscoe Village

-May 12th, community center, Bricktown

Today was the 15th, 3 days after the last fire. If the pattern continued—and unfortunately, I couldn't see why it wouldn't—we were due for another one. I dropped my feet to the floor and pulled out a map to mark out the locations of the incidents. There wasn't anything telling about them, but they were clustered around North Center.

I tapped my chopsticks on the container, thinking while I chewed. I looked back at the spots again and dated them. They were heading somewhat from North to South. It was a bit of a stretch but something to watch.

Setting the map to the side, I switched to a fresh page in my notepad. I was a paper-and-pencil kinda girl. I had tried to use an online note program, but it just never stuck. I pulled up Dr. Millwood again, searching a few sites for information on his previous work, but still nothing. I pushed back from the laptop while I thought of other ways to find information on him. Even the background-check service I paid for had zero results. Maybe he was operating under a fake name with a false license.

Focusing back on my Kung Pao, I dug through it for the peanuts; they were my favorite. A little tricky with the chopsticks, but it gave me time to think.

Setting the half-empty container down once more, I grabbed my cell. He answered on the second ring.

"Hello," came a voice as slimy as I remembered it.

"Hiya, sugar," I answered in my disguise. "It's Moll. We met this morning at Arlington?"

"Of course!" he replied excitedly. "I was hoping you'd call."

"Well, aren't you the sweetest!" I rolled my eyes even as my voice dripped with honey. "I was just thinking over our discussion and was hoping we could chat more about the services you offer. Could I meet you at your office? I'd love to see your facility and hear about your success stories! I always do love to see a man at work."

"Well, I typically meet clients at the stables," he hedged. "I have a very secure facility, and I have to protect my clients' information. You understand, of course. How about we meet for lunch sometime?"

"Sure, we could do that." I allowed my disappointment to show. I was hoping to find his office, but maybe I could still get some answers. "I'm free tomorrow."

"Perfect! Are you near Arlington Heights?"

"I live in Uptown, dear. But I can meet somewhere in between."

"How about the Shallots Bistro in Skokie at noon?"

"Sounds lovely! I'll see you then," I replied, hanging up the phone and resuming picking through my lunch. They never did give me enough peanuts.

Meanwhile, from a comfortable and carefully appointed home office,

"I'm telling you, Dad. Something happened," Marco explained, the sound of his feet scraping the alley behind Mantovani's audible over the phone. "You didn't hear anything?"

"No, nothing. What do you think happened?" Dom asked. He loved it when his kid called on break. It was getting harder to find time to talk to him now that he was grown and was making his way on his own.

"I'm not sure, really." His son paused, thinking. "You should have heard them. It was obvious Uncle Peter had something over on Aunt Shelly for her to apologize like that. You would have had to hear it and see their body language. And she announced she wasn't going to be comanaging anymore, either."

"Look who's being observant." He chuckled approvingly. "So, what else have you noticed?"

"Well, we also had new help, a redhead named Mal, for a few nights here and there. And now, she's quit and Shelly's out."

"Okay."

"Mal was really friendly and did a decent job, but she also asked a lot of questions."

"What else do you know?" he prodded gently.

"Well, Phil's been irritable, and Sally's been stoic, but neither of those things is new. There was some tension with Uncle Peter. Cash was coming up missing. But I don't really know how much."

"Really?" Dom perked up; maybe he was on to something.

"Yeah, I thought someone was making mistakes, but Uncle Peter was getting pretty upset about it. Definitely not his typical friendliness."

"This was about the time that Mal started?"

"Yeah, that's right," Marco said, his voice betraying a lightbulb-click moment. "You don't suppose he brought her in to find out what was going on?"

"I think it's a good possibility," Dom offered. He was pretty proud that his son was learning to watch and listen. It was a good trait for the Poggiali family, even if he didn't want his son in the business in the same capacity. Marco had a college education and a chance at an honest life. Still, there were qualities a man should have, he thought. Marco would do well for himself.

"And then with Aunt Shelly apologizing, the tension between them, and her leaving like that. I'd almost say she had something to do with it," Marco said.

"Shelly, Shelly, Shelly," Dom sighed, shaking his head. He had a sneaking suspicion of what his sister was doing.

"You know, Dad. I was actually kinda impressed with Uncle Peter," Marco said, a smile in his voice. "You shoulda seen him. He was in charge, you know? He pushed back, and she crumbled! Uncle Peter's growing some balls!"

He chuckled. "Imagine! I never thought I'd see the day…So, tell me about Mal. What do you know about her? What does she look like?"

I went home a little early, having exhausted my research efforts. I had also spent a couple of hours trying to get my finances in order. It seemed like I never had time to get it all done. The bills just kept coming in, and I kept paying them. The worst part was I wasn't really certain I could cover them all the time. I tried to keep my work checkbook balanced, but it was always the last thing on my mind. *Probably because I hated doing it.*

Bills always wore me out, and I thought a cup of coffee would be perfect to perk me up. Locking my front door behind me out of habit, I chucked my shoes off and walked into the kitchen to make a pot of coffee.

I poured water into my dead plant on the counter and slid open the sliding door.

It was a beautiful day out on the balcony, and I let myself sit for the first time in a while without anything to do. My brain was shot. I watched the clouds in the sky, waiting for the coffee to perk.

Unable to wait any longer, I stole from Mr. Bunn mid-brew and took a sip of the beautiful thing before going back outside. Letting out a deep sigh, I felt my caffeine level rise back to an acceptable degree and relaxed a bit more.

I really should get a pet to talk to at home. We always had one when I was younger. Mostly dogs, but with an apartment, a cat would be easier. Then I thought about my ivy plant on the counter and decided it wasn't that good of an idea anyway.

I needed a new case. I was still busy with Suzy's, and I was still tracking down these fires, but I would eventually need another income coming in. I thought I had made enough on the Mennon case to last me a bit. He had given me a nice bonus, which I still didn't feel comfortable accepting. It had dragged on longer than I planned, but it was my own fault, really, not following up on Jeremy's work sooner. I wouldn't take even more money from Sam. It just didn't feel right. I would have kept on the case regardless.

Looking up into the sky, I noticed an odd cloud, maybe a plume of smoke, off to the south. Yep, it was darker than it should be, definitely smoke.

Alarm spiked through me. Damn it, another fire!

The alarms went off in the distance, but I was already out of my chair. Shoving my feet back into my boots, I dumped my coffee into an insulated mug and was out the door.

Chapter 13

It was hard to know where to turn. I was in my Jeep, peering up through the windshield, turning right and left to get closer to the source of the billowing black smoke. But the wind kept blowing it around, and it was hard to see where it was thickest.

I finally heard sirens and saw a few cop cars race by, already several blocks in front of me. I flicked on my turn signal to change lanes and follow, but gritted my teeth when I got a red light.

I banged the palm of my hand against the steering wheel in frustration before the light changed, and I turned left in pursuit of the responding officers. Finally, I saw the fire trucks ahead and cop cars blocking traffic. Dark plumes rose from a brick building, soiling the sky. The traffic was heavy, and I found a place to park a block down a side road. I hurried back to the spot and slid into the crowd to blend in.

I knew there wasn't much I could do about the fire itself. The fire and police departments had already responded. It wasn't Station 56, but I found myself checking for Rhodes anyway. We were too far away from Bricktown. There wasn't any chance he'd be here, so why was I looking? I was supposed to be searching for clues. Shifting my gaze to the crowd, I scanned it for interested parties, but I was also taking a page from

Rhodes and trying to identify what was missing from the scene, if anything.

It was amazing how quickly people gathered at the scene of an accident or tragic event. Everyone wanted to get a peek at the unfolding drama. Funny how no one seemed to want to do anything about the problem, but they sure wanted to make sure they *saw* it. A few of them had their cell phones out, videotaping everything. These people were particularly interesting to me. I slid along the back of the crowd, getting closer to a woman who was recording the transpiring events.

"See, Darren? The fire is out of control!" the woman screamed into her smartphone. She was bouncing from foot to foot, eyes wide in a mix of horror and excitement.

I passed by her and moved along, writing her off as a bored housewife. Several onlookers were simply transfixed, gasping as the firefighters came in and out of the building. They waved at the smoke blowing in our direction as a few of the police officers yelled at the crowd to keep back.

"Oh, man! This is terrible! We just got the place set up and have taken several donations already," a man said, toeing the line set in place by the police. He was pulling at his hair and jumping to see around the cops.

Another guy had his phone in the air, too, but he was farther out. He didn't look as stressed, but he was definitely unhappy, bordering on angry. I edged closer to him, watching the fire. The firemen got busy running a hose into the building.

"Do you know if anyone's inside?" I asked the stranger nonchalantly.

He glanced over at me while filming, grimaced, and looked like he was going to ignore me. "No, I don't think so. The place isn't open today."

"What is the business?" I asked.

"It's a collection facility for a work program. People donate office wear and supplies. In this neighborhood, they've gotten good donations so far. I guess that's all wasted now, though." The guy looked sad and put his phone away.

"That's terrible," I replied. "Do you work with them?"

"No, well, not really," he answered, sighing heavily. "I work for an insurance company. The one insuring this place." He gestured angrily at the building.

"Oh, that sucks," I said, commiserating with him.

"You don't know the half of it. We've insured several of these community programs and are going to be shelling it out," he said, shaking his head in anguish. "I'm not sure we're going to be able to stay afloat."

"Any idea what happened?"

"No, they're under investigation," he answered, eyeing me.

"Well, good luck." I nodded to him. He had shut down and wouldn't say anything else. "Hope it all works out."

As I stepped away and back to scan the area again, the man relaxed somewhat. The firefighters were slowing down. Smoke was still coming out of the building, but much less than when I first arrived. Fire hoses were being pulled back out of the building. They must have got it put out already. I was impressed by their timing.

There was still a lot of activity, officials walking around, and equipment being put away. Lots of discussions between the firemen and the police officers were taking place, and I edged forward to see if I could hear what they were saying.

But to my far left, at the very back of the crowd, I noticed one guy break away. He had a grim, determined look to him that seemed out of place. He was a tall black man in his early forties. His jeans and worn flannel shirt stood out in this neighborhood—the NW outskirts of Lincoln Park. He glanced back toward the officials, jaw ticking from grinding teeth. He gave a short shake to his head and stalked off, hands stuffed in his pockets.

I wasn't sure what it meant, but it was interesting. Glancing back at the crowd and the cops, I made a quick decision. No one else looked overly suspicious, and the cleanup was well underway. Stepping away, I kept my head down and followed the man.

He stalked down the center of the road, since traffic wasn't moving yet, then up onto the sidewalk to take a right at the next street. I followed slightly behind, staying close to the buildings on the right. There was less street traffic and few pedestrians in this part of the commercial district. He didn't seem to be paying attention to much, just kept walking determinedly, leaning forward, his posture resonating with anger and frustration. The few people we passed moved out of his way to avoid him.

I lagged behind more when he paused at the convenience store. He headed in, and I continued on past the store to cross the street and looked at magazines at a newspaper stand. I perused covers as I kept my peripheral on the door he had entered.

Before long, he came back out, paper sack in hand. It had the distinctive shape of a tall 40 oz, but he kept it wrapped as he crossed the street to where I was standing. I ignored him, pretending to shop until he was nearly out of my vision, then turned lazily and crossed the street in pursuit.

He walked another block, slowing down a bit. This area was more residential, and I stuck closer to the few trees lining the sidewalk. He started to slow, but his jerky, tension-filled movements indicated he still had some pent-up frustration to work out.

Pausing, he scanned the street. I turned and walked up to a ramen shop that was tucked between two apartment buildings. I stood there, pretending to consider the menu, then subtly glanced back to see he had crossed the street again and was heading to a dark-blue sedan with rusted wheel wells.

Turning, I crossed the street as quickly as possible, trying to close the distance. I was determined to get the license plate. I just had to get a little closer, fast. His car edged out, but I was still too far away, so I broke into a run, not worrying about my cover at this point. I was afraid I wasn't going to catch it.

A screech sounded, and I jerked my head to the left to see a sports car coming down the road a little too fast. The blue sedan braked as the sports car honked and careened around him. The sedan paused a couple of seconds longer, and I heard shouts coming from inside, then it pulled away.

It was the few seconds I needed to get close enough to get the plate. A42 1781. I had it. My next stop would be to the station tomorrow to ask for a favor to find the owner. I headed back to my Jeep to write down the plate number before I forgot it.

As I drove back home, I tried to figure out my next move. I wanted to poke around the preschool in Ravenswood to see what I could find out about. I still didn't have any evidence on Dessi, but I had lunch scheduled the next day with Dr. McSleazy and would hopefully get a lead from that.

I also had dinner with Rhodes the next night. Damn, I wasn't sure what to do about that. I was surprised by how much I was looking forward to it and a little uncomfortable with that fact.

I also realized Jen and I never got around to lunch last week. With the craziness of Suzy's rescue and wrapping up Pete's case, it just escaped my mind. It was with this thought in my head that I made an impulse decision to swing by Hungry's.

It was early enough in the evening that they had a local band on stage, but I bypassed that and headed toward the back. The rear patio was why we all loved this hangout so much. When the weather was nice, we'd sit outside until they closed the place down. Well, I used to. My old colleagues probably still did. I felt a small pang of something slightly resembling regret about dropping out of the academy.

It didn't last long, though. I was much happier on my own, with my own schedule, even if I didn't have the security of a steady job with a pension, vacation time, sick time, and a 401k. Ugh, I would *not* let myself regret my decision. Ultimately, I much preferred my life. I could take cases that mattered to me. It's just that I missed the camaraderie with the crew. It was a family, and I sometimes missed being a part of it.

I stopped by the bar before I stepped outside. I wasn't in the mood for a beer tonight, so I asked for a Negroni instead. Hungry's had some great cocktails. The bartender was fast and efficient, and I was soon outside in the cooling early evening.

Scanning the crowd, I found a few officers I knew, a few I didn't, and several civilians cross-mingling with them. It wasn't strictly a badge bar, but its location practically across the street from the cop shop meant it was a favorite hangout.

I finally spotted Jen and let out a short sigh of relief. I'd just been taking a guess that she'd be here on Monday night, her least favorite day of the week, and was glad I was right. Not that I couldn't bullshit with the others long enough to enjoy my drink, but it had been a while since I had seen her, and I didn't want to lose the friendship. It was one of the few I had time for. *Made time for, if I was being honest.*

Jen's face split into a large grin when she noticed me. She jumped up from the wrought-iron patio table to envelop me in a hug.

"Geez, Jen," I complained halfheartedly, hugging her back. "You'd think you hadn't seen me in weeks."

"It's been over a week, for sure!" she replied, still smiling. "And much longer since I've seen you here."

I just grunted in reply but was flattered she was so pleased to see me.

"What brings you here? Are you having a crappy Monday, too?" she continued.

"It didn't start out that way," I replied, pulling out a chair to sit down. "I just got back from a fire near Lincoln Park. I think it's related to the others in the neighborhoods."

"Fires?" Jen asked, intrigued. "I know there's been a few more than normal, but they're related?"

"Well, I think so," I replied, taking a swig from my cocktail. I really liked the gin and Campari.

Jen took a long pull of her pint of beer and settled back further into her chair to relax. "What do you know?"

"Not much so far, but this makes the sixth fire in the past few weeks, and they are all city-funded programs," I filled her in. "And all of them are also supported by Fire Chief Sullivan."

"That's interesting," she replied.

"Yeah." I nodded. "Not sure how it's all related, but something's going on."

Jen nodded, frowning slightly. "Do you know who's working the investigation?"

"Not yet," I replied. "But if you have any ideas, that would be helpful."

"Not sure they could give you too much information if it's an open investigation, but I'll see what I can do," she promised. "You've consulted with us before, so it really depends on who's on the case, you know."

"Yeah, I know." I grimaced. I hated the bureaucracy.

I relaxed a bit, easing deeper into my chair, matching Jen's pose.

"So, what else is new," I asked, eyebrows raised.

"Well, Charlie started soccer last week. He's very excited about it." She laughed. "I see a summer of sitting in the hot sun."

"There are worse ways to spend your evenings," I replied. Charlie was Jen's nephew. He was the only kid in her extended family, and she doted on him.

We laughed our way through catching up and finished our drinks. Just when we were getting ready for seconds, a pitcher of beer slammed down on our table with a stack of cups. Several other police officers had decided we'd had enough private conversation and helped themselves to the table.

"Mal! How the hell are you?" Stevens bellowed, throwing an arm around my shoulders and a glass of beer in my hand. "I haven't seen you in Hungry's since you and Alex broke up."

I shook my head, my grin slipping at the mention of his name.

"I'm doing fine, Stevens," I replied, elbowing him in the arm to give me some space. "How is Melissa?"

"Melissa's good." Stevens nodded, smiling.

Walker and Bradshaw slapped me on the arm as they came around to fill their drinks. They crowded around the table, pulling up chairs and pouring beer.

I smiled and shook my head at them. It seemed I was still close enough to be part of the family on occasions like this. It made me happy. I accepted a cup and joined in the conversation. They were teasing one of the rookies for losing his lunch because of a motorcycle accident earlier that day. I was glad nothing had changed.

It was just the evening I needed. It didn't even kill my mood when I noticed Detective Dillhole at another table farther down the patio. I just ignored him and enjoyed the company.

Much later, as I was heading home to write down my notes for the day, realization struck me; the fire tonight put their locations in a fairly predictable pattern: South. I frowned, waiting at a light. What, then, were they headed towards?

Meanwhile, at a much more peaceful Italian place,

Peter opened the cash register, humming lightly as he tallied the night's receipts and cash. The rest of the crew was busy with cleaning and other closing duties.

"Holy damn!" Peter shouted, banging a fist on his bar. The drawer had come up $200 short compared to the cash receipts for the night. Apparently, Shelly had struck again, one last time, since she wouldn't have access to the money after tonight. A final retaliation against his modest expense budget.

He sighed, stuffing the cash in the bank envelope, noting the discrepancy. Letting out one last growl of frustration, he slammed the door shut, stomping off to his office to finish the deposit.

Phil and Marco glanced at each other, frozen by Peter's outburst. Sally didn't even look up; she just continued drying a glass behind the bar, then put it away to grab another.

Chapter 14

It was early when I woke, unable to sleep in despite my unusually late night out. I grabbed my laptop on the way to the kitchen to make coffee, anxious to check the news. I wasn't surprised that last night's fire wasn't brought up in the Tribune or that the only mention I could find on it was on the local Inside-Booster. The article didn't have much more information than what I had already observed at the scene, except for more detail on the program itself.

The center had just finished getting up and running. Donations had been made over the past few weeks, and they had just opened to start accepting applications to the program, which let participants select a free outfit for job interviews. Should they get the job, they would then get four more outfits, for a full week's worth of clothes, meant to last them until they started getting paychecks.

It appeared to be a good program, and it was disheartening to hear the fire had damaged so many of the outfits. Those not burnt were full of smoke, and heavy cleaning would be required to see what was salvageable. There was concern that the funding wouldn't even cover the losses and cleaning expenses, but I was encouraged to hear that two of the local dry-cleaning business had already stepped forward to help.

Part of the program's application process required the participants to be enrolled in at least one course of the continuing-education facility in Uptown, but since that had burned down almost two weeks ago, they had to waive that requirement until they got back on their feet, assuming they would be able to.

I was still surprised by the lack of connection drawn between the fires in the news. It was highly unlikely that the reporter hadn't made the connection yet. I noted the name of the article's author. Interestingly enough, it was the same one who had covered several of the other local fires. The only story written by another journalist was in the News-Star, regarding the incident in Uptown.

I went for a short run to clear my head, then headed out to follow up on some leads.

Travel mug in hand, I pulled onto a street in Uptown, parking in front of Adult Learning Center, the continuing-education facility. This was the site of the first fire, according to my assumptions. A few weeks before, there was the dumpster fire in Edgewater, which was North of Uptown, fitting the Southern-moving pattern. It might have been an initial arson test, but it could also just be a coincidence. Dumpster fires were far from rare.

This incident had happened only two weeks ago, and there was still evidence of the flames. Soot covered the front of the old brick building. A plywood door had been nailed to exposed beams where there was once a doorway.

A sign on the plywood announced it was closed until further notice and left a phone number for questions. I gave it a quick call.

"Hello?" came a man's voice on the third ring.

"Hi. I just stopped by ALC in Uptown and was wondering if you had plans to rebuild and reopen?" I asked.

"Oh, well, we're really not sure yet," he replied. "Are you a participant?"

"Not exactly. I was looking to donate to the cause."

"Oh, that's good news. We haven't been able to reach every participant yet since they don't all have phones. We were hoping they'd see the sign at ALC and find a way to contact us. I can give you an address to send donations if you'd like," he offered.

"That would be great. Thank you," I said. I took down the PO Box he provided. It was still a good cause, and I was happy to contribute.

"Did you hear about the fire near Lincoln Park yesterday?" I asked.

"Unfortunately, yes," the man sighed.

"Seems like a string of bad luck," I prodded.

"Yeah, seems like," he replied, his voice flat as though he didn't quite believe it.

"Just doesn't make any sense. Why would anyone want to put an end to these services?" I nudged just a little more, hoping he'd give me something.

"I know, it's such a shame. We put so much effort to get these off the ground, you know?" he answered passionately. "Most of the effort is in setting everything up. After that, it's just keeping things afloat. I tell you, no one is more upset than Sully, uh, Chief Sullivan. He put in so much effort, fundraising and helping us maneuver the political waters."

"Really? Are there a lot of politics around the center?" I asked.

"There's always politics involved with city-funded programs," he replied. "Chief Sullivan really knows his way around the city and all the players, if you know what I mean."

Hmm, I raised my eyebrow.

"Well, I'm sure an investigation has been made into these fires. Any idea what they've determined?"

"Uh, not really." He paused. "They don't really tell us much, but Sully did say they were looking into it."

"Well, I sure hope everything works out," I replied, thinking I'd gotten as much as I would out of him. In an afterthought, I added, "Tell you what. I'm happy to assist wherever I can. If you want to take down my number, you can call me if you need some help getting back on your feet."

I gave him the information and hung up. My interest was twofold. I was interested in joining the cause but also thought if I was embedded in the efforts, I could get more information out of the volunteers.

I headed into Roscoe Village to stop by the police station. The parking lot was fairly empty of cop cars at this time of the day. Most were already out on their rounds. It didn't take me long to find Jen; she was back at evidence again.

"Mal! Long time no see!" She laughed, throwing an arm around me.

"Good to see you too, Jen," I said, returning her hug.

She was a perpetual optimist, with perky blonde hair and sky-blue eyes. Hell, she even had dimples. She was good for me. I wasn't terribly touchy-feely, but for close friends, I made an exception. Jen met those requirements.

"I'm so glad you stopped by last night," she said. "It was great catching up."

"Yeah, it was," I agreed, tucking my hair behind my left ear. "It was good to see the guys, too."

"See?" she teased. "I told you it would be fine. Alex didn't even bother you."

"You were right," I admitted, hanging my head in defeat.

"You should listen to me more."

"Don't push your luck," I said, teasingly elbowing her.

"Fine, fine." She laughed. "Hey, I got that name for you," she said, pulling a slip of paper from her pocket. "Detective Harris is the police officer working the arson investigation. I didn't find out who was the arson investigator with the fire department, but Harris would know. Don't know if he'll share it with you, but he'll know."

"Thanks, Jen." I nodded, taking the paper. "I know he can't tell me much, but it's worth a shot."

"No problem." She smiled. "He's down on 19th, in Uptown."

I spent a few more minutes chatting with her before making my way back to the offices. I wanted to stop by and see Rodriguez. Well, I didn't really *want* to see Detective Dillhole, but I wanted to know if he had any updates for me.

He was sitting at his desk when I showed up at his door. It was a shame he was so good-looking. His Mexican heritage looked good in the blues. *His mom must have been so proud of him when he made detective*, I thought wistfully, remembering her kindness. It felt like such a long time ago. Too bad he was unfaithful and so very full of himself.

"Mal." He slowly smiled, rising to his feet. "I didn't expect to see you here. Not that I'm complaining."

"Relax." I held my hands up, not wanting him to come toward me. "I'm not staying. I was just stopping by to see if you had anything new on Jeremy or Dessi."

"Unfortunately, no." Alex frowned, tucking his hands in his pockets. "Not since Dessi denied everything, we have nothing on him. We didn't find anything in Jeremy's empty car. There's still an APB on him, but if we haven't found him by now, he's lying low or left the area till things cool down. There's really not much we can do."

"Yeah, I figured but thought I'd check." I wrinkled my nose. "You could put a tail on Dessi and see what he's up to."

"We did initially, but, Mal, you know how it is. We can't follow him around forever." Alex put his hands up in surrender. "He'd call us in on harassment. He's got enough pull to cause problems. We don't need that."

"You mean *you* don't need that," I accused, eyes narrowing. I knew he couldn't realistically keep a tail on Dessi without compelling evidence, but it was satisfying to give him shit.

"Geez, Mal." He ran his hand through his thick black hair, gaze pleading. "Give me a break."

I rolled my eyes and turned to leave.

"I did call and check in with the Mennons earlier this morning, though," he offered. "Suzy seems to be doing good. Sure did hold up well for being underground so long."

"Suzy's a tough one," I agreed, turning slightly back, hand on the doorway.

"Nice couple, although the husband's a little nerdy." Alex grinned.

"Sam's great and never gave up on her." I leaned in to make the point. "He helped me find her."

"Yeah, for sure. I'm just saying he's a funny guy. Very smart, though," he backpedaled.

I rolled my eyes again. They were getting quite the workout today.

"It was nice to see you last night at Hungry's. I know the guys were happy to see you there."

I paused, not sure how to respond.

"Thanks. It was nice seeing everyone," I admitted, crossing my arms.

"I didn't say hi. Didn't want to ruin your mood," he said offhandedly, shrugging.

I had a bubble of emotion rise up but squashed it pretty quickly. I wasn't going to feel sorry for him. He'd screwed up our relationship, not me.

"Thanks for that." I raised my head a notch. I had lost some of my anger, though.

"It would be nice if we could be social with one another without biting each other's heads off," he said, watching me closely. He actually looked a little regretful.

"Maybe someday," I agreed, head tilted. "But not today."

I turned and left, this time without waiting for his response. I still wasn't ready to let go completely. Maybe I never would. I didn't let my guard down easily, and when I did, he'd crapped on it. Part of my anger was at myself for trusting him. Great, I was angry at myself because of him. *That's healthy.*

I left the station and found the Jeep, seeing her dark-green hood by the side of the road. I didn't have time to make it to Uptown before lunch, so I headed northwest instead.

Luckily, I pulled into the lot a bit early. Unlocking the back of the Jeep, I rooted around in the duffle bag I kept back there, finding a nice button-up shirt and a long necklace I was able to put on over my fitted V-neck T-shirt. The navy blouse was flowy and loose enough not to show the layers underneath.

I found a large statement ring to slip on my first finger and ran my fingertips through my wavy red hair. I tried to tame down the curls as best I could, to give me more of a sleek do instead of the running-through-a-wind-tunnel look that it currently had. I guess I shouldn't have driven with the windows down.

When I had done the best I could, I grabbed a tote I kept on my back seat, threw my keys inside instead of clipping them to my belt, and tossed my wallet in as well. I settled the tote in the crook of my arm, put my sunglasses back on, and adopted a slower, relaxed pace as I strode into Shallots Bistro to meet Dr. McSleazy.

I scanned the place, slipping my sunglasses on top of my head. I didn't see my lunch date in the dimly lit room but did see a bar, so I walked over and slid onto a stool.

The bartender raised his eyebrows and smiled. "Can I get you something?"

I smiled sweetly, cover already in place. "That'd be great, sugar! I'll take a Sauvignon Blanc."

The bartender nodded and pulled out a glass. I took note of the place a bit while he poured. It was a nice restaurant, a little fancier than I typically went for.

He slipped the drink in front of me. "Would you like a menu?"

"No, thank you." I smiled, taking a sip. "I'm meeting someone. He hasn't arrived."

The bartender nodded and returned to cleaning glasses.

I nursed the wine slowly for a minute or so until I saw the doctor's sandy-blond head come in the building. He had fine hair and wore it a little long so that it feathered where it parted and brushed across his forehead to hide the receding hairline. I could see him searching the interior for me, and a smile crossed his overly tanned face when he found me at the bar, glass in hand.

"I hope I didn't keep you waiting," he said, walking up to me.

"Oh, not at all." I smiled. "I only just got here."

"Shall we get a table?" he asked.

"Definitely." I nodded, laying cash on the counter for my drink.

Dr. Millwood gave the hostess his name, and she led us to a white linen-covered table. He held my chair as I sat down. I rolled my eyes to myself as he waited to scoot it in for me, then plastered on a smile as he came around to join me.

It was a nice place, the stone walls giving it an upscale feel. I scanned the lunch menu while sipping on my wine.

"Get anything you'd like," Dr. McSleazy crooned, waving a hand. "It's on me."

"Oh, aren't you generous," I purred, leaning forward while vomiting a little inwardly.

They had decent food options, and I settled on a grilled steak wrap and a side salad, while the good— uh, bad—doctor got the schnitzel sandwich. Leaning back, I toyed with my wine glass's stem.

"It's *so* good to see you, Doctor," I drawled.

"Oh, my dear. Please call me Edward."

"Edward," I said, smiling like it didn't curdle my stomach. "I've been just so excited about us working together. I can't wait to get started."

"Me too." Edward smiled, looking too smug in his black turtleneck and mushroom blazer.

I glazed over a bit while he went on and on about the weather, the traffic, and his intense knowledge of wine. I just kept smiling and nodding my head. This went on through the lunch itself until we were nearly finished. I knew business was generally conducted after the meal, but it was a stupid tradition.

"That's fascinating, Edward! It's obvious you are an accomplished man. I'm so glad to have found you. I would love to hear more about your incredible veterinary care." I nodded, eyes wide in appreciation.

"Well, Moll, it's not just veterinary care. It's personalized *medical science* based on the equine's specific DNA and blood type," McSleazy corrected me.

I hit a nerve with the vet comment.

"I can come up with the perfect mix of supplements to enhance a racehorse's performance.

Completely natural and legal, of course," he added offhandedly.

"Of course," I murmured in agreement. *My ass.*

"I can even guarantee the horse's improvement." He nodded emphatically.

"That's incredible." I put a hand to my chest.

"Have you and your husband decided on one yet?" he asked.

"Well, not quite," I hedged. Then brightly said, "Would you happen to know of any good racers for sale that would be good candidates?"

"Like I said, I can improve ANY horse," he boasted. "But I think I can come up with some good options for you if you'd like. And remember, my dear, *anything's* for sale if you want it enough!"

I squealed with excitement and rolled my eyes inside. He was playing right into the persona I was lying down. And it was disgusting. I couldn't believe people really talked like this.

"Can I ask with whom you've worked in the past?"

"I do take my client's confidentiality very seriously, but...let's just say I've worked with some of the big *families* in Chicago, those who have a long-standing interest in the grand tradition of horse racing." He all but patted himself on the back with his statement.

It sounded like he could be referencing Dessi, and I was relieved to find a tie to help firm up the Stand Up And Dance comment Suzy had heard.

"Yes, of course. So, once we decide on a horse, we hire you to get his supplements and training set up?"

"That's right. I have a standard contract, of course, but don't you worry about that." He grinned at me. "It's just boring legal paperwork."

"Sounds wonderful." I smiled. "And we'll have the best hands taking care of the newest member of our family!"

Dr. McSleazy gave a slight frown. "Yes, well, I do have a team helping support me. One of them is an outstanding young man, Ty, who is my physician's assistant. I've been grooming him, you understand."

"But I want *your* specialized care, Edward." I shook my head and looked sad.

"Oh, please understand you will be receiving only the *best* care and that I will be personally involved every step of the way." He oozed. "I have a very *hands-on* approach."

Ugh, shoot me now.

"Ty is my protege, you see. He's just so very much like me at that age. I've taken it upon myself to help him succeed in this business," Edward said, preening himself to the point of petting. "So I help guide him, and he gets the official sign-off. Just for establishing his own records, you understand."

"How very kind of you," I answered.

I was getting very tired of the charade, but since we were getting somewhere, I stuck it out a bit longer.

McSleazy talked more about his process, testing, and diet, but in the end, I didn't find out anything else on the matter. He promised to call me the following day with a few names of horses and contacts to investigate. I thanked him profusely, fussed over his kindness in paying the bill, and made my way to the parking lot to word vomit all the nasty things I wanted to say to him in person.

As I headed back to town, I made a shortlist of things to do. I needed to investigate Ty and find out why he was signing off on everything. Was Dr. McSleazy just the marketing guy, getting new business, with Ty being the brain behind the science? Or maybe there was something wrong with Edward's license to practice medicine?

My gut told me it was a third option, that the bad doctor was doing bad things and getting young Ty to put his name on it. I shook my head. I hated it when innocent people got bulldozed like that.

I could investigate the first two just to write them off, but I was betting pretty hard on the third option. I intended to go back to the office to look into this Ty guy, but on a lark, ended up swinging into the parking lot at Insideonline instead. It was the Jeep's fault; she was curious as hell. I patted her hood as I rounded the corner to walk up the steps of the office.

Chapter 15

I pulled my glasses off when I walked in from the bright sun to find a busy little office. The middle-aged receptionist greeted me, and I introduced myself and asked to talk to Paul Whitfield, the author who had written the articles about the fires.

A strained look came over her face at Paul's name, but she was polite when she directed me to the waiting area near her desk.

Picking up her phone, she spoke low and carefully into the receiver. Her brow furrowed, and she repeated her muffled noises, delivered more pointedly this time. I couldn't quite get what she was saying, but she ended it with a snap of the wrist as she plunked the receiver back on its cradle.

She lifted her head to me and said, "He'll be right out, Ms. Malone."

Sure enough, less than a minute later, a soft forty-something man with sandy hair came around the corner looking frazzled and tense.

"Uh, Ms. Malone?" he asked as if he was hoping I was someone else.

"Yes. Hi, Mr. Whitfield." I stood and held out my hand to shake his. "I just have a few questions if you have a moment."

He glanced at the receptionist, who just gave him a firm look over her glasses.

"Sure, yes," he replied, casting his eyes down to his feet. "I have a few minutes. We can go to my office."

I nodded, confused at the exchange, and followed him into a brightly lit room scattered with papers and clippings. Taking a seat in front of his desk, I watched him nervously shove his hand through his hair and pace a bit before he sat down.

Weird.

"Mr. Whitfield—" I was cut off before I could finish.

"I know what you're going to say, but it's my job!" he exclaimed, spreading his hands on his desk. "I report the news. It's what I do!"

"Okay." I nodded slowly, unsure what to say.

"Can you please tell your boss to stop sending people? I'm only avoiding you guys because I can't *do* anything for you! The article has been published. It's done!"

"Mr. Whitfield," I tried again, holding up a hand to stop him. "I believe you have me mistaken for someone else. I was not sent here by anyone."

Stopping suddenly, he frowned at me.

"Then, what do you want?"

"Look, Paul. Can I call you Paul?" I asked, trying to get him to relax. "I just wanted to ask you about the articles you wrote, covering the fires."

The pained look crossed his face again, and he rolled his eyes.

"I *told* you! It's my *job*!"

"I realize that, Paul," I said, frowning. "That's why I'm here. I want to know why you're the only paper reporting on it. Why they're not in the Tribune."

We both stared at each other expectantly for a moment.

"You're not trying to talk me out of writing the articles?" he finally said.

"No, I'm not. I'm glad you did," I said, still trying to reassure him. "Who's trying to talk you out of it?"

Paul slumped in his chair and ran his hands over his face.

"I'm not sure exactly," he replied. "I've had several visitors highly *encouraging* me to stop writing articles about the fire."

"Threatening, you mean?"

"You could call it that."

"Any idea why?"

"Well, I haven't quite figured that out, but they're very motivated about it." He gave me a wary expression. "Are you *sure* you aren't here to talk me out of writing any more articles?"

"I'm sure." I smiled. "I'm trying to figure out why everyone else *isn't* reporting on them as well."

"Well, for starters, probably the same reason they're trying to talk me out of it," he said, leaning forward, his voice lowering. "It seems, Ms. Malone, that we've stumbled upon something big."

"I would have to agree with you. I'm trying to figure out what that is. That's why I'm here." I leveled with him. "Whoever started the fires needs to be stopped."

"That's right!" he slammed a hand down on his desk. "If we don't report on the news, no one will know what's happening. That's what's really going on here. They're trying to brush it all under the rug. And I won't be a part of it!"

"Do you know why they're trying to cover it up? Or who 'they' are?"

"Not exactly."

"Well, what did they say to you about it?" I asked. "The people who tried to talk you out of it."

"Oh! I took some notes on it to figure it out," he replied, pulling out a notepad similar to mine. "But I can't quite connect the dots. I was approached after the first article came out on the fire. A young businessman in a suit. He told me his boss sent him to talk about the piece I wrote. He wanted me to retract it. He said it was impeding the arson investigation."

"Was he a cop?" I asked.

"I don't think so. He implied he was working with them, though."

"Fire?"

"Not sure. He didn't give me any personal information, not even a name. He mentioned the articles were giving publicity to the arsonist, which is what he—the arsonist, I mean—wants."

I leaned back in my chair, listening.

"It makes some sense, but freedom of speech, and all that!" he replied, throwing his hands up. "I told him I'd be more conscious of what details I published next time and sent him away.

"After the next fire, I received a phone call asking if I was going to write another article. I told the guy on the phone that I had to report the truth. Like I said, It's my job. They offered to make it worth my while. I refused them again and was told I would regret the decision. After that, a few other people showed up at the office, asking to see me. I rejected them at first, but they caused quite a scene, and Judy, the receptionist, told me to deal with my own mess. But I snuck out the back door and went home early."

Paul put his head in his hands. "Judy was so pissed when I came in the next day. I thought she was going to throttle me."

"Why didn't you tell security?"

"We're a small newspaper. We don't have security."

"In Chicago?" I asked incredulously.

"We have had to cut a lot of staff," he replied. "More and more people every year are subscribing to the Mighty Tribune."

I explained who I was and that I was looking into the fires and pulled out my list to compare with his.

"Have you talked to the other newspapers?" I asked.

"Yes, and they were very tight-lipped about it. Said they didn't know what I was talking about," he said, slumping. "I'm guessing they took the bribe. I only know of one article that was published by another paper, but then nothing."

"Do you know of other fires?" I asked.

"I heard there were others, but I don't know where or when." He shook his head. "I couldn't get any more details from my usual sources."

I sighed, trying to think of anything else helpful to ask.

"Are you going to write an article about this? Exposing the Tribune for covering up stories and being bribed?" I gestured to him.

"Well." He squirmed in his chair. "I'm not sure. It's one thing to write about something that people know is happening, but I'm afraid if I target the

Tribune, I'll really be in trouble. I don't know what they'll do. I don't have kids or anything, but my parents would be crushed if anything happened to me."

He looked at me, eyebrows drawn tightly together in worry. I wanted to judge him for not pushing more, but I got it. My path wasn't the same as everyone else's. But still, I expected more from a journalist, someone wanting to report the truth.

Thanking him for his help, I left my card for him to call if he needed anything. I wrote Jen's number on it, too, in case he wanted to report the threat and encouraged him to do so.

I tried to go to the office again, but the Jeep still didn't listen to me, and I found myself sitting in the police station parking lot in Uptown. I shrugged and headed inside to find Detective Harris.

The officers here weren't familiar with me, so I had to wait quite a while before I was walked back to an interrogation room to meet with him. I rolled my eyes at the formality.

It took several more minutes before Harris finally graced me with his presence.

"Sorry to keep you waiting, Miss Malone," he lied as he shook my hand and took a seat.

I raised my eyebrow at him. "Detective Malone," I corrected.

"Oh, right." He smiled, glancing at the papers he held. "My mistake."

"No worries," I lied.

"So, you wanted to talk about some fires?"

"Yes, about the arsons that have been happening around the city."

"We can't confirm they're arson at this time, you understand," Harris replied.

"I realize the investigation is underway," I conceded. "But surely, the link to the city-funded programs is no coincidence."

Detective Harris leaned back in his chair. "We're currently looking into every piece of evidence. I can't confirm any links have been made."

I was getting nowhere and fast.

"Don't you think it's just a little strange that every program was personally backed by Chief Sullivan?" I threw that fact out.

A micro frown crossed his face for a split second, followed by a bland smile.

"Miss Malone, I appreciate your dedication to this great city, but I think it would be best if you let the City Police handle this. I'm sure you wouldn't want to impede the process of investigation."

I was struggling to control my temper.

"But if you hear anything else, feel free to give me a call. Don't try to follow up on any leads yourself," he said, leaning forward to slide a business card across the desk."

"Gee, thanks, Harris," I said, taking the card. I was being excused. "Fuck you, too."

I stalked out of the office and the building, directly climbing in and slamming the Jeep door before I could do something that would cost me my license. Shaking internally, I took several deep breaths with my hands tight on the steering wheel. I try not to drive angry...anymore.

After envisioning my fist through his face, I felt much better and headed back to the office. But first, I swung through HERO for a cappuccino with cinnamon on top. I felt like rewarding myself for not shoving Harris's face into the table. Progress.

Chapter 16

I ended up bypassing the office for my apartment. I had lost track of time and nearly forgot about my date with Rhodes. Sighing, I glanced at my laptop with longing. I knew if I called him to cancel because of work, he'd probably understand, but it was a little late to do that at this point.

This was why I didn't date. I got too absorbed in my job for most guys. That was why things had worked so well with Alex—at first anyway. I sighed again at my disappointing history with men and went to freshen up with a quick shower. I had spent too much time in the company of slimy men to feel clean enough for a date.

I dressed a little nicer than normal in a deep-red flowing blouse and black jeans. I ran my fingers through my hair to loosen the waves, swiped on some mascara, and was ready to go.

Luckily, I was able to make it to Rhodes' house on time, but only barely. I hesitated in the drive, wondering what I was getting myself into. After a minute or two of indecision, I chastised myself for being silly about a simple date, shook it off, and swung out of the Jeep. I barely made it to the front door before it opened and a beautiful, broad-shouldered man leaned against the doorframe.

"I'm glad you decided to come in," he said simply.

I shifted, slightly uncomfortable that he knew I'd been sitting in my Jeep all that time.

"Sorry," I replied with a small shrug. "Like I said, I don't date often."

He opened the door wider, grinned, and headed to the kitchen.

I stared after him, confused. Shutting the door, I followed him in.

Rhodes' house was distinctly masculine, with large wooden and leather furniture, but also some slightly feminine touches. A candle here, a wreath there, sage-green and taupe walls. It made me wonder if a previous girlfriend, Mom, or sister had added the warm accents. A loft with a wooden railing looked over the living room from what I assumed were upstairs bedrooms. It was somewhat spacious for a brownstone.

He was cutting carrots and cucumbers for a salad when I walked into the kitchen. He nodded to a glass of red wine on the bar.

I picked it up and tasted it, nice and spicy, but not overly dry. Leaning against the counter, I watched him curiously. Rhodes had a denim apron on that said "I like it hot!" and was carefully chopping veggies and ignoring me, totally at ease in the kitchen. I suddenly realized he was giving me some space.

He glanced up at me as I sipped my wine, catching my gaze. Unable to help myself, I grinned and shook my head at him. He smiled back, wiping his hands on his apron, and turned to check a big pot of what smelled like stew. You know, if stew was the most heavenly scented aroma in the world. That kind of stew.

"Sorry I didn't bring anything."

He glanced up. "You brought yourself. That's enough." He winked and went back to his work.

Flirt.

"Smells good." I smiled sincerely. It was hard to not like him, with his easy smile and warmth. Not that I was *trying* to not like him. Really.

He stopped chopping for a minute to take a sip of his glass, finally shifting his attention directly to me for the first time. "I hope you like Guinness Stew."

"Definitely," I said earnestly. *So that's what smells so heavenly.*

Rhodes walked around the center island to where I stood next to the bar. My heart rate ratcheted up as he got closer, and I could smell his cologne, a woodsy leather scent that fit him. He stopped a foot or two away.

"You look really nice tonight," he said.

I tried not to squirm under the intensity of his stare.

"I'm really glad you decided to come," he continued.

"I told you I'd be here," I said, frowning slightly.

Rhodes tilted his head and lifted one eyebrow in a lighthearted challenge. "You considered calling to cancel."

It was my turn to lift an eyebrow. "So sure, huh?"

"Yep." He smiled.

"You're right," I admitted with a sigh.

"Like I said. I'm glad you decided to come."

"Thanks for going to the trouble." I motioned to the kitchen.

"No trouble. I enjoy cooking."

"Do you always cook at the firehouse?"

"Most of the time," he replied. "Course, cooking for a firehouse is a lot different than this."

"Bigger meal?"

"That, and I'm not trying to impress them," he said honestly, then turned to go check the oven. He pulled out a loaf of sourdough that had been warming and set it on the top of the range in a bread bowl with a towel to keep it warm.

"I think we're ready," he said. "If you want to grab your wine and the salad, I'll bring the bowls."

"Works for me," I replied, grabbing the big wooden salad bowl and following him into the dining room.

A scented candle sat in the middle of the table. It was a cedar scent that worked well in a man's house. The table was nice and big with a bench on either side. I slid in opposite from him, setting the bowl between us.

Rhodes tossed the salad and served us both generous amounts. It looked great, filled with blue cheese, chopped walnuts, and a lot of chopped veggies. There was a light vinaigrette on it that I wondered if he'd made himself.

We chatted a bit about the week we had. I told him a bit about Suzy, Sam, and the case. Well, what parts I could without betraying any confidence. A lot of the case had been on TV and wasn't confidential, so I could share that. Besides, Sam was so happy to have Suzy home he'd been sharing the news with everyone.

After the salad, Rhodes went to the kitchen and brought bowls of the stew, then went back to get the sourdough. It was strange having someone wait on me, but I appreciated the few moments to myself. Rhodes was a great guy, but I wasn't used to having anyone's full attention like that.

"Oh, Lord." I sighed, eyes rolling back. "This is even better than it smells if that's possible." The stew included bits of browned bacon, root vegetables, pearl onions, and large seared hunks of beef. The base had a nice Guinness flavor cooked down into the sauce. "It's really delicious."

"Thank you," he said, pleased, blowing to cool a bite of stew himself. "It's one of my favorites. Thankfully, it was still cool enough tonight to make it. Pretty soon, we'll be out of stew weather entirely."

"That will be a shame," I said around a mouthful.

"You'll just have to stick around till next fall, then, I guess."

I actually, genuinely liked the sound of that. It felt good and nerve-wracking at the same time.

"What will you cook when it gets warmer out?"

"I typically grill out when the weather is nice," he replied, pointing to the brick patio outside the dining room slider door. He had cracked it open to let the cooler air in, keeping the kitchen from getting too warm. "Burgers, brats, chicken, salmon, pretty much any meat. I have a decent smoker out there too."

"I love smoked salmon," I replied.

A slow grin spread onto Rhodes' face. "Next time, then."

"Sounds good," I replied. And meant it.

The wine and good food warmed and relaxed me a bit. I settled back in my chair as we swapped stories and laughed. Me talking about some of the crazier PI cases, and him talking about some of his wilder calls, leaving names out to protect the innocent, of course.

"Are you still going to look into the fires now that Detective Harris has ordered you not to?" Rhodes asked.

"Of course." I nodded. "Someone's got to figure out what's going on."

"It's probably just standard procedure for him to not share case details," Rhodes gently reminded me.

"Sure, I know that," I conceded. "But I could tell he had already looked me up when he came in the room. He knew my background working with the Department and could have made calls to vouch for me. He just chose not to give it any credit." I shook my head. "Some people just don't like outsiders."

"We get that on the job as well." Rhodes nodded. "Different departments, volunteer firefighters outside the city, it's all the same."

"And I'm really stuck on why the Tribune isn't publishing articles on the fires! Feels awfully shady to me."

"You would be surprised how much doesn't make the paper." Rhodes raised an eyebrow. "It's not just the fires."

"But why?"

"Well, sometimes it's just because there's more interesting news. Downtown events tend to outshine the suburbs, good or bad." He toyed with his empty wineglass. "Sometimes it has to do with politics and influence, and sometimes it's simple feuds between the paper or journalist and whatever they're reporting on."

I sighed. "I guess I get that, but this is bigger than that. Eventually, people are going to notice.

Besides, in this case, someone is threatening the journalists not to write the articles."

"Agreed. So it's not just a case of *better* news." Rhodes raised his fingers for air quotes around "better."

"And I intend to find out exactly what's going on," I stated matter-of-factly.

"I just bet you will," he replied, half smiling, watching me carefully, then he glanced down. "Just be careful, will ya, Columbo? I'm getting kinda fond of you."

I smiled, warmed by that. "I always do."

He nodded, satisfied.

"Want a cup of coffee?" he asked, standing up to clear the table.

"Have you met me?" I replied, laughing. I stood up to help and carried dishes into the kitchen.

Cleaning up, Rhodes pointed to the coffeepot.

"I got it ready if you want to hit the start button," he said.

"Thinking ahead. I like that," I replied, leaning over to hit the button.

Rhodes was mid-reach for a plate and brushed my side. He watched me but wasn't smiling. I looked at him questioningly. Taking a step to his left, he positioned himself in front of me, eyes level with mine. He breathed in and waited a beat, looking at me. Asking.

I stood still, unsure what to do. Or really, unsure what I *wanted* to do. He lifted a hand to trace the skin along my collar, then to my chin. He raised it a fraction of an inch, watching me the whole time. He was giving me space to stop him. Again, I didn't. Finally, I leaned forward slightly, meeting him halfway, and his lips lightly brushed across mine. It was a soft, gentle kiss that deepened slowly, ending all too soon.

Then he smiled and stepped back, returning to stacking dishes in the sink and wrapping the salad for the fridge.

I caught my breath and stood there for a minute, just watching him, surprised by the retreat.

"Do you take cream or sugar?" he asked, standing next to the fridge.

It didn't feel like a rejection, really. It was more like he was just taking his time.

"Just cream, please," I replied, clearing my throat.

Rhodes placed it on the counter and pulled out two coffee mugs to join it. Ladling the rest of the stew into a glass container, he set it out to cool on the counter.

"Have you talked to anyone at the Tribune yet?" he asked.

"Not yet." I shook my head. "Honestly, I'm not sure how far I could get there. I've tried to talk to them in the past and never got farther than the front lobby. I'll probably wait to see if I'm out of leads before I do that. I'll probably follow up with Paul again for more details on last night's fire. I meant to ask him what else he heard on the police scanner that didn't make the article."

"Last night?"

I nodded. "In Lincoln Park, on the outskirts. I followed it to find out what happened but didn't learn much except overhearing some talk about insurance. I have a few questions to follow up on." I leaned against the counter to wait for the coffee to finish brewing. "I may go see Sully again and get his take on it."

"How did that go?" Rhodes asked, wiping down the counters.

"Well, I stopped by, a couple of days ago, to find out more about the fires." I nodded, checking the coffee. Almost done. "You were right, though. He didn't give me much to go on. Only talked about the community projects a bit. They all seem like good causes. Still can't quite figure out who would want to ruin them."

"I agree. That community center was doing good work."

"Course Sully disagrees that the Tribune is covering up the stories, and tried to dissuade me from following that lead," I said blandly, rolling my eyes. "He seems to think it's just because Downtown isn't concerned about a little fire in Bricktown. Why would he be covering for them?"

Rhodes shook his head. "Sully's a good guy, Mal. I don't think he's covering for them."

"But we do know someone is pressuring Paul to withhold articles. And the guy at ALC said Sully was helping with political red tape. Between all that and how he avoided my questions, it all just seemed a little shady to me."

"He works with the city officials, so he gets involved in politics from time to time," Rhodes replied, looking down at the sink and frowning, then up at me. "I'll admit that he acts a bit like a politician sometimes, but he isn't a bad guy; It's part of the job. I really doubt Sully would be pressuring the papers to withhold articles."

I wasn't sure what to say. I was still investigating it for myself.

"Is Sully one of those leads you're looking into, or are you just reaching out to him for information?" Rhodes asked, turning to lean back against the counter. "I mean, are you asking other people *about* Sully?"

"It's a lead," I said, half shrugging. "I have to consider everything. I'm not trying to implicate him or anything. I'm just asking questions with an open mind."

Rhodes considered that a minute. "Questions can get people talking." He shook his head and stepped closer, watching me intently. "Sully and my uncle went through the academy together. I know him. He's a good guy."

"I'm sure he is, Rhodes." I looked at him, head tilted. "I appreciate your take on it, but I have to find out for myself."

"It sounds like you've already made up your mind, Mal." Rhodes crossed his arms. "You could cause problems for him, especially as a white-shirt, a manager. If people start to think something's up—look, that kind of questioning gets Internal Affairs investigating, and they don't stop until they find *something*."

"What if something *is* up?" I asked, trying to reason with him.

"Not with Sully, Mal."

"Okay," I replied slowly. "I'll be careful who I ask what. I will pay more attention to how I conduct this investigation. But, Rhodes, you know I can't just assume he's not involved."

"Mal," he said. "It's not even a real investigation. You don't have a case."

I stepped back. "Not a real investigation? Just because I don't have a paying client doesn't mean it's not a real investigation or a real case." I didn't like where this conversation was heading. "Something is going on here. In our city! A police investigation is going on right now anyway. Apart from mine."

"And they're not doing a good enough job?"

I took another step back, bigger this time. "Really?" I bristled, good mood gone. "Are you implying I should sit back like a good little girl and let the *real* police officers handle it? I was told that once today already, and it still doesn't sit well with me."

"That's not what I meant, Malone. It's just that you don't have to be the one managing it. I'm sure the police have it."

"The police didn't have Suzy," I argued. "Good thing I didn't just sit on my hands for that one. I know what I'm doing."

"Do you?" Rhodes asked. "How much do you know about the fire-service politics?"

"I don't really care about politics," I countered. "I care about the city and stopping these fires."

"I don't like politics, but they do exist. I'm staying on the suppression side of the fire department, and not the management side, because I don't want to deal with them, but they exist nonetheless." Rhodes spread his hands wide. "If you're going to work with politics, you need to understand them."

I could see where this was going. "That's why I'm asking questions, Rhodes. I'm trying to learn and find out what's going on." I moved to get my jacket, disappointed at the change of tone, his earlier jovial attitude gone.

"I think I should head on out," I said, slipping into it.

Rhodes stood there watching me, eyebrows furrowed. He nodded tightly. It appeared he was fighting with himself, but he didn't reply.

I nodded, thanked him for the nice meal, and headed out.

I sat in my Jeep for a minute, gripping the steering wheel. I was frustrated at his insistence to take his word on Sully when everything was screaming that his superior was hiding something. I was pissed he'd questioned my abilities. I also didn't like that it mattered so much to me. I hit the steering wheel. *Damn it!* I was also pissed because I missed out on coffee.

Well, that was one situation I could manage. I let the Jeep drive me where she liked to go best: Grounds.

Chapter 17

Luckily, by the time I got to my favorite coffee shop, it was getting late and only a few patrons were left in the building. Maurice looked up from wiping down the counters.

"Hey, Mal! Having a good evening?"

I gave him a grimace.

"That good, huh? Tell Mo all about it." He patted the bar over where the barstools sat.

"Eh, not much to tell," I hedged. "Dinner date that ended badly. Big surprise."

"You went on a dinner date?" He grinned from ear to ear. "With whom?"

I fidgeted a bit. "A local firefighter I met the other day."

"From the fire down the street?"

"Yep."

"Really?" He stopped, frowning. "And why haven't I met him yet? Did you take him to another coffee shop?"

"How did you know I had coffee with him?" I replied incredulously.

"It's you, Mal. Of *course*, you had coffee with him before agreeing to a dinner date!" Maurice shook his head, laughing, his salt-and-pepper side part bouncing with the belly laugh. "Tell me the coffee sucked, and I'll forgive you."

"Of course it sucked, Mo!" I chuckled, bad mood forgotten. "It was like drinking dirt."

Mal winked at me, sliding across a perfectly crafted cappuccino. "That's my girl."

I sprinkled on a smidge of cinnamon and readied myself for the first sip of a perfect cup of coffee. It didn't disappoint.

Mo didn't ask me anything else about Rhodes, and I didn't offer it up. He knew I'd say something if I wanted to. Instead, we talked about my previous case with "the pizza guy."

At closing time, I settled up with Mo and headed out. Some people sit at a bar late at night. Most of the time, I was sitting at a coffee shop—if I wasn't working. Yep. I was a real party animal.

The ever-present road noise hit me when I stepped into the cool night air. I raised a hand to Mo, who was locking the door behind me. Zipping up my jacket, I juggled a to-go cup of coffee. One couldn't have too many, *am I right?*

I noticed a black car pull up in front of me— between me and where my Jeep was parked. I glanced back to see Mo had already disappeared into the back office. Sliding my hand into my jacket pocket, I wrapped it around my ASP expandable baton. The passenger car door opened, and a large man wearing a business suit stepped out.

"Detective Malone?" the man said, not quite asking.

"Who wants to know?" I said, widening my stance. I glanced around, but didn't see anyone else on the street.

"My boss would like a word with you." He nodded to the back seat.

I took a step back, and the man put his right hand on his suit jacket lapel, angling it slightly. I could see the butt of a gun. *Crap!*

I didn't give away the ASP I was clutching, but it wouldn't do much against a gun. I glanced at the parked car to my right. I was next to the passenger door, not quite close enough to make a dive for it to hide behind.

I stood there, weighing my options, when a voice came from the car.

"Malone, I would like to speak with you but a moment." The disembodied voice didn't sound malicious, but still. A threat had been made.

I didn't have much of a choice in the matter, so I made nice and walked to the car door, peering in.

"Would you please join me?" A palm patted the seat next to the dark figure.

I put a hand on the hood, glaring at the brute who had moved to shove me in. He backed off for a second, so I slid into the car. The door immediately locked. *Double crap!*

"Thank you for agreeing to speak with me," he said with the friendly smile of a politician, his perfectly pressed suit completing the picture. It looked expensive, not that I knew much about suits. But it looked cut to fit well.

He looked vaguely familiar. He was large, like the brute in the seat in front of me, but with less of a stomach over his belt. His graying hair was combed back, slick. He wasn't unattractive, really, exuding an air of power that was hard to ignore.

I glanced at the door and raised an eyebrow.

"Sorry about that. I won't take up much of your time," he continued in the most nonthreatening way, as if I had a choice.

I watched him dubiously.

The car pulled away from the curb, and my eyes went wide, going to the handle reflexively.

"Just taking a trip around the block." He smiled. "I wanted to personally thank you."

My eyebrows went up in blatant surprise. "For what?"

"For proving my son's innocence, of course." He chuckled.

It took me a beat to put it together. "Marco?"

He smiled appreciatively.

Holy Jesus, this man was Domenico Poggiali. As far as I knew, he was the patriarch of the Poggialis. I took a deep breath, face draining of color. I knew working with family members could be risky, but Marco seemed like such a normal kid. It was easy to forget who his father was.

"I appreciate both your investigative skills and your appreciation regarding the sensitivity of the issue." He nodded, no longer smiling. "Our family's reputation and name are very important, you understand. If others doubt our honor in a business deal, well, it doesn't end well."

I nodded, still not saying anything that would change his mood.

"Detective Malone, is it?" he asked.

I nodded again.

"I understand you also discovered Shelly's hand in all of this?"

I went still, unsure if he was upset at me for outing his sister.

"I very much appreciate your stealth in that as well." He shook his head. "Shelly has been a bit spoiled; I will admit. I thought she'd do well with Peter, him being such a kind soul, but it seems he's been too soft with her."

"He said he was going to have a talk with her," I said. I didn't want him angry with Peter.

"Oh, he did. Not to worry." Domenico chuckled. "He made her apologize to the crew and quit the comanager sham. Good boy! How I would have loved to have seen that."

I smiled a bit and waited for him to continue.

"What it comes down to, Detective, is that I am in your debt."

"Oh, no." I shook my head, not wanting any tie to the mob. "Peter paid me fairly. We're square."

"Nonsense." He shook his head. "When someone helps one of mine, I take care of them. Now, what can I do for you? I could offer you a job. I'd be happy to have someone like you on retainer."

"I really don't need anything," I stammered. "And thank you, but I am busy enough anyway." I really needed to get out of the car before I got roped into something.

"Well, how about I owe you one, then?" he replied. "If you get in a jam, you give me a call."

"I can definitely do that." I nodded, grateful.

"You know, if you need somebody *taken care of* or something," he added with a wink.

I blanched visibly, and he burst into laughter.

"Oh, you are a peach, Bugsy," he said amid laughter.

"Bugsy?" I sputtered out, then mulled on it. "Oh—Bugsy Malone." I rolled my eyes, then thought better of it and glanced at him.

He was still chuckling at my expense.

"Relax, will ya? I'm just offering you a favor." He gave me a friendly smile. "Honestly, though. I sincerely appreciate your aid in this matter. Marco's name is saved, Shelly's indiscretion has remained private, and my family is in your debt."

I nodded. "You're welcome, sir, but honestly, I would have done the same thing even if it wasn't your family. No offense."

"No offense taken. I appreciate your honesty and that you didn't try to use it as leverage. That's why I'm personally thanking you. Now, you remember my favor and call me if you ever need anything."

We pulled back up next to the Jeep, and the *probably*-bodyguard opened my car door for me. I looked back at the scarily powerful man next to me.

"And call me Dom, please." He smiled, holding out a hand.

"Call me Mal." I smiled back, shaking his hand.

"Oh, I don't think I will, Bugsy." He winked a second time.

I got out, and Bruiser handed me a business card with the name Domenico scrawled across it.

They pulled away while I stood there, frozen in the middle of the street, holding the business card in one hand and my coffee in the other. I shook my head in disbelief.

Just then, Mo opened the front door of Grounds, locking it behind him.

"Hey, Mal," he said, tilting his head. "Whatcha doin' still hanging around? You need something?"

Palming the card, I turned to him. "Nope. Just took a bit of a walk."

I waved goodbye and got into the Jeep, gulping down my cooling coffee in an effort to jump-start my heart.

What a day, I thought and headed home.

Chapter 18

The following morning, I headed into the office, once again a little tired from the night before. I had stayed up late, searching for news on the Lincoln Park fire. In the end, the only article I could find was Paul's.

The headlines in the Tribune were regarding legalizing marijuana and a new tollway. *Yep, definitely bigger news than a measly fire.* I rolled my eyes.

But when I pulled up to the building, I noticed the Sentinel Security van parked outside. I slammed the Jeep door. After last night's surprise visitor, I was less than excited. The same security guys who had been at the Mennons' house were sitting in the front seat. They waved and nodded toward my office building. I hurried up the steps, worried about Suzy and Sam.

Opening the outer door, I was surprised to find the hallway empty. It wasn't until I walked to my office that I saw them, Wyatt, Suzy, and Sam, waiting in the reception area. Apparently, Wyatt had let himself in.

"Just make yourself at home," I said, head cocked. My voice dripped with sarcasm.

He just shrugged, unapologetic. "Safer inside."

I rolled my eyes and turned to the Mennons.

"Everything okay?"

"It's so good to see you, Mal!" Suzy moved to hug me.

Her sweet smile was too contagious. Any irritation I had drained away, and I leaned in to hug her back.

Sam moved to hug me, too, and I halfheartedly sighed. *What the hell...*and hugged him too. It was a regular hug party in my office. I wasn't sure what it was about these two, but they had certainly gotten under my skin.

"Everything okay?" I asked again, looking from Suzy to Wyatt.

Wyatt nodded.

"Sure, everything's fine," Suzy said. "I just had to get out of that house. I wanted to see you."

"I would have stopped by if you'd have called," I replied. Someday, I'd get a receptionist.

Wyatt looked over at the two, eyebrow raised. It looked like he had indicated the same sentiment to them.

"I was going to call you today anyway, but this works. I checked out that lead. I found out a Dr. Edward Millwood has *Stand Up and Dance* on 'specialized supplements.'" I used air quotes. "I met with him, pretending to be in the market for a horse."

"Really!" Sam crowed. "You went undercover?"

"And all I did was sit around at home." Suzy sighed.

I thought about Dr. McSleazy and waitressing, smelling like pizza every night.

"Not as exciting as one might think," I murmured.

"Still, it has to be kind of fun," Sam prodded.

"It has its moments." I smiled. "But then there's the bookkeeping and trying to pay taxes and figuring out what to do with a 1099 form."

"That's just a miscellaneous earning form, silly." Suzy laughed at me. "You just have to log it into your Schedule-C as income."

I looked at her like she had two heads. "That's it? Then, why don't they just say that?"

Suzy laughed again. "Hey! If you won't take money to keep looking into the case, let me help you out with the bookkeeping!"

"You'd want to work out of the house. For now, at least." Wyatt jumped in finally.

Suzy waved her hand. "That's not a problem. I can do it wherever."

I told her I'd consider it, and I meant it.

"Boys, why don't you let us girls have a moment?" Suzy shooed the guys out of the room.

I stopped her, indicating my office off the lobby. We could speak privately there instead.

Settled in my office, she sat down and leaned forward, elbows on my desk.

"Now, spill. What's going on? You're stressed."

"I'm stressed?"

"Definitely." She nodded. "I mean, you were before. You work too many hours. But something else has happened since then."

"Something else?" I thought back, considering. Turns out, I had no control around Suzy; I spilled like a broken mug. "I had a crappy dinner date, then was approached by the mob. Maybe something like that?"

Suzy just blinked

"Huh. I was thinking more like a bad haircut."

I frowned and touched my wavy hair. It was a bit unruly today, but it wasn't that bad.

"Tell me about the guy." She settled down, grinning.

"The bad date? *That's* the one you found interesting?" I was in disbelief.

"It's always about a guy," Suzy said, waving her hand.

"You really don't know me." I shook my head. "It's nothing, really. Just a date that went bad."

"Went bad?"

"Yeah, it started out good. It was going really well, actually. Then it took a turn for the worse, and I ended up leaving before coffee."

"What happened?" She frowned sympathetically.

"Well, he tried to get me to stop my investigation into a fellow firefighter."

"He's a firefighter?" Suzy's eyes went wide. "Tell me more!"

My eyebrows drew together. She really was adorable. "Yes, and I think the assistant chief may be behind some of these fires we've been having. I've been looking into it. Doesn't all make sense just yet, but there's something there."

"And he doesn't think it's the assistant chief?"

"Nope, says he knows him, and it couldn't be him. Doesn't even want me to ask questions. Could cause a stir." I held up my finger. "Best part is that he questioned my looking into it at all and said to let the police handle it! Like I wasn't even qualified or capable."

Suzy gasped, and I felt validated. Surprised, I shook my head. What was I turning into?

"What's his name?" Suzy asked.

"Rhodes, Marlon Rhodes," I replied. The words just kept coming out. I'd never had a friendship quite like this. "He works over in Bricktown."

"How'd you meet him?"

"I wandered into the fire over in Roscoe Village when I was frustrated by the lack of leads on your case."

"Was it love at first sight?" She sighed.

"Not exactly." I laughed. "But I'll admit he did look good out there. I ran into him again at Mariano's, and we got to talking."

"It wasn't with Sam and me either." She waved it away. "No worries. I fell for his charm soon enough."

I smirked at that. Sam, full of charm? But I guess he did have a likable nerdy quality to him.

"Oh, don't look at me like that." She raised an eyebrow. "Sam may be eccentric, but he's the sweetest guy ever!"

"And he loves you like crazy." I smiled.

"Yes." She grinned back. "He does. Me too. We've been through a lot together. But when you find the person it clicks with, well, it just works."

It was getting a little sappy, even with Suzy's own brand of charm.

Probably time to get on with my day. I stood, telling Suzy I would let her know what I found out from McSleazy and hugged her goodbye. *Hugged?* I was really getting soft, I thought, shaking my head.

I didn't like the growing feeling of regret I had around Rhodes. It's not like I had forgiven or forgotten what he had said the night before, but I couldn't get over how bad I felt about the whole thing.

Chapter 19

After they left, I got online and tried to use my search engine to find the owner of the license plate from the fire, but didn't have any luck. I really didn't want to call and ask Jen for help. Harris had already made it clear I should leave the case to the professionals, and I didn't want to put her in a bad position. I hoped he hadn't given her too much crap about giving me his name.

Pulling out Dom's card, I considered calling in my favor. I was certain he had a way to run plates. But I wasn't so sure I really wanted to go down that route. It could just tie me deeper to the family. Probably better to just let it ride. I tucked the card into a spot at the back of my drawer. Just in case.

My phone buzzed on my desk.

"Hello?" I answered.

"Moll!" came a voice dripping with hair grease and plastic.

"Hiya, Doctor!" I replied, slipping into my guise. "I'm so glad you called!"

"Miss me already?" He preened.

I vomited, metaphorically of course.

"I have the name of a couple of horses I think you'd be interested in, but really, there's one in particular I would recommend."

"Ooh, I'll definitely want your recommendation," I oozed with phony excitement.

"*Black Magic Fever*," he announced triumphantly.

I remembered seeing that name on a plaque in the horse barn. I also remembered the couple arguing near it. I wish I could have heard what they were upset about.

"Sounds mystical. I love it!"

"I had a feeling you'd like it," he preened. "The horse has already been winning races, but the owners have decided to sell."

"Why are they selling if the horse is winning?" I asked.

"Maybe they needed the money," he answered, brushing me off. "I don't know, really, but the horse isn't doing nearly as well as he *could* be. I could give him *real* potential. I already talked to Mr. Baird, and I think you can get a good deal on him."

He gave me Mr. Baird's number so I could contact him to inquire about the sale, and I promised to follow up soon.

After I got off the phone, I went to the bathroom to wash my hands. Creep.

I made a pot of coffee and sat back down to look up the regulations on drugs and horse racing. After a couple of hours of good research and several cups of coffee, I found out that racehorses were thoroughly tested for a wide range of performance-enhancing substances and the list expanded all the time.

There was a zero-tolerance policy, and racing authorities took it very seriously. I wondered how McSleazy was getting away with his "supplements." Maybe it was a new drug, not yet identified. I also tried to do more research into the doctor but found nothing new.

I considered going over my books again and pushed away from the desk. I had been sitting long enough. I needed to get out of the office. It felt like I was circling the drain on this case. My leads weren't going anywhere concrete.

Soon, I promised myself, picking up my phone. Might as well follow up with Mr. Baird first.

"Hello?" He answered on the third ring.

"Hiya!" I kept my persona up. "I'm Moll. Dear Dr. Millwood gave me your number about that beautiful horse, *Black Magic Fever.*"

"Oh, yes!" Mr. Baird perked up. "Give me a moment while I go into my office. Okay, sorry about that. So, you're interested in buying a racehorse?"

"Oh, definitely," I assured him.

We talked a bit about lineage, and Mr. Baird gave me a dollar figure.

I didn't know much about it, but it seemed a little low to me, especially for a winning racehorse.

"Sir, excuse me for asking. But can you tell me why you'd want to sell him?"

There was a pause on the phone.

"Well, it's just the right thing to do right now for our family," he replied. "We have some family issues we're dealing with. Better to not have to worry about a horse in the mix."

"Oh, I get that." I nodded, even though he couldn't see me. "Let me talk it over with my husband and get back to you. Give us a little time to think it through."

"Well, don't sit on it too long," he pushed. "I can't exactly hold it, not at that price."

"I completely agree," I promised. "Thank you."

I still didn't know how I could get the owner of the license plate, but at least I had a connection to someone working with Dr. McSleazy. Maybe I could find out why they were selling or what they were arguing about.

I climbed into the Jeep to see where she would take me today and found myself pulling into the parking lot at News-Star, one of the other local papers for some of the neighboring burgs. I patted the hood of the Jeep; she always took me to interesting places.

I wasn't sure which reporter would have covered, or *not* covered, a story like that, but since a paper like the News-Star was fairly small, I just asked to speak to whoever covered the police and fire articles and told them I had a story idea to pass along.

The receptionist gave me a calculating look and told me to sit down. A few minutes later, a slim blonde woman edged around the corner. She was mid-to-late twenties and looked more than a little nervous.

"Hello." I introduced myself because she didn't look like she was going to. "I'm Mal. Do you handle police and fire?" I smiled to put her at ease.

"Uh, yes?" she answered with a question, wringing her hands slightly. "I'm Erin Stone."

"Is there anywhere we can talk, Erin? I just had a news story idea I wanted to run past you." I smiled again, reaching out to shake her hand.

She looked at the receptionist, then down to an empty hallway with a windowed meeting room. She pointed to it, the receptionist nodded, and I followed her in.

I was getting a little suspicious.

"You have a story idea?" she repeated back to me, sitting down slowly.

"Yes, in fact, I do," I replied. "But I also wanted to talk to you about the fires we've been having."

Erin shot back to her feet. Bingo.

"Easy," I said, standing as well, my hands raised to appear less threatening. "I have no agenda here. I just have a few questions."

She remained standing, eyeing the door.

"I can tell something happened here, but I assure you. I am not those people."

Considering me, she slowly sat down on the edge of the chair. I had a suspicion she would bolt if I made any loud noises.

"Then, what do you want?" she asked.

"I know you published an article about a dumpster fire a while back, but I'm wondering if there were other fires in the area that you *didn't* write an article about."

Her face blanched, so I added, "I know Paul over at Inside-Booster was threatened. He's a friend of mine."

Erin's eyes widened. "Is he okay?"

"Right now, yes," I assured her. "He's not taking many visitors at the office."

She nodded. "Mary is helping me out front. She's on the lookout. But since I haven't written anything, I haven't gotten any more visitors."

"Who came and when?" I asked.

"I can't tell you that!" Erin's voice rose. "I promised."

"Can you tell me why they came?" I prodded. "Was it because of the dumpster fire?"

"No," she said, shaking her head. "I don't think so."

She looked around the room and out the window to the hallway, considering.

"Someone came by to ask about an article I was writing on a fire in Edgewater," she finally said. "They said they had insider information for me. Naturally, I was interested.

"But they didn't want to give me any information at all. They threatened me, like Paul." She spread out her hands to explain. "I have a daughter at home. She's two. I can't risk her."

I nodded, understanding. These guys had to be stopped. It wasn't right, pushing people around like that, threatening their kids.

"Did they say anything specific?" I asked.

"They said I couldn't talk about it to anyone," she replied, leaning forward, voice lowered. "And that I wasn't to report on any fires for the foreseeable future."

"Just fires in general?" I asked.

"Any fire, any community center, or anything condemning the mayor."

"The mayor?" I frowned. *That was new.*

She nodded. "And I haven't."

I knew she wasn't going to give me anything else, so I thanked her.

She nodded her head but stayed seated, looking too nervous to move.

When I walked through the lobby, I noticed their newest paper sitting on the coffee table and picked one up. Dessi was smiling back at me on the cover.

Startled, I asked the receptionist if I could have the copy. She nodded, and I headed back to the Jeep. Once there, I flipped through the article. It was on the Arlington Racecourse and the most recent wins. It was a generic piece on the season and the upcoming Derby party next month. But most interesting was the picture on the cover.

Fabian Dessi was standing with his arm around a winning horse. According to the caption, it was *Black Magic Fever. Curious and curiouser.*

Meanwhile, in a heavily guarded and technologically advanced fortress,

"Heya, Suz?" called Sam, face buried in his computer.

"What's up, hon?" Suzy replied, coming around the corner.

"I found some info on that doctor Mal was telling us about." He pointed at his computer.

"Really, what did you find?" She leaned over his shoulder.

"Well," Sam said, rubbing his hands together. "Dr. Millwood used to specialize in sports medicine. Sounds like he was trying to expand his career with athletes by using DNA testing and therapy. He was trying to find some venture capitalists at one time, not sure how that worked out, but it seems he was trying to break into a niche market. He got in trouble for using drugs without proper trials. There were some charges against him, and his license was suspended."

"What happened?" Suzy asked, her eyes rounding.

"Well, nothing really. That's what's weird. The charges were dropped, and his license was reinstated, but there's no record of anything happening. And now, all of a sudden, he's working on horses, but I'm not finding his name tied to any of their veterinarian records."

"Sam, you're a genius!" Suzy said, wrapping her arms around his shoulders from behind his chair. "You've got to call Mal!"

"Wait, you haven't heard the best part." He grinned.

"What's that?"

"I found his name in one place online recently, but only one." He held up his index finger.

Suzy leaned forward expectantly.

"On the list of doctors who manage the drug testing for the racehorses."

Suzy's eyes went wide, and she grabbed the phone to dial Mal.

My head was spinning by the time I got off the phone with Sam. It looked like the doctor was cleaning the records for "his" horses. I bet this was why he was using his "physician's assistant" Ty. The poor kid was probably signing off on everything the good for nothing doctor was doing. If they got caught, he wouldn't take the fall.

Dessi was such an ass. Dr. McSleazy was a bad guy, sure, but Dessi played at being a good guy, and I was sure he was orchestrating the whole mess.

Sam had really impressed me. I knew he was good with computers, with his successful business and all, but he was also good at putting together important information. Research was a different skill.

I decided to run out and get a late lunch, stopping by home instead of Mariano's today. If I was being honest with myself, it was because I didn't want to run into Rhodes. *Good thing I wasn't.*

Entering my apartment, I dropped my keys in their spot and watered my dead ivy. I still had some cold coffee sitting, sadly dejected in Mr. Bunn, so I set to warm it in the microwave while I pulled out some lunch meat, eggs, and an avocado half. It was a quick, easy meal.

I ate at my kitchen counter, between slugs of burnt coffee. *I really needed to get a life.*

My cell rang. I glanced at the name to see it was Jen.

"What's up?"

"Mal! Just calling to see when you'd be free for lunch," came my friend's voice.

I glanced at my empty plate. "Just finished eating."

"You just now ate lunch?" Jen said in disbelief.

"Yep, eggs," I replied, smiling.

"Yuck." I could hear Jen roll her eyes. I'd seen it enough.

"Eggs are good," I said defensively. "And good *for* you."

"Eggs are breakfast food."

It was my turn to roll my eyes.

"How about tomorrow, then?" Jen asked.

"Can't," I replied, slugging more coffee. "I'm in the middle of hot leads."

"Well, I'm going out of town this weekend to see my folks. My grandma's getting a knee replacement, and I told my mom I'd come help out for a few days."

"That's nice of you," I replied. "How about next week? I could probably do Monday."

"Monday's good. We can go to Cuba 312 for ropa vieja. It's been forever since we've been there."

My mouth drooled at the thought of Cuban food even though I had already eaten.

"Sounds great." We decided to meet at noon, and I wished her good luck on the weekend.

"I heard you talked to Officer Harris," Jen said before I could end the call.

"What an ass," I interrupted.

"Sorry about that," Jen apologized. "I didn't know he was going to be like that."

"No worries," I reassured her.

"I've never actually met him myself," she insisted. "I'd have warned you had I known."

"I believe you, Jen," I said. "It's really not your fault. Some people are just jerks."

"Anyway, you should stop by the bar again sometime, too. The guys really liked seeing you," Jen said. "I did too."

"It was fun," I agreed, not pleased that I would eventually have to coexist around Rodriguez. Great, now I had two people I was avoiding. But it was worth it to see Jen and the guys. "I'll try to," I promised and hung up.

Chapter 20

I drove back to the office to do more research there, just to be available if someone wandered in needing a PI. I needed a new case. I didn't quite have the time, but I could use the cash flow.

Sitting at my desk again, I jotted down all the notes I had on Dessi and Dr. McSleazy. I needed to get the doctor on tape saying that he was the mastermind behind Ty. I also needed to get him to implicate Dessi. Otherwise, McSleazy would hang and Dessi would walk, yet again.

I called Dr. McSleazy back and scheduled lunch for the following day, grateful I had left it open just in case. This time, however, I'd be wearing a wire. If I could just get him to repeat most of what he'd said at our first lunch and dig into the Dessi aspect a bit, I'd be set. Now that I had the newspaper, I had reason to bring him up.

Pulling up some of the articles on the city programs, the ones Sully had been supporting, I finally noticed something I had missed before; the mayor was also supporting them. It made sense, being a city-sponsored program. But something about how chummy he and Sully looked in the pictures online had me curious. I wondered what the story was there.

I had no trouble finding articles on the mayor. The Tribune had several glowing pieces on him. It only made my suspicions grow even more.

Making another pot of coffee at the office instead of walking over to Grounds, I thought about a way to find a tie between the Tribune and the mayor.

I tapped my pencil against the desk. Frustrated, I tried shifting cases. If I could run the license plate, I could at least follow up on that lead.

Duh!

I smacked the heel of my hand to my head, cursing myself for not thinking about asking Sam earlier. Picking up my phone, I called him.

"Hello?"

"Hi again," I said. "You know, Sam, you really are a researching rock star."

"Thanks, Mal!"

"I bet you could find anything online," I said, crooning.

"Alright, alright." Sam laughed, getting my angle. "What do you need?"

"Well, I have a license plate number…"

"Hold on while I hack in!"

I laughed, shaking my head.

A few minutes later, Sam had a name for me: Jermaine Lewis.

"Uh, Mal?" he said thoughtfully as I jotted the name down.

"Yeah?"

"I also found an article here about Jermaine that I think you'll be interested in, but I think you'll want to read through it yourself. How about I email it to you?" Sam asked.

"That'd be great, thanks," I replied, hanging up.

I chuckled as I checked my computer. Sam really was a funny guy, but he was a good person, too. His email had already popped up in my inbox, and I settled back into my chair to look through it.

The article talked about Jermaine Lewis, who had been arrested the previous year for violently attacking James Koch, current mayor of Chicago. It didn't really say why he had attacked him; all it said was that it was unprovoked. Jermaine was arrested on assault and battery and sentenced to six months.

Huh, there's the mayor again, I thought, tapping my pencil once more.

There was a picture, so I was able to confirm Jermaine's identity. I was pretty sure he was behind the incidents; I just wasn't sure why.

All I had on him was that he was at the scene of the last fire and that he had assaulted the mayor last year. The mayor was also backing the community programs, which were getting burned. Maybe he was targeting the sites to get at the mayor. I nodded, considering. *Yes,* that felt good enough to go on for an arrest. Or at least to take him in for questioning.

I looked back at the email Sam had sent. Sure enough, he had also included a current address and phone number for Jermaine. *Sam, you beautiful man.*

I debated calling Harris but decided he didn't deserve to get this one. And probably didn't want information from someone who was obviously not competent enough to handle a case. I was certainly not calling Rodriguez, and Jen would suggest including him. I hoped she wouldn't be too mad.

I picked up my phone as I headed out the door. It took me about thirty-five minutes in the afternoon traffic to get across town. Officer Jill Mathews and her partner were already waiting at the curb when I arrived. I hadn't seen her since the fire in Roscoe Village, but luckily, she remembered me when I called.

I had filled her in on the way here, giving her what info I had and my suspicions on the mayor and Sully. Thankfully, she had agreed it was enough to take Jermaine in for questioning. As a police officer, I knew she'd be careful to accuse a government official or a city employee without just cause.

We approached the door cautiously. Mathews knocked as I stood to the side. Her partner, a tall older guy, went around the back in case he made a break for it.

Jermaine answered on the second knock, took one look at the two of us, glanced at the police car by the curb, and said, "It's about damn time." He just turned, shuffled back into his house, and plopped down into an old recliner.

It looked like he had been sleeping; a tall beer sat on the side table next to him. Several empty ones piled on the floor around us where we walked in.

Looking up at us through bleary eyes, he said, "You can have the guy around back come on in, too."

I frowned.

"There's always a guy around back." He shrugged.

"Jermaine," I said. "Do you know why we're here?"

"Of course I do," he replied, looking at me like I was an idiot. "Will my arrest make the paper?"

I glanced at Officer Mathews, who nodded.

"Arrests are public record," she replied. "They're all listed."

"But the arson story?" he said. "Will it make it? Was it big enough?"

"You started the fires just to make the paper?" Mathews replied incredulously.

"I don't think that's quite what he's saying," I answered. "Jermaine, why don't you fill us in."

He nodded at me. "It all started last year." He teared up a little. "My little girl, just three years old, was accepted at the new preschool that had opened up in Near North Side. It was a big deal, the new school, geared towards people with learning disabilities and all. My little girl, you see, was a little developmentally behind. Just in reading, but it was enough to get her some extra help."

He looked up at us and pointed. "She wasn't dumb, mind you. She was born prematurely. My wife had trouble carrying her." He swiped at his eye with his thumb. "She's gone now."

"Your daughter?" I asked.

He nodded. "Yes, both actually. My wife left after she disappeared. She couldn't take the pain."

"Disappeared?" I asked again.

"She was kidnapped. My baby girl was kidnapped from that school." His eyes flashed in anger. "They opened too fast, trying to make a timeline, and didn't have security in place!"

He rose from his chair. "The cops never found her. They tried, but they never did." He began to pace around the room. "The story was kept out of the paper because of him."

"Because of who?" Mathews asked.

"Mayor Koch, of course." He turned on us, pointing. "He kept it out of the paper because it was his baby, the first big community project he had worked on. Didn't want the bad publicity. He's trying to make a name for himself to get re-elected."

Mathews and I glanced at each other.

"What about Sully—Chief Sullivan? How does he play into this?" I asked.

"Sully?" Jermaine replied. "I don't know who that is. But it's the Mayor's fault she's gone. He backed it. He signed off on it when it wasn't ready. They hadn't even finished installing the security system! No buzzers on the door, no badge access like they have today.

"Mayor Koch hired friends to do work for the city. Friends that are paying him well. He's also taking money for passing on business licenses," he continued.

"Do you have proof of that?" Mathews asked.

"Well, no, but I know he did it," Jermaine said sharply. He was getting agitated.

"It's his fault my wife left, too." He turned and collapsed back in his chair. "She couldn't take the stress. Couldn't take me when I lost it."

"So, you attacked the mayor?" I prodded him.

"Yes, and I paid for it, too," he replied. "*He* was the one who took everything from me, and *I* was the one who went to jail. It's his turn to pay."

"Why did you start the fires, though?" Mathews asked. "You could have hurt someone."

"I didn't want to hurt anyone," he mumbled, hands on his face, rocking a bit.

"I think he was trying to get in the paper, expose the mayor for what he did with the preschool. Make him look bad," I told Mathews. "But the Tribune wasn't publishing on it, and the reporters for the local papers were being threatened to keep quiet."

"I didn't know about the threats. I didn't know why they weren't publishing. Figured he was paying them off," he replied, coming back into the conversation. He looked at us, eyes wide, a little crazy. "There's some kind of conspiracy going on here with the Tribune!"

Mathews appraised the room. "We'll get to the bottom of it, don't worry, Mr. Lewis."

"You can arrest me. Shit, I don't care what happens to me, but my story *has* to make the paper!"

"We need to get you downtown, and you can give your official statement." Mathews moved to take Jermaine in.

"You need to promise me my story will make the paper," Jermaine continued, voice rising.

"Mr. Lewis," Mathews said. "Arrests are public record. Your story will be in the paper regarding the fires. But I can't guarantee how much of the connection with the mayor will make it."

Jermaine started to get violent, waving his arms around. I stepped back to let Mathews and her partner restrain him. I wanted to give him some kind of reassurance. I was pretty sure I had enough of a story to get published, but I didn't want to lie to him.

"Jermaine," I said, putting a hand on him. They had handcuffs on him and were heading him to the front door. "I'm working on it, okay? I've been looking into it."

Jermaine gave me a hard, measured look. Finally, he nodded and allowed himself to be led outside and into the cop car. Not like he had a lot of other choices, but I was glad he went willingly.

Getting into the Jeep, I put my hands on the steering wheel. I had found the arsonist, but I didn't feel much better. The fires would stop now, but the mayor was still guilty of signing off prematurely on the school, and other corners had possibly been cut in other projects. Jermaine's daughter hadn't been avenged. I prayed we'd be able to implicate the mayor.

Chapter 21

At the station, Jermaine detailed the fires he had started, including a few that didn't make it to the papers. Those were ones outside of the burbs Paul covered. The dumpster fire in Edgewater was his work as well, from when he was just learning about accelerants. I was glad Officer Mathews let me sit in on the investigation. I had given her the tip, but it was an "unofficial" case.

Jermaine showed remorse over shutting down so many good projects aimed at helping people and was glad to hear some of them had plans to reopen. I really think losing his daughter and his wife broke him somehow.

Mathews called in Harris, who arrived sometime during the questioning. I got the absolute dirtiest of looks from him, which I found profoundly satisfying. He directed his questions to the accused, ignoring me as much as possible.

After Jermaine signed off on his official statement, I made my way out of the office. Harris took over the case, and Mathews hung back with me.

"We don't have any hard evidence for a warrant on the mayor yet," she said. "The judge won't want to cause the publicity stir until we're sure."

I raised an eyebrow. She had been in that office with me, hearing Jermaine's statement. There was no way he was lying.

"I know, but you know how it is," Mathews replied, shrugging.

I nodded. "So, what's the next step?"

"Business permits are public property. We're pulling them now. If they have the mayor's name on them and show the proper security measures weren't checked off, then we should have enough. We'll talk to Paul and the other reporters, too. See if we can ID who threatened them."

"Perfect. Let me know if I can help with anything."

Walking out of the station, I pulled my phone out.

"Hello," answered Paul.

"Have I got a story for you," I started, a little swagger in my step as I made my way to the Jeep.

I laid the entire story out there for Paul, as much as I knew of it anyway. He listened intently, only interrupting me for a few questions here and there. I could hear him scratching down notes.

"So, you want me to publish a story against the mayor?" Paul asked breathlessly. I could hear the panic forming in his voice.

"What do you think should happen?" I asked him, trying to keep my promise to Jermaine. I didn't have to follow the same protocol as the police. It was a little insurance in case the evidence didn't materialize.

"Well, yeah, I agree." Paul struggled to speak. "But should it be me?"

"It's the story of a lifetime." I dangled the carrot. "The Tribune can't ignore that. Just imagine the publicity you'll get."

Paul mulled it over for a beat. "But what if they come back? They've threatened me before."

"When you're ready to publish the story, you can call this number." I rattled off Officer Mathews' line. She had given me permission to pass it along to Paul. "You'll have a tail for a few days, just to make sure no one comes calling."

Paul eventually acquiesced, and I was smiling as I climbed back into the Jeep. I felt a little better, knowing this case, official or not, was finally getting wrapped up.

Just then, I saw a blonde head in the parking lot, hands on hips. *Crap.*

"Hi, Jen." I waved, getting back out of the Jeep.

"You didn't call me," she accused. "You called Mathews? Why?"

Double crap.

"Jen." I sighed. "I'm really sorry. I just figured you'd insist we bring Rodriguez in on it. And I'm just not ready to work with him."

Jen wavered a bit. "Well, Rodriguez *is* the detective on duty."

"See?" I said, eyebrow raised.

"Yeah." She squirmed a bit. "I guess. But you could still have told me about it."

"I was planning on it," I promised. "I just had a few loose ends to tie up first. I'll make it up to you."

"Okay." She smiled suggestively. "I guess I'll let you do that."

"What do you want?" I asked, knowing that tone in her voice.

"You can buy me a drink." She smiled triumphantly, cheerfully swinging into my Jeep. "I just got off shift. To Hungry's!" She raised a fist in the air.

"You know we can walk there," I said, pointing across the street.

"Yeah, but you're here. You can drive." She smiled.

I climbed back into the Jeep. She had won, and I was off the hook. *Works for me.*

I just hoped this time the evidence wasn't destroyed before it could be collected.

Hungry's wasn't quite busy yet, so we had a few minutes to catch up over a drink. However, it didn't take long before a few of the other boys in blue joined in, all fresh off shift.

I was a little disappointed but not terribly surprised when I saw Rodriguez saunter in. I was still nursing a celebratory tequila with lime when he approached. My muscles immediately tensed.

"Heard about the big bust," he said, leaning in. "Why didn't you call?"

I swiveled around; no way was he going to stand at my back.

"Now, why would I do that?"

"You probably didn't know it was Harris' case," he said.

I shot a short glance to Jen, trying to keep the edge of my mouth from inching up.

"But I don't know why you didn't call Jen and me," he finished, looking slightly hurt. "It would have been a good arrest. And you know us. How do you know Mathews?"

"I ran into her at the fire in Roscoe Village. We're practically old friends," I elaborated. Thankfully, Jen wasn't as self-promoting as the man in front of me. She liked evidence and wasn't trying to make rank.

I finished my drink and gave her a hug.

"Gotta go. Still have some planning to do tonight." I stepped around Rodriguez.

"Thanks for the drink." Jen smiled, doing a little happy dance in her seat. She was obviously pleased with herself.

I laughed, shaking my head at her.

Rodriguez looked back and forth, confused and put out that he wasn't in on the conversation.

I settled for a nod at Rodriguez and headed back out the door. *Look at me being a well-adjusted grown-up.* I hadn't even made any snide remarks.

Settling in at home for the night, I spent the rest of the evening getting my surveillance equipment ready for lunch the next day with Dr. McSleazy.

The morning was much warmer than usual, and I took the time for a long run, glad I was able to forgo my winter gear. I had enough time for a few weight exercises when I got back before showering and heading out for the day.

I had another long blouse on, with black leggings this time. I really hated slacks; they were so difficult to run in. Thankfully, the current legging craze gave me another option. I slipped my feet in some comfortable but dressy black flats. Heels were out of the question when I was working. It wasn't worth the risk if I had to make a quick exit.

I had time to stop by Sam and Suzy's house on the way out of town for a quick update. I wanted to thank him for his help in finding Jermaine Lewis and let them know how it all worked out.

The ever-present van was in place, but with new faces today. It took a minute to explain who I was. They had me wait until Wyatt came to the door to clear me.

"Morning." He nodded, letting me in.

"Morning." I nodded back.

"They're in the kitchen."

I walked in to see Brian sitting at the computer again. I was pretty sure it was Brian. I gave him a friendly smile as I walked through.

Rounding the corner, I found Suzy frying eggs and bacon while munching on a piece of toast. She was wearing her yoga pants, probably just finishing her own workout. Sounds of Elton John's *Crocodile Rock* mixed with the frying food filled the room with a comfortable air.

Sam sat at the table, still in his robe, nursing his coffee. His hair stuck up in all directions.

"Good morning, you two!" I waved, smiling at them.

Suzy waved back, smiling and moving her hips to the music. Sam simply grunted.

"He's not a morning person," she explained, winking, and gave her husband a sweet smile. "He stays up late, working on his computer."

Suzy left her stove for a moment to give me a hug.

"Coffee?" she asked, pointing to the pot and mug stand.

"Always," I replied, grabbing a cup and filling it. "Thanks." It tasted like heaven, more specifically, like Lavazza Armónico, based on the slight hazelnut note. I sighed in pleasure, glad I hadn't added cream. It was perfect this way.

"What's up?" Suzy asked.

"Just wanted to update you two," I said. "I'm on my way to lunch with Dr. Millwood. I'm trying to get evidence on him, hopefully enough to implicate Dessi as well."

"Do you have backup?" Wyatt asked from the doorway.

I turned, not realizing he was still in the room.

"Not really. It's just lunch." I shrugged, explaining. "I've had lunch with him before."

"But you're wearing a wire, right?" He frowned. "You'd have to be if you were trying to get anything solid."

"That's right," I replied, fighting to not adjust my top. No way could he have seen it. I had it well hidden.

"You don't have someone on standby at least?" he continued his questioning, arms folded.

"Um, no," I hedged. "I don't have a partner. But I don't expect any trouble."

Wyatt shook his head and pulled a card from his pocket. He walked to me to hand it over.

"Take this," he said. "Call them before you go in, let them know where you're going and when you think you'll be done."

I took the card, looking down at it. It said Sentinel Security: Wyatt's business.

"Thanks," I said.

"If you get into trouble, just hit redial. I have a few guys in different burgs scattered around. Depending on where you're headed, it's likely someone could get there pretty fast. If they don't hear from you, they'll come looking or send the police."

"I appreciate it," I replied sincerely. "I'm headed to Skokie."

Wyatt nodded. "Yeah, I've got guys near there today. Shouldn't be a problem."

I considered Wyatt. "Why are you offering to help?"

I wasn't stupid or stubborn enough to turn it down but wanted to know if I was setting myself up to owe him a favor. I didn't mind paying it back, but I needed to understand the deal and timing. If I was balls-deep in a job, I wanted to give it first priority.

Wyatt raised his chin towards the Mennons. "It's part of their case. Which means I am invested. I always take my work personally."

I nodded, satisfied and grateful for the extra help. Taking your work personally wasn't always a good thing in this line of work, but I couldn't say anything. I did it myself. I slid the card in my back pocket.

"Thank you for your help yesterday," I said to Sam. "We were able to arrest Jermaine Lewis as the arsonist in the neighborhood fires. He admitted to everything. Signed statement and all."

Sam perked up. "Really? I helped get a bad guy off the streets!" He looked to Suzy, who came over to kiss him.

"Nice work, honey!" she said. "You too, Mal. I'll bet it feels good to put a stop to the fires."

"It does." I agreed. "But it's not quite wrapped up. There's something else going on there, with the mayor. Jermaine was targeting his community work to draw the focus to him and some shady business deals. The fires were Jermaine's way to force awareness, nearsighted as it was.

"With the arrest and publicity, I'm hoping the police will be looking deeper into the mayor. In the meantime, I'll continue to as well."

Sam nodded, thinking. "That's the reason for the assault charges."

I nodded.

"There was nothing written about why he attacked Mayor Koch."

"No. The Tribune doesn't seem to be publishing anything negative on the mayor. And the neighborhood papers have been pressured not to, either. I haven't found out if the Tribune got the same pressure, but they're a much larger business. It would be harder to threaten them. You'd think they'd love the opportunity to expose a rotten public official."

"Especially in Chicago," Suzy added.

"Exactly," I agreed. "So, I'm not sure why the Tribune is withholding articles."

"Probably a political motive," Sam said.

"Maybe," I agreed. "But one this large must have something big behind it."

He nodded thoughtfully, still nursing his coffee.

I finished mine and thanked them before heading out, promising to let them know how things went at lunch.

Wyatt nodded to me, letting me out the front door.

"I already talked to the guys. They'll be expecting your call."

I nodded my thanks in return and waved at the new guys in the van on my way out.

Chapter 22

Walking into the restaurant—the same one we met at for our first lunch—I scanned the room for Dr. McSleazy.

I had my wire on, double-checked to make sure it was recording on my phone app. Jim with Sentinel Security had answered my call from the parking lot. True to form, he had been expecting me and confirmed he had team members in the area, on standby, if needed. I had let him know I'd be about an hour at the most and that I'd call back when I got out.

People had my back. It was an unusual feeling for me, at least for the past few years. A little uncomfortable, but I liked it. Suzy had even sent me a text on my drive over. All it said was "Good Luck!" but it made me smile knowing someone was rooting for me. Such a sweetheart. I would do anything I could to protect her, which meant nailing Dessi to a wall.

Seeing the doctor wave at me from a table, I made my way over to him.

"Dear! It's so great to see you again," I crooned, leaning in to give him an air-kiss.

"The pleasure's all mine, I assure you," Dr. Millwood preened. "But you're spoiling me, allowing me your company twice in one week!"

I played at batting at him with my napkin as I sat down. "You're such a flatterer."

I laid the napkin on my lap and regarded the menu, making sure I was turned toward him, ensuring clean audio.

"I hope you don't mind taking the time away from your important work," I said. "It's just that I really wanted to get your opinion on *Black Magic Fever*. And I hoped we could talk over the details of your business once more. Get a plan in place."

"Of course, my dear!" He leaned forward and gave me a slimy smile.

Gross.

"Did you talk to the owner yet?"

"Yes, I spoke with him yesterday." I nodded. "And I think we can come to an agreement on a price, but I just value your opinion so much."

Dr. Millwood gave me a look like the cat that ate the canary. He smoothed a hand over his wispy hair and settled back in his seat.

"I do have intimate knowledge about the horses at Arlington Track," he explained. "*Black Magic Fever* is no exception. I can guarantee his performance will increase under my *personal* care."

"And it will be *you* taking care of him, correct?" I asked, prodding him to talk about the arrangement with Ty.

"Oh, yes, of course." He patted my hand on the table. "Don't you worry yourself."

Dammit.

"But you mentioned an assistant," I said in concern. "I was worried he would end up being the one treating my new baby. Something could go wrong if he's in training!"

"Oh, please, don't worry your little head about that!" The doctor frowned. "It's all under control. I guarantee it will be me, not my assistant. Although Ty is in training and I am molding him to be an excellent physician. I am with him *every* step of the way.

"You may see his name on emails or records now and then, but you have my assurance that I'm overseeing *everything*. There's not a drop of medicine, er, *supplements*," he corrected, "that will be given without my express permission. You have to trust me on this."

Satisfied he had given me enough to clear Ty's name when this all went down, I sat back in my chair and nodded sagely at him.

"Thank you so much. I feel so much better. I'm so glad I ran across you that day at the track," I mused. "Whatever would I have done?"

"I am the lucky one," Dr. McSleazy said, patting my hand.

I smiled and moved to take a sip of water, suddenly wanting to wash my hands.

When the waiter finally arrived to take our order, we asked for salads, and I listened to him expound on his prowess with the horses. Boy, did he like to talk about himself.

After we got our food, I let him continue, asking questions a bit now and then, just to keep up the conversation. It didn't hurt to go along with the evidence for the case. Eventually, I tried to find a good way to drop Dessi's name into the conversation.

Toying with my salad, I said, "I forgot to tell you the other piece of news I had!"

He looked up expectantly.

"While I was out yesterday, I noticed a local paper with an article on horse races." I leaned over excitedly. "You'd never guess who was on the front cover!"

Dr. McSleazy leaned back in his seat, chuckling patiently like to a five-year-old child.

"I can guess, but you tell me."

Patronizing asshat.

"It was *Black Magic Fever*!" I finished with a flourish, struggling to maintain my phony playful exterior.

"I did tell you he'd been winning races, my dear," he cajoled. "You'll find that even more commonplace once you're the new owner. Particularly once I'm managing him."

I eyed him discreetly. He was so full of himself. I couldn't wait to give this guy his due. And I had solid evidence on him. *Now for Dessi.*

"But do you know who was in the picture next to him?" I asked, eyes wide. "Fabian Dessi! He's quite well known in the betting world." And beyond, I thought but didn't add.

McSleazy stopped in the middle of his self-congratulations to watch me closely, then used his napkin to dab at his mouth.

"Yes, well, he is known for betting on the strongest contenders," he offered, less enthusiastically. "I would assume anyone who spends as much time at the track as he does to have *some* knowledge of which horses are in good shape."

He exculpated him so completely I was trying to decide if he disliked him or if he was just trying to divert the conversation.

"Do you know him?" I asked, still pouring on the excited-school-girl act.

"Well," he hedged, clearly trying to decide how to reply. "You can't be around the racecourse without encountering Mr. Dessi at one point or another."

"He's somewhat of a celebrity," I added, pressing on his vanity.

"True," he chuckled, pausing again. "We are a bit familiar, you know. Mostly swapping horse stories." He brushed lint off his sports-jacket lapel. "He has valued my opinion from time to time, to be honest.

"But I assure you," he continued. "I am very discreet about my client and business confidentiality."

I nodded sagely. "I would never think otherwise, Doctor."

Taking another sip of my water, I watched him finish his salad. He didn't offer any other information on Dessi. I had to be careful I didn't push this too far.

"I'm not surprised, though, that he values your opinion. Well, I'd bet you know just about all there is about horses."

"Oh, you flatter me, my dear." He smiled but didn't argue.

"It's just amazing that Mr. Dessi doesn't have horses of his own and that you aren't working with him as well."

"Oh." He eyed me directly. "You know I wouldn't be able to tell you. Even if I was."

"Ooh." I pretended to be impressed. I knew that, publicly, Dessi didn't own any horses at all. Likely due to a conflict of interest, since he runs the offtrack betting shops.

I toyed with my lunch a bit more. "Well, just so you know. I would be happy to do business with him as well. If the opportunity ever came up."

I glanced up to find Dr. McSleazy eyeing me too carefully.

"I'm not quite sure what you're implying," he said, head cocked and eyes narrowed. "I didn't say I was doing any business with Mr. Dessi. I simply said we spoke from time to time."

Crap. I probably pushed a little too far. It was like walking a tightrope. I had to take some risks.

"Oh, I didn't mean to imply anything," I hastily covered up. "I just always try to keep an eye out for good opportunities."

"It would be very unethical for me to be giving out leads." He steepled his hands in front of him. "Unless you were suggesting that games are somehow *fixed*. And I very much doubt that someone like Mr. Dessi would be resorting to that sort of information."

I'll bet, I thought, but replied, "Oh, Doctor, I want you to know that I would *never* think you'd do anything like that! You spend all your time helping others." I widened my eyes in my best Bambi impression. Holy cow, this was getting deep fast.

McSleazy was still watching me a little more intently than I liked.

"I never got your last name," he finally said. "You know, when I was talking to the Bairds, I could only give them your first name, Moll."

He chuckled a bit, but his smile didn't make it to his eyes.

Time to go.

"I'm sorry, dear." I tried to regain the previous ease. "It's Cameron," I lied easily. It was a name I used now and again.

"And you and your husband"—he lifted his voice at the question—"are looking to buy the racehorse?"

"Oh, yes, of course," I reassured. "My husband, Walter, and I have a new interest in racing. He's a bit older than me, you understand. The races are something we can do together."

"So, he's gone with you to see races at Arlington?" McSleazy pried further.

"Well, yes, once or twice," I replied, thinking fast. "But he'll be joining me more once we get *Black Magic Fever.*

"Speaking of Walter," I continued, checking my watch. "I really need to get back. We have an appointment this afternoon. So sorry to rush!"

I had trouble reading the doctor as I fumbled with some cash.

"I've got it." He brushed my money away.

"Well, thanks so much, hon." I rose to go. "I'll be calling soon."

He stayed seated, watching me leave.

Crap on toast. I was pretty sure I had blown my cover. I definitely gave him a reason to doubt. I made my way out to the lobby and checked my phone. I was still within the hour I gave Jim. Hurrying out, I made it to the Jeep before the doctor could follow me.

Once there, I stopped my recording and saved it, sending it to my email just in case. Then, I called in to let my backup know that everything was fine. I may have put my cover at risk, but I got some good dirt on Dr. Edward Millwood and some implications towards Dessi.

Pulling out of the parking lot, I headed back towards Roscoe Village. I called the Mennons on my Bluetooth to let them know how the meeting went.

"Everything all right?" Sam asked, tension in his voice.

"Definitely," I replied. "I may have blown my cover, but I think I got some good evidence. I have Millwood and enough to clear Ty if it comes down to that."

"That's good," he agreed. "But anything on Dessi?"

I could hear I was on speakerphone.

"Nothing hard," I admitted. "But I did get him to talk about him. He indicated some shady dealings, but when I pushed harder, he turned the conversation on me and started asking questions."

"Oh, that's not good."

"No, but at least I got some of what I came for," I replied. "I can still try to follow Millwood to get stronger evidence on the Dessi tie."

"Did you check for a tail?" came Wyatt's voice.

"Yeah, I was paying attention," I promised. "Nothing."

I heard Wyatt grunt in reply. He was a man of many words.

"I'll send you guys the tape and see what you think about it. You may hear something I didn't."

"Thanks, Mal," said Suzy's voice.

"No problem. I'm going to head back into town and see what I can dig up on Dessi's wins."

"I can look too," Sam promised. "See if there are any owners related to the Dessis."

"I was thinking that, too." I grinned at Sam's line of thinking. He was a natural.

"One more thing," Sam stopped me before I could hang up. "It's just that after you left, I couldn't quit thinking about Mayor Koch."

"Okay?" I asked, curious.

"So I did some digging," Sam explained, obviously proud of himself. "The Tribune's newspaper editor, Arthur Blake, was a lead supporter of the mayor's campaign. He's from a wealthy family. The Blakes have had political ties for the past few generations at least. It looks like Arthur significantly helped to fund Mayor Koch's campaign."

"Holy crap, Sam!" I exclaimed. "Did you hack his financial records?"

"Uh, no," Sam said dejectedly, then explained. "Campaign contributions are public record."

"Oh," I said, relaxing. "I had no idea."

"But still, I knew where to look," Sam rebutted, trying to regain my good impression.

"That's great work, Sam." I smiled. "You're becoming quite the detective."

"Yeah?!" Sam asked excitedly.

"Most definitely."

Chapter 23

I made a left and used my voice command to dial Mathews' number.

"Hey, Mal," she answered.

"Hey, yourself." I was feeling pretty good after wrapping up the business with the fires and getting some solid evidence where Dr. Millwood was concerned.

"It's a good thing you called. I have some news for you," she offered. "We pulled the business licenses, and at least two of them have solid evidence that Mayor Koch was signing off without all the inspections being completed. One of those being the security for the school, which is a requirement for all schools. There are some other questionable items, but those are the strongest. We have enough to get a warrant and to bring him in for questioning."

"That's great work," I congratulated her. Satisfaction filled my chest that justice was being done.

"Well, Harris got the physical warrant, but he's letting me stay on the case."

"Good enough." I smiled, pulling into my office parking space. "I'm sure Jermaine will be pleased to hear the mayor will answer for his part in this."

"Yes," she agreed. "It's a bit bittersweet, to be honest. Meeting destruction with destruction."

"Agreed. Not really the ideal situation." I nodded, disconnecting from my Bluetooth and walking into the office.

"They put him into psychiatric care. From what we can tell, he wasn't like this before the incident with his daughter. I think a little extra help will go a long way for Mr. Lewis."

"I'm glad to hear that," I replied sincerely. "When you're working through your investigation, you should check the mayor's campaign funds. Looks like Arthur Blake, the newspaper editor at the Tribune was a heavy supporter."

I knew she'd just pass the news along to Harris, but that was okay with me. I'd rather he hear it secondhand.

"Really? Well, that would explain why he's never had the bad press other mayors have experienced."

"And the reports of the fires as well," I agreed, sitting down. I leaned back and crossed my feet on my desk. "It's bad publicity after all of those donations. I wouldn't be surprised to find out that the mayor was behind the threats to the other local newspapers."

"We've got someone looking into that," Mathews promised. I could hear her shuffling papers in the background.

"So, did you find anything connecting Chief Sullivan?" I asked.

"Honestly, no," she replied. "I mean, he definitely supported the projects, but he wasn't physically on the board. Chief Sullivan's involvement centered on fundraising and networking. He did a lot of public-awareness work. They were using the mayor as a figurehead for city support, but the chief was seen as one, too, just because he was such an active supporter."

She paused. "Look, Mal, I know you were looking for a connection there. But there doesn't seem to be one. Sorry to disappoint you."

I put my feet on the ground and sat up. "I wasn't looking for a connection," I stammered. "It just seemed shady. It looked like there was one."

Had I been looking for a connection? I knew a few things didn't quite feel right, but I thought I was keeping an open mind. Wasn't that what I'd told Rhodes?

"Isn't it a bit odd, though, that Sully—I mean, Chief Sullivan—has been involved in the same work Mayor Koch worked on."

"Not particularly," Mathews explained. "Sullivan has a passion for outreach efforts on the fire department. It's an auxiliary function he runs. And the mayor has been actively trying to influence the polls for re-election."

I winced. I had a bad feeling that I had been a little quick to jump on a lead. It wasn't like me to not probe a little deeper into someone's background before I judged them. The worst part was that it looked like Rhodes was right about Sully and I had pushed harder to prove my worth as a detective. I was just so tired of people thinking I wasn't competent.

My dad never thought I could hack the academy, and he'd nearly been right. Part of the reason I dropped out wasn't just because I wanted to get further away from Rodriguez. I liked to blame him, but part of it was because I thought I was taking a harder path, doing it on my own. If I could do this, I could prove to everyone that I made it because of me. Despite my gender or family affiliation to the force.

I leaned an elbow on my desk and propped up my temple.

"Anyway, we're still digging through the evidence," Officer Mathews continued. "If I find anything different, I'll let you know. But we're not actively pursuing a connection."

"I understand. Thanks for staying open-minded," I replied. "I'm starting to think maybe I haven't."

"Eh, we all do at one point or another. It just depends on what you do from now on that will shape you."

"I'll definitely be more open in the future," I promised. There was something else I could do, too. But that was a lot more unpleasant than simply admitting it to Mathews and myself.

"I would anticipate a hearing will be scheduled in the near future to look into this issue and the other projects as well. Because of this turn of events, we put Paul in protective custody. His article is being published tomorrow morning."

"Thanks for doing that," I said, sitting up. I was glad Paul would be safe from retribution.

"There's a good chance he'll need to stay there until the investigation is over, though."

"How does he feel about that?"

"He's excited beyond words." I could hear the smile in Mathews' voice. "Something about good publicity."

I chuckled a bit, happy to hear Paul had gotten his scoop. He deserved it for fighting to publish the truth. At least things had worked out for some of the people involved. Jermaine would be getting the help he needed, and it sounded like the mayor was getting what he deserved.

There was just one more thing to do. I sighed, pushing up from the desk. I really didn't want to do this part. Grabbing my keys again, I shoved my hands through my hair, probably sending it in all directions, and stalked determinately out the door.

For all my decisiveness at the office, my resolve started to wane when I turned my engine off in Bricktown and sat, staring at the fire station. I weighed my options, but even if I weren't trying to fix this thing that had developed with Rhodes, I would probably come and apologize. It wasn't about fixing what had broken; it was about doing the right thing.

It was enough to get my legs to swing out of the Jeep and walk up to the fire station door. The young firefighter who opened it up gave me a big smile.

"Rhodes here?" I asked. I had already swung by his house, but he wasn't home. That would have been easier, less public, but I wanted to get it out of the way. Some things, you just don't do over the phone.

He nodded and hollered Rhodes' name over his shoulder.

I saw a familiar bald head and broad shoulders lean out from a room to the left. The smile on his face dropped a bit when he saw it was me. I swallowed hard, feeling even worse.

Rhodes walked toward the door; a hand towel draped over one shoulder. He must have been cooking dinner. He gave the firefighter a look that made him slide past and into one of the back rooms, giving us privacy. Approaching, he eyed me in a curious way that wasn't altogether welcoming, but not quite reproachful.

"Looks like you're busy with dinner," I hedged, a little unintentionally.

"A bit. Everything okay?" He filled the doorway, wiping his hands on the towel.

"Yeah." I shifted on my feet a little. "I just need a minute. If you have it."

He gave me a long look. "Sure," he said and stepped out the door, motioning towards the bench out front.

I walked over but didn't sit down, turning to face him, hands twisting. Forcing myself to stop, I dropped my arms to my sides.

"We got the arsonist," I started.

"That's good news," he replied, giving a short nod. He didn't sit down, either. "I'm relieved to hear that. We can use fewer fires in the area."

He was still giving me a polite look. It wasn't exactly a good thing. Rhodes *never* gave me a polite look. Gone was the playful banter and suggestive glances. Gone was the easy way he carried himself. It felt like he had shut an invisible door between us.

Well, it didn't matter, really. I needed to do this, even if he didn't forgive me.

"It seems the arsonist was trying to frame the mayor, to expose some mismanagement that led to the loss of his daughter. They're continuing to find questionable actions to look into." I waved my hand in the air. "There's more to the story than that, but that's the gist of it."

"Okay," Rhodes said, tilting his head, arms crossed. "So what brings you here?"

My heart sunk a little more.

"Well, to set the record straight." I straightened and looked him right in the eyes. "You were right. There's been no connection found to Sully. Even though I had them look."

"You had them look?" he asked, frowning.

"I felt there was enough pointing in that direction," I explained. "But I was wrong."

I could tell Rhodes was trying to decide what to say. His jaw was shifting like he was chewing his words.

"Somewhere, I lost sight of maintaining an unbiased opinion. It's important to look at facts and make assumptions in my line of work," I tried to get him to understand. "But I climbed the decision ladder too quickly. Some of my opinions were unfounded."

"I appreciate you telling me," he finally said. "I'm glad Sully's name is untarnished. He's a good guy and doesn't need the bad press."

"You're right," I agreed.

"But I am still a little surprised you suggested the cops look for a connection without further evidence." He raised a shoulder. "I thought you were still just asking questions."

"Well, I was," I admitted, not liking that he had used my words against me. He really wasn't making this easy. "But at that point, I thought things were wrapping up, and to be honest, I was feeling pretty good about myself. The officers were pulling documents, and I wanted them to know which leads I was looking into."

I wasn't getting anywhere.

"Look," I leveled with him, adjusting my stance. "I know that doesn't help much. I realize how bad it sounds, but I'm not going to just blow it off and leave it unsaid. I do realize I was in the wrong here."

Rhodes considered me and slowly nodded. "I get that. And I do appreciate you being honest with me. You didn't have to give me all the details." He looked down at the ground, then back at me. "But these guys are my family. We've been through a lot together and look out for each other."

I nodded in understanding. It was like that on the force, too. That had been harder to walk away from than my stable career. It was also why I clung so tightly to my friendship with Jen.

"I understand." I backed away from Rhodes, surprised by how much his rejection hurt. I took a deep breath. "Thanks for giving me a chance to explain. And to apologize. I'll let you get back to your dinner."

Rhodes frowned and slanted forward as if to stop me. But just said, "Mal."

I stopped mid-turn and looked at him, resigning myself to the fact that I may not get a second chance.

"I'm not saying no, Mal." He looked at me directly, head inclined. "You put my family in jeopardy, though. I tend to be a bit protective."

I froze, listening, then dipped my head in understanding. My hands were worrying my keys.

"I forgive you, but I can't just jump back in where we started."

I nodded again, not having a lot to say. I turned to go.

"Give me a little time, alright?"

I glanced back to see him giving me a small smile. I returned one as well, barely more than a corner turned up. My stomach was in knots.

"Thanks," I said, looking right at him. "I appreciate that."

He inclined his head again and watched me as I turned to go. He didn't stop me this time.

I didn't have the impression I'd be getting a phone call from him anytime soon, but at least, I wasn't worried about running into him at Mariano's anymore.

Oh well, what's done is done. I did the right thing about the whole mess in the end. He had, too, because he had been honest with me. I valued that.

I drove to Mariano's because it was still on my mind and picked up a salad with extra cheese and a container of olives. I needed a new job. I had a couple of emails for potential cases I hadn't answered yet. I'd head back to the office and go through them. At least one of them would likely pan out.

As I walked back out to the parking lot, I couldn't help running back through the conversation with Rhodes in my head. I was still glad I said what I said. Honestly, I wasn't sure what I had expected. I just missed the easygoing Rhodes, full of confidence and with laughing eyes. I shook my head, a sad smile on my lips at the memory.

Finally spotting my Jeep at the end of the lot, I made my way around a black van. But just as I was aiming the key for the lock, I heard the vehicle's door open and was grabbed from behind.

I let go of my groceries, arms flailing in surprise. Then I dug my heels in and tried to drop to the ground, attempting to make it difficult to manage. But I had someone on either side, and one of them had a hand over my mouth. Unable to stop them, it didn't take long before I was being pulled toward the van. I couldn't get my arms free to fight back or to grab my ASP.

Twisting and jerking to break free, I was finally able to get the hand over my mouth to budge and bit down as hard as I could. The attacker howled, and I filled my lungs to scream when another hand came down on my face.

I had gotten turned back around a bit in my struggles and got a glimpse of my assailants. They had hoods pulled down over their faces, and in the dark, I couldn't see a lot. Just that it looked like two men.

The one to my left was cursing about his hand and hit me in the head. I got a punch to the kidney when I kicked out. I was still fighting to get away when my feet were knocked out from underneath me, and I hit the ground hard. Another blow came to my head, and this time, darkness followed.

Meanwhile, in a state-of-the-art house mixed liberally with superhero memorabilia,

"Sam. She's still not answering," Suzy called from the kitchen.

"I'm sure she's just on a stakeout or something," Sam replied, trying to calm her.

Suzy walked into his office. "She could at least text me back. It's really not like her."

"You text Mal often?"

"Well, I *have* texted her." She shrugged her shoulders defensively. "We've had girl talk. We're friends."

Suzy crossed her arms and leaned against the doorframe.

"When I tried her earlier, I left a text message inviting her to dinner," she explained. "So, she would have texted me back. I just tried again, and it went straight to voicemail. It's nearly ten o'clock."

Sam walked over to Suzy and rubbed her arm.

"I'm sure everything is okay. Mal is a busy lady."

"I don't know, Sam." Suzy sighed. "I just have a bad feeling about this. She had that lunch with Dr. Millwood, and he was questioning her story. It just makes me wonder if something bad happened."

"Well, do you know any of her other friends?" Sam asked. "Doesn't she have some cop friends? She knew Detective Rodriguez."

"True." Suzy nodded. "But I didn't get the impression she liked him very much. I think there's some baggage there."

"Well, I didn't see her talk to anyone else at the station. And I don't really know anyone else she knows. We could run by her place. See if she's there or at her office."

"I'd like that." Suzy nodded, gazing up worriedly at Sam. "I'm probably being silly, but it would make me feel better."

"I'll go ask Wyatt to get the car started," Sam said, heading out of the room.

Chapter 24

I awoke with my face pressed against a hard surface and my hands tied behind my back. I didn't know if I was alone, so I stayed as still as possible. Which was fine because my vision swam for several minutes. The room smelled like stale, unwashed bodies and didn't help the nausea from the hit to my head.

Once my dizziness quieted somewhat, I cracked an eyelid to see the wooden floor that I was resting on. A thin film of dust covered the ground. It was dark, and I hoped it was still Friday night. I didn't know how much time had passed. I couldn't see enough to tell if I was alone, but I hadn't heard any sounds. I risked rolling my shoulder to see if anyone was waiting for me to wake.

Nothing made a sound, but pain shot up through my elbow to my shoulder. Slowly, I turned my face to look around, my neck sore from lying at a bad angle. I was in a bedroom, on the floor, next to a bed. There was a tattered blanket covering an old mattress and box springs. I could see a window, but it was boarded up from the outside. Only a sliver of moonlight came through it. As I slowly scanned the room, I confirmed I was alone.

I rolled back facedown and struggled to get my knees pulled up beneath me without the use of my hands. My muscles ached, and I stifled a groan, feeling a sting on my lip. I had to scoot them just a bit farther up and finally had enough leverage to press my forehead up and off the ground.

As I struggled to get upright, my head went back to swimming. It must have been a pretty hard it. I edged the tip of a tongue out to feel my lower lip. It stung in confirmation, adding a split lip to my growing list of injuries.

Nothing felt broken, but the spot on my head felt swollen. I wiggled my eyebrows and felt stiff, painful skin in reply. It felt like dried blood, but I couldn't tell for sure with my arms behind me. I twisted my wrists; in this position I had a little space between my arms. The thin bite of my bindings made me guess they were zip ties, and thick ones, harder than hell to snap.

Rolling to my hip, I slowly slid my legs out in front of me. I moved to get my heels under me to realize I had lost one of my shoes. *Of course,* the one day I don't wear boots would be the day I got kidnapped. I rolled my eyes and winced at the pain.

Struggling for a few minutes to pull my hands under my butt, I conversely wiggled and grunted through the pain in my shoulder. I was pretty sure it wasn't dislocated, but it sure felt beat up. I finally managed to slip my arms under my legs and in front of me and had to sit for a few minutes to regain control of my breathing. I yanked at the ties again, but they weren't loose enough to slip off my wrists.

Standing up slowly, still trying to not make a sound, I moved to the door. I didn't see any light coming from underneath it and still hadn't heard any sounds from the house around me. Glad to have the use of my arms again, I grabbed the doorknob, pressing it against the doorframe so it wouldn't jiggle. Slowly, I tried the knob to find it locked. *Figures.*

I moved to the window and was only able to make out a patch of grass through a slit in the wood. I tried opening it, but it was painted shut. I might be able to break the seal, but it wouldn't be quiet.

Leaning against the wall, I tried to come up with a plan. It didn't look so good for me. I wondered what the hell I was going to do.

Meanwhile, in a fully decked-out security van,

"She's not there, either," Suzy said, concern fully setting in. They had driven by Mal's apartment, but her Jeep wasn't there and no one answered the door. There was still no sign of the Jeep at her office either, and the lights weren't on.

"She could be visiting a friend or on a stakeout," Sam offered.

"She didn't say she was following up on any more leads. And she's been keeping us in the loop on the case. She, just yesterday, arrested the arsonist. I don't think she's on any other cases."

"Suzy," Sam said, grabbing her hand. "Mal doesn't tell us everything."

"But we're becoming friends," Suzy argued. Surely, she would have mentioned something.

Sam smiled at her. "Even friends don't tell each other everything."

"I know." She huffed, slumping in her seat. "It's just that something feels off."

They drove back out of town, and as they passed the Roscoe Square shopping center, she saw Mal's Jeep.

"There she is!" she shouted.

"There's her Jeep, at least," Wyatt corrected, directing his guys to drive into the parking lot.

All five of them piled out of the van when it pulled to a stop.

"See, she was just shopping," Sam said, smiling.

"They're closing," Wyatt said, starting to frown. "She should be coming out if that was the case."

They all turned as one to the store, waiting for people to exit. No one came out except one clerk.

"This doesn't look so good," Sam said.

"Nope," Wyatt agreed, walking up to the Jeep to look inside. But it wasn't until he walked around it that his shoulders fell. "It doesn't look good at all."

Suzy and the rest rounded the car to see the crushed bag from Mariano's with a broken container of olives spilling out. Her eyes went round, and she leaned back into Sam.

"What was that detective's name again?" Wyatt asked, looking up.

"Rodriguez. I think he and Mal had history," Suzy offered. "But I also thought of one other person we could call."

They all looked at her expectantly.

"She was dating a city firefighter by the name of Rhodes."

"Mal's dating someone?" Sam asked, surprised.

Wyatt turned towards her. "Do you know which station he works at? We could try him first just to see if he's heard from her. The groceries could be a coincidence and he picked her up here. If not, we'll put a phone call in to the detective. A current boyfriend would be more likely to know her whereabouts than an old one."

They all looked down at the grocery bag, crushed deli container, and olives. No one really believed it to be a coincidence, but they kept quiet.

"Bricktown, I believe. I think he's the captain."

I pushed away from the wall, done feeling sorry for myself. I wasn't ready to give up and wasn't going to wait to be found. I scanned the room. They had taken my jacket and my ASP baton with it. There was a crate against one wall with a broken chair next to it. I tried its legs and was able to wiggle a wrung.

It wasn't much, but it was better than nothing. I stopped periodically, as I wasn't quite as quiet as before, but still heard no sounds. I was hoping that wherever I was, my captors were either gone or asleep for the night.

The window seemed like my best bet, so I tried it again, using the chair wrung to lightly tap against the dried paint. It was hard going with my hands tied in front of me, but I was able to get some of it chipped off and edged the window open about 3 inches when it screeched in protest.

Hurrying back to the door, I pressed my ear to it to listen for movement on the other side. Still nothing, so I went back to the window to try again. I put the blanket between my hands and the glass to muffle whatever noise I could. I eventually had to give it a short, sharp shove, which resulted in a squeak loud enough to wake the dead. At least it seemed that way to me. I stilled to listen for sounds. And again, there were none.

The window, finally open enough for me to get through, laughed at me. Because, although I had gotten it open, the wooden slats lay over it, trapping me inside. Since it was nailed from the outside, I couldn't pry the nail head, but I could push. I tried a wide board, placing the heel of my bound hands near the edge of the slat and shoved. It didn't give at all.

Frustrated but not ready to give up, I pulled the crate closer to give myself some leverage. I stepped up on it and put my foot on the wooden board between me and my freedom. But even gripping the window frame, I didn't have enough leverage to move it.

So I centered my weight, readied myself, and gave the board a strong, firm kick. The window frame rattled a bit, and the board wiggled a little. I tried it again. After three tries, the plank came free on one side but hung from the other. I scrambled over to pull it free, bringing it inside instead of letting it drop. I didn't want to step down on those nails when I went out the window.

A nice, large six-inch gap in the window gave me hope for more. Leaning forward, I got my first full glimpse outside. My heart sank when I saw I wasn't on the ground level. It looked like I was on the third floor of a brick building with concrete directly below. The grass I had seen was a small square in the side lot.

I staggered back from the window, looking around for another solution. No way could I jump from here. I looked back out, trying to determine if there was another window ledge I could use to climb down. I could only see one below, but I wasn't sure if I could reach it. It didn't look very wide. Last resort, then.

Meanwhile, at a fire station in Bricktown,

"I saw her earlier tonight," Rhodes replied, frowning at a frazzled Suzy. "Is something wrong?"

"She's missing," Sam supplied, waving his arms around.

"What time was that?" asked Wyatt.

"We can't find her," Suzy said, eyebrows drawn.

"Wait, what?" Rhodes said, standing up.

He had been sitting in front of the station with a cup of coffee, relaxing after a call, when a van pulled up. No sooner had it shut off than five people poured out. The nice-looking brunette and slim nerdy guy hadn't worried him, but the sandy-blond-haired guy looked like he had training. The two muscle-bound twins looked less concerning, but he hadn't made up his mind yet.

All at once, they had descended on him, asking for "Rhodes." Ever since he had identified himself, they had peppered him with questions about Mal.

"What do you mean she's missing?" Rhodes asked, concerned. He walked toward them, trying to sort out what was happening.

Wyatt answered, hands raised to calm the firefighter. "We don't exactly know she's missing."

"We went by her place," Sam said.

Rhodes turned to face the guy.

"She wasn't there or at the office," Suzy continued.

"We did find her Jeep at Mariano's," Wyatt explained. "But she wasn't there."

"She could be with a friend," Rhodes offered, trying to be reasonable. "I can't see her leaving her Jeep at Mariano's, but you never know."

"Agreed." Wyatt nodded. "Also, there was a bag of groceries left next to the Jeep."

Rhodes frowned. "Groceries? Just left sitting there?" He crossed his arms and searched their faces for answers.

"Crushed, like someone had stepped on them," said one of the gym rats in the back.

He froze; that didn't sound good. "What was in the bag?"

"Looked like some olives and a deli salad," offered the other guy.

"Shit," Rhodes said, rubbing his head. "She likes Mariano's salad bar."

"We wanted to check with you first. To see if you had seen her," explained Wyatt, focusing on the facts. "Did she say where she was going, or if she was working on another case?"

"No," Rhodes replied, dialing her number with his phone. He had to see for himself. "We had a short conversation. I know she just wrapped a case, but I don't know any particulars."

When her phone went straight to voicemail, he paced for a bit, deciding. "We should call the police. She has friends there."

"Yes, we were going to call Detective Rodriguez next," Suzy filled in. "It's just that they have history, and we wanted to try with you, first."

"Some kind of old boyfriend," Sam explained.

"Old boyfriend?" he turned, frowning.

"Don't worry," Sam continued. "I don't think she's back with him or anything. She hates him."

"What?" Rhodes asked, trying to follow.

"We just thought he may know other friends of hers to try," Wyatt offered, twitching his eyebrows at Sam to indicate that he should be quiet.

Rhodes looked around, trying to find an answer, but feeling helpless. One of his least favorite predicaments.

"We're going to the station to let them know what's going on," Suzy said, putting a hand on Rhodes' arm. "You're working. Why don't you give me your number, and I'll call you and let you know what we find out?"

Rhodes fought with himself. He rubbed his head again, trying to decide what to do. He wanted to go with them. Hell, he wanted to go by Mal's place and see for himself. See the Jeep. He knew they were telling the truth, but he'd feel better at least trying.

"Okay," he finally said. "But please call me the moment you hear anything. I can call in a replacement if needed. I can be anywhere in a matter of minutes."

"Definitely," Suzy promised, taking his number.

Wyatt nodded, and they all piled back in the van.

Weighing my options with the door, I tried the knob again, more forcefully this time. I checked the hinges. Maybe if I could take them out, I could escape.

It was then I heard the first scrape of noise from outside the room. I heard footsteps coming closer and ran to grab the chunk of wood with protruding nails.

The steps stopped in front of the door. I waited on the other side, frozen, listening.

Finally, a hand banged on it. Then a key scraped in a lock. I readied myself, board clutched between zip-tied hands.

When the door opened, I was ready. I swung, leaning forward to add all my weight. The man on the other side caught my hand, but not quite fast enough. The nails scraped at the side of his face.

He let out a bellow of pain and backhanded me against the wall. I slid down and struggled to get up before he could hit me again. I swept out a foot to trip him and was able to jump out of his reach as he went down. Giving him a shove, I leaped over him, heading out the door.

Swinging around the doorframe, I took a moment's glance to find the quickest way out. Spying a door at the end of the hall in front of me, I took off for it. Out of the doorway to my right, another goon came, rubbing the sleep from his eyes. He stood there, in jeans, no shirt, and a chest holster fitted with a firearm.

"What the hell?" he said.

As soon as he saw me, he reached for the gun. I didn't think I'd make it to the the end of the corridor, so I grabbed a chair sitting in the hallway and swung it at his face. He dropped his weapon but made a grab for me. I continued my path to the doorway, grabbing for the knob, but it was locked.

Fumbling with the handle, I felt a hand rip me back from the door. I hit the ground hard and rolled to get back up, but it was hard to get leverage with my wrists together. My attacker dug his fingers into my hair and shoved me back to the floor.

He pressed my face into the wood. "Forget about it, you stupid bitch," he spat out. "You're not getting out."

My strength was starting to fail me as I tried to struggle against his much stronger frame. My scalp burned from the tight twist he had in my hair. Vision swimming, I tried to gather my energy. Just before I passed out, the front door burst open.

A large man in a suit leveled a gun at the shirtless man at my back, who dropped me instantly. The man jerked his head toward the door, and I scrambled up and behind him. I was instantly at his side.

He nodded at me and backed up with me behind him. I took the cue, not caring who he was or why he was there. We were moving away from my captors.

Exiting the building, I rushed down the front stairs of an apartment lobby, the concrete steps biting into the skin of my bare foot. The brute motioned to a car waited at the curb. He opened the door and ushered me in. I went willingly.

He got in after me, pulling a knife to pop the ties around my wrist.

"Thanks," I said, rubbing my sore skin. "But who are you?"

He nodded to the driver, who handed me a phone.

I stared at it for a moment, then put it to my ear.

"Bugsy," came a voice on the other line.

"Dom?" I asked, adrenaline still rocking through my system.

A chuckle came through the receiver. "That's right. I told you I owed you one. You can't go dying on me, you know. It would make me a welcher. Now we're square."

"But how'd you find me?" I asked, grasping the phone like a lifeline, hands starting to shake.

"My guys keep an eye on Dessi's guys," he explained. "Good thing, too. The tail notified me, and I sent my men to get you out."

"Could have been a little faster," I drawled, lightly touching my brow.

I heard another chuckle resound. "At least you're alive, kid."

I nodded at that, then, realizing he couldn't hear me, said out loud, "Thanks."

"As I said, now we're square. I owed you one." Dom paused. "However, if you're ever looking to make a buck, I could use someone like you on the team. You're very resourceful. And you don't back down when you've got a scent."

I appreciated what Dom had done, but I really didn't want to get mixed up in the mob. No more than I already had, anyway.

"As much as I do appreciate the offer, Dom," I replied. "I have my own business to run."

"I figured as much, but keep it in mind. Keep my card, too. If you ever need another favor, I'd be happy to trade again."

"Will do," I replied, smiling slightly.

"The driver will take you anywhere you need to go, but I'm assuming the station is where you're headed," he guessed.

"That's right."

"I figured you for the type to press charges. I tend towards a more personal approach."

I thanked him again, not intending to ever put myself in his debt.

"Heal up quickly, Bugsy," I heard over the phone as I passed it over to the driver and told him to head on to the police station in Roscoe Village.

Chapter 25

I didn't recognize the officer behind the desk. *Must be a new guy.* A look of surprise flashed across his face when he glanced up at me. I probably looked like I had been run over. Surely, he'd seen worse. Then again, I hadn't seen myself yet.

"Is Officer Mathews still on duty?" I asked, doubtful. She'd be long-since at home unless she was on call or on an active case.

"No, ma'am," replied the officer. "Can I help you?"

"I'm Detective Malone, PI," I answered. "I'd like to report a kidnapping."

The funny thing was that it wasn't the word kidnapping that caused the young officer to grab his phone. It was my name. I looked at him curiously as he leaned back toward the offices behind him and spoke urgently into the receiver. *What was going on?*

I was still looking at him, confused, when the door opened and out poured a group of people. Suzy and Sam led the way, with Jen not far behind. Wyatt and Detective Rodriguez, plus Wyatt's guys, and a few other officers I had worked with previously. My eyes widened at their sudden arrival. *What were they even doing here?*

Gathered around me, they chattered furiously, gasping at my appearance. I smoothed my hair, trying to regain some semblance of order. I was peppered with questions all around and hurriedly assured everyone that I was all right. I told Rodriguez where I had been held, and he sent a squad car to apprehend my attackers.

When it all slowed down, I sat in a room with everyone and recounted my story. However, I left out the part where Dom's men got me to the station. I just told them I had called a taxi. Apparently, they found my Jeep at Mariano's and had been looking for me. I was amazed so many people cared. I had always been a bit of a loner, and this was the first time I had more than one or two people in my life who cared about me. I was stunned.

The officers returned without an arrest. Apparently, the kidnappers had hightailed it out of there after I got away. All they found was an old abandoned apartment building and a few furnishings implying someone had used it as a safe space, but there was nothing personal to tie it to anyone. Nothing personal but my leather jacket tossed into a corner. It was enough to make me feel a little better, just pulling it on, certainly glad to have it back. Checking my pocket, I was surprised to find my ASP baton and phone still in there. Things were looking up.

I had shared my suspicions about Dessi and Dr. Millwood, figuring the doctor had called Dessi to tell him I was asking questions. I must have been causing them too much trouble and he sent someone to get me out of the picture and to find out what I knew. I just prayed I had enough on Dessi.

Pulling up the audio on Millwood, I emailed it to Rodriguez. It should be enough for his arrest once they confirm everything. Hopefully, once they got a warrant on Millwood, they'd find more connections to Dessi. Millwood would spill; I didn't figure him the type to put others ahead of himself.

Before I put my phone away, I noticed seven missed calls and a slew of messages. I looked up to see Suzy staring at me sheepishly.

"Sorry," she said. "I got a little worried."

I grinned, leaning in to hug her. It was nice to have friends.

When I finished my official statement, Suzy stopped Rodriguez short.

"Don't you have enough? We need to get her to the hospital. She needs some rest."

Exhausted, I didn't argue with that point and let them take me there.

It was early morning by the time they had me cleaned up and resting in a hospital room. Suzy, Sam, and Wyatt stuck around although the other two security guys were camped out in the van. Jen and Rodriguez stayed at the station, working on the case, but had posted a policeman at my door.

I had gotten stitches along my eyebrow. Luckily, my shoulder wasn't dislocated, but it did get a massive bruise. I would have a sling for a few days while the swelling went down. My kidneys still hurt from the blow to them, and it ached with every deep breath I took. The crack in my lip still stung, but the ointment helped. As bad as I felt, the safety of the bed and the comfort of friends gave me a little relief.

"You should really head on home," I told Suzy, noticing her tired eyes. I suddenly felt the need to take care of all of them and send them home to rest.

"Home? I can't leave you here," she replied. "You're here because of me!"

"What? No way," I argued. "You are *not* taking credit for anything Dessi does. He's responsible for his own actions."

"It's just that you wouldn't have been looking in on him at all if it weren't for me." She looked down at me with incredibly sad eyes.

"Hey, I wouldn't have been looking in on him at all if he hadn't had you kidnapped in the first place," I assured her, taking her hand. "He's the bad guy here."

"Still," she said, patting my hand. "I just want to make sure you're all right."

I laughed and winced at the pain it caused in my side. "I'm as safe here as I'll ever be."

She nodded, then glanced at the door. Turning to see what she was looking at, I saw Rhodes standing in the doorway, his jaw ticking as he took in the sight of me. His eyes filled with a quiet fury as they moved from one injury to another. I shifted uncomfortably under his inspection.

He slowly came to the bed, still wearing his uniform. Suzy stepped back to where Sam was sitting by the window. Wyatt stood next to him, leaning against the wall, quietly watching the interaction.

I frowned at Suzy, unsure why Rhodes was here. She looked down at the floor in a telling glance. I struggled to sit up more.

"You okay?" he asked, eyebrows furrowed sharply as he moved to help me.

"Right as rain," I answered, trying to give him a grin. But it ended up looking more like a grimace when my kidneys screamed. My split lip pulled, and I put a hand up to make sure it wasn't bleeding again.

Rhodes' face got even more stony. "Who did this to you?"

"Dessi's guys, I'm pretty sure," I replied. "They were gone by the time the police got there, but they've got an APB out."

His eyes traveled over my face and body, jaw clenched. "Why'd they come for you? Because of your investigation?"

"Yes," I admitted. "It seems I stumbled onto something. The police are looking into it now."

He nodded tightly. "How bad are you hurt?" he asked, his eyes searching me with an intensity I'd never seen on him.

I shook my head. "Not what you're thinking. They roughed me up a bit, is all. Most of this came when they were getting me into the van."

"At Mariano's?" he asked.

"Yes. I went there to grab some dinner after I left you."

"Fuck," Rhodes said, turned away, and paced a foot or two. He moved back to the bed. "Suzy and Sam came to the station last night, looking for you."

"They did?" I looked at Suzy incredulously. She glanced up and gave me a half smile that didn't quite reach her eyes.

"They wanted to know if I knew where you were. Mal," he said, taking my hand and searching my face. "I felt so helpless. Is there anything you need?"

I patted his hand. "I'm okay, Rhodes. Honest. Just give me a few days, and I'll be back at it." I gave him a light smile and a wink.

Another voice came from the hall. "Mal, how are you holding up?"

I looked up to see Rodriguez standing in the doorway. He and Jen came in, carrying a take-out container of coffee. Rodriguez caught sight of Rhodes standing intimately by my bedside, still holding my hand. He bristled and stepped forward, invading the space.

Rhodes looked back and forth between us and dropped my hand. I struggled again to sit up farther, and both men moved to help me. They glanced at each other, and Rhodes stopped. Rodriguez kept moving, and I waved him off with a frown.

"Knock it off, Rodriguez." I gave Rodriguez a nasty look. He had no right to be jealous. I smoothed the blanket from the hospital over my lap and checked to make sure my hospital gown was still in place. "Any update?"

"Yeah, actually," Rodriguez answered, straightening. He sent another short look to Rhodes and continued.

"You'll never believe what happened," Jen said, coming to my side, elbowing Rodriguez out of the way.

I looked back over to Rhodes, who was regarding the whole exchange with interest and a little irritation.

"Jeremy Jones turned up," Rodriguez said.

"What?" I asked.

"Where?" Wyatt asked, suddenly coming to life.

Suzy stood up as they all moved closer to me.

Rodriguez shook his head. "He's at the precinct. He was found wandering around with a black eye. Looks like he had been beaten up pretty badly. He's saying he orchestrated your kidnapping. Yours and Suzy's."

Jen and I exchanged looks.

"That's not right," Suzy argued. "He's no angel. He definitely needs to be put behind bars, but he wasn't behind it. Dessi ordered it."

"Of that, we have no proof," leveled Rodriguez.

"But Jeremy told me he did," Suzy continued.

"I know it, and you know it, but if his story checks out and we don't find any hard evidence on Dessi, he *will* walk."

"Again," Sam ground out, finally joining the conversation. He had moved to put his arm around Suzy's waist.

"We're bringing Dessi in right now for questioning," Jen offered. "Like Alex said, he'll probably walk, but you never know. We may be able to trip him up somewhere."

"We'll try again with Jeremy after we get him cleaned up," Rodriguez said. "Maybe he'll soften once he hears how many years we could get on him. And once he's away from Dessi's influence."

We all knew Dessi had forced his confession. He likely had one of his goons beat him up, too. I bet Dessi had never even lifted a finger. Asshole.

"Hey, Jen," I shot out. "What are you doing here? I thought you were going out of town."

Jen just smiled and touched my arm. "You're crazy if you think I wouldn't come straight back once I heard you were missing."

I looked at the group surrounding me and noticed that, somewhere near the end of the exchange, Rhodes had slipped out the door. I wish he had stuck around a few more minutes.

I was surprised he came; it made me hope that, over time, we may actually become friends. I wasn't stupid enough to expect more. Hell, a week ago, I wasn't even sure I wanted more. I had seen the look on his face, and the wall he put up was pretty thick. I shook my head to clear it and focused back on my friends around me and on Rodriguez.

"Does that make me more or less safe now?" Suzy turned toward Wyatt.

"Hard to say." Wyatt shrugged. "Depends on if it goes to trial. If Jeremy turns against Dessi, then you'll be a key witness. At that point, you'll need to get off the grid entirely. May be a good idea to get you to a safe house now."

"I doubt he'll do that," Rodriguez said. "Dessi's got his hooks in pretty deep. I'm not so sure what he threatened Jeremy with, but he didn't waver."

"But there's always a chance," Jen said.

"True."

Suzy and Sam looked at each other.

"I'd really rather wait and see what happens," Suzy said, leaning into Sam, who tightened his arm around her protectively.

"The house is secure." Sam nodded confidently. It wasn't the first time his eccentric nature ended up being a good thing. Besides, he loved the fact he practically lived in a literal Batcave, minus the alter-ego.

"Actually, I don't disagree," Wyatt said thoughtfully. "I would typically argue, but your house is a freaking fortress. Although being out and about like this will have to stop. You'll need much more protection when you leave the house. I'll want several men on you."

Suzy just sighed.

"We should know something before too long," Sam consoled her.

"Hopefully," Rodriguez nodded. "But sometimes court cases can drag on forever."

Sam gave him a look that said he wasn't helping, and rubbed Suzy's back.

"Well, we'll at least know where Jeremy stands soon," he conceded.

"Alright, everyone," I announced. "I appreciate everyone's concern—and you, Alex, for stopping by—but visiting hours are over." I rubbed my good eye. "I'm exhausted, and I'm sure you all are too. I have a police guard. I'll be fine."

"Mal," Rodriguez said, looking hurt. "I'm concerned, too."

I eyeballed him, recalling his betrayal and his actions toward Rhodes. Then sighing, I admitted, "You didn't have to come all this way just to give me an update on Jeremy. But I'm sure you're tired too." It had been a long night, and none of us had gotten any real sleep.

"Thanks, Alex," I conceded.

Still not friends, though. It took another twenty minutes to hug everyone and get them out of there. I smiled again at my luck. They were nice people. I didn't really deserve them in my life, but I'd take it.

I wouldn't screw it up, either. Not like with Rhodes.

Chapter 26

They didn't let me check out of the hospital until Sunday morning. They wanted to keep me a full twenty-four hours to make sure I wasn't hemorrhaging. Jen stopped by sometime Saturday evening to check on me. I got several update texts from Suzy. She said Wyatt and Sam "strongly suggested" she didn't leave the house for a little while. She said she was going to come unglued. I just shook my head.

Wyatt offered to send a guy if I wanted someone to drive me home and walk through the apartment, but I politely refused. I had an assigned guard who would do that. Rodriguez had set him up to watch my place for at least a few days.

By the time I finally got home, it was already late morning. I was glad it was a guard I didn't know. I would have hated for one of my old crew to see me wincing and limping this bad. I loosened up a bit after I got moving, though.

I got an odd look from my neighbor, Noelle, when she saw me in the hallway. I didn't know if it was my appearance or the armed guard. Either way, she just gave a quick "hi" and an even quicker exit. I shook my head. What she must think of me at this point.

The guard gave a cursory look through the apartment and left me to myself. It felt good to be home. I relished the quiet of the place after all the noises at the hospital. I mean, it was still Chicago, and street noises were a constant reminder of that, but they were my normal and felt good.

I slowly lowered myself to the couch and ended up taking another nap, curled up in the corner. Resting at home was better than in a hospital.

When I got up, it was past noon, and I was dying for a cup of coffee. The one Jen and Rodriguez had brought was great, but that was twenty-four hours ago. Hospital coffee was terrible.

Making a pot, I showered and dressed in clean leggings and a comfy oversized sweater. I decided I would stay in for the day. No sense in trying to accomplish anything today. I'd make it into the office tomorrow. A fresh start to Monday.

And I surprised myself by doing exactly that. I did answer a few emails and set up some meetings for the coming week. It looked like I had some new cases to look into. It felt good to get moving again. However, I was interested to hear how things went with Jeremy and Dessi.

I made a light dinner and relaxed on the back patio with a blanket and a glass of scotch. I was a little disappointed that I hadn't heard from Rhodes again.

After my scotch was empty, I thought about refilling it, but didn't want to chance it with the pain meds still making their way out of my system. Besides, I was already tired. I crawled into bed early and slept like the dead.

Meanwhile, at a fire station in Bricktown,

"Rhodes," said Sully, walking into the station.

"Hey, Chief," replied Rhodes, turning around from where he had been heading in to write up a report. He put his hands in his pockets and raised his eyebrows, waiting to see what Sully needed.

"I don't know if you've heard the latest, but the mayor was arrested," Sully explained, concerned.

"I had heard, thanks," Rhodes said, nodding.

"Well, it looks really bad," Sully said, shaking his head. "It looks like he may actually be guilty. There's talk downtown. All associated with the community projects."

Rhodes just nodded again, unsure what to say.

"I can't believe it, really," Sully continued. "I had no idea."

"You couldn't have known," Rhodes finally replied.

"I just hope this doesn't stop the projects. They're helping so many people."

Rhodes walked over to put a hand on Sully's shoulder. "I'm sure it will work out. Let's go get a cup of coffee."

"We are still working to clean up the ALC facility," Sully said, walking into the kitchen. "I heard we may have to re-submit the licenses to the board for inspection."

"That's not so bad," Rhodes replied, getting mugs out of the cabinet and filling them with dark, black coffee from the station pot. "At least you can ensure it's all above board."

"Yeah," Sully replied, nodding as he leaned against the counter. "So, I heard you've been seeing that red-headed detective. Malone?"

Rhodes shrugged, mug in hand, but remained silent.

"Well, she came in, poking around about the projects a while ago. I was worried she was a reporter trying to run a story and put it all in a bad light. But actually, I just found out from the ALC crew that she's slated to help out with the cleanup next week." Sully shook his head and grimaced. "I guess I really misjudged her."

"Oh, don't feel bad about it, Chief." Rhodes slapped him on the back. "We all do it now and then."

Rhodes took a sip of his black coffee and wrinkled his nose. "Teddy!" he hollered. "Did you make the coffee again? I thought I told you not to touch the machine!" He put his mug down and shook his head. "Damn Probie. Non-coffee drinkers should *not* be allowed to make coffee."

"Sorry, Cap!" came a stuttering voice from the living room. "I *know*, but, but, but the guys told me it was my job and you'd get mad if the coffee pot went empty!"

The sound of giggling adult males could be heard from other parts of the station.

Sully took a testing sip from his mug and shook his head, too. Rhodes sighed and poured the black sludge down the sink.

"Don't worry about it, kid. I'll make more." He shook his head and moved to get a tub of coffee grounds from his locker. He didn't like the cheap ones they bought with cookshack, the money they all chipped in for food basics. "Just let me make the coffee when I'm on shift."

Sully clapped Rhodes on the back, laughing. "The other guys must have set him up. Some things never change."

Rhodes just rolled his eyes.

The next morning, after sleeping in well past nine, I dressed and made my way to the office. I was moving a little easier finally, and my lip was looking a little better. Unfortunately, my eye was still a putrid shade of puce. I patted at it lightly; it didn't hurt too much, but there was nothing I could really do with it. I wasn't much of a makeup wearer and didn't have any concealer. Honestly, I wouldn't know what to do with it if I had any. The officer parked behind me outside my office, and I waved at him as I walked inside.

I spent a couple of hours doing a little housekeeping. I paid a few bills, thought about balancing my ledgers, and looked through my emails. That counted, right? I made some notes in my files to wrap up my cases on the fire and on Suzy and filed them in the drawer. Suzy's case was in the court's hands. At least for now.

I stretched a bit and decided I needed a cup of coffee. Glancing at my coffee maker, I frowned, wanting something stronger. I hated for Mo to see me like this, but the desire for a cappuccino prevailed. Heading outside, I stopped by the officer's door and pointed across the street.

"I'm just running in there for a cup of coffee," I told him. "You want one?"

"Sure, sounds good," he replied, fighting off a yawn as he moved to get out of the police car.

I shook my head to stop him. "Don't worry about it. I've got it. You can see the door from here. I'll be right back."

He considered a moment, then nodded in agreement. "Alright. If you take longer than ten minutes, though, I'll go in."

I agreed and headed across the street a little slower than normal, limp almost hidden.

Maurice was busy with lunch-hour customers and gave me a frown when he saw my black eye. I moved to another barista's line since his was so long and placed my order. If I was being honest, I'd admit I was intentionally avoiding him. I was glad the place was so busy. It made it easier to delay the impending conversation.

I thought back to the day, only a few weeks ago, when I was headed back outside Grounds, trying to find a lead on Suzy's case. It was the day I first met Rhodes, too. I had a small pang of sadness at that thought, but smiled just the same.

The barista waved me aside after she took my order. "It's been paid for."

I looked at Mo, who was busy with a customer but was still giving me an eye. The barista shook her head and pointed to a seat at the back. I followed her finger to find Dessi sitting as cool as could be, sipping from a cappuccino. He had a newspaper out, his legs crossed, decked in an expensive suit. Lifting his drink, he winked at me.

A wave of fury rose within me, and I made my way over to his table.

"Careful, Detective," he chided me. "Wouldn't do to make a scene."

"You had me kidnapped," I ground out. "Suzy, too."

"What? Me?" He placed a hand to the vest of his three-piece suit. "I'm an innocent man. Jeremy was the mastermind behind all of that."

"You want me to believe Jeremy came up with the whole thing?" I asked. "Have you met him?"

He gave a low chuckle. "I see what you mean. Honestly, I was surprised myself. Please sit." He indicated the chair opposite to him. "You have a few minutes before your order is ready and the officer across the street starts to miss you."

I glowered at him but didn't have any recourse. I was curious to find out what he had to say, so begrudgingly, I sat. I tried to slip my hand in my pocket to start the audio recording.

Dessi gave me a look and shook his head.

"I have found I have enjoyed this game we're playing." He smiled at me.

"This game?" I started, then looked around us. Mo was watching me closely. "This may be a game to you, but it's my life. And Suzy's."

He waved away my words. "This has been quite fun. But it seems I won this round."

"You won?" I asked. "You lost your gopher, Jeremy."

I didn't bring up Millwood, not sure if they had gotten a warrant for his arrest yet.

He sighed. "That idiot? He wasn't good for anything anyway. That was always, uh, temporary."

"Temporary. That's one way to look at it."

"You may have gotten me out of the horse races for a while, but Millwood will take the fall, as he should."

I just looked at him. I wasn't giving him anything.

"That's okay," he admitted. "I needed a new pastime. The betting shops are still in operation. That particular one will just be managed by another idiot." He picked up a biscotti that was sitting on his plate and took a small bite.

"What about Suzy?" I asked, folding my arms.

"You're worried about Suzy. How sweet. She no longer matters," he said, waving it away. "Consider it a gift."

"I'm not taking any gifts from you," I replied, leaning across the table. People were starting to look. Mo was making his way to us. He was bringing my order personally.

"Looks like my time is up," Dessi said, rising elegantly to his feet. He brushed the crumbs from his slacks.

He leaned in, almost affectionately. "This has been fun. I'll be seeing you." Then he winked and sauntered out the door, leaving the rest of his coffee and biscotti at the table.

I sat there, mouth open, not knowing what to do.

"Mal, who was that?" Mo asked, approaching me to set my coffee down.

His hands went to his hips, eyebrows drawn in concern.

"Fabian Dessi," I replied, standing up to follow Dessi.

"Dessi? Mal, what's going on?"

"Nothing," I said, looking back at Mo. "I'll come back later and fill you in when it isn't as busy."

He moved as though to argue.

"Promise, Mo."

He paused, then nodded as I hurried out to follow Dessi.

I stepped out on the street outside Grounds and watched him get into a black car parked a couple of buildings down. The officer watched me exit and followed my line of sight to Dessi. His eyes went wide as he straightened up and jumped out of the car.

I motioned for him to be still. There was nothing he could do.

Dessi gave me a little finger wave as he passed by.

When I got back into the office, I called Rodriguez to fill him in. He said Jeremy had signed an affidavit to his statement. His story checked out; there was no way they could argue. They didn't have enough against Dessi. Jeremy Jones was going down for Dessi's crimes.

They had Dr. Millwood and were questioning him later today. But already, the evidence they had dug up was pointing overwhelmingly against his favor. He was being charged for the admittance of controlled substances, drug trafficking, and almost assuredly would lose his license. Arlington had already distanced themselves from him, citing breach of contract.

They also had evidence he was selling leads on "winning horses." I was relieved to find out Ty's reputation had remained intact. By his own admittance on the audio file, Dr. McSleazy was doing it all himself, and Dessi had no intention of interfering. He would be going to prison for a long time.

Mathews called to confirm Mayor Koch had been officially arrested, and a public statement would be made later in the day. I was relieved to hear Chief Sullivan had been cleared of any connections.

They were still finding evidence against the mayor, documents signed without all the required inspections and illegal agreements promising subsidies to companies that didn't meet the requirements but who were funding his campaign.

I called the Mennons to fill them in as well. They were silent while I recounted my story with Dessi.

"Does that mean I'm safe?" Suzy asked slowly.

"I'm not sure," I admitted. "But it sounded like he wasn't going to pursue you any longer. He said you posed no threat."

"Hmmph," came from Wyatt, who was listening in.

"What do you think?" Sam asked him.

"I wouldn't trust it," he said. "But maybe we can lighten security a bit."

Suzy squealed in happiness.

I was still worried about her, but it seemed the looming threat was at bay. They decided to keep a security detail for a while but to lift their self-inflicted house arrest. Suzy was ecstatic.

Wyatt came on the line. "Hey, Mal. Let me know if you need any help in the future. We're always available for backup."

I thanked him, grateful.

I called Jen to apologize that I had forgotten about our Monday lunch. She just laughed it away, saying she didn't expect me to be up and about yet anyway. I told her I thought she knew me. After filling her in as well, we rescheduled for a Friday lunch. By then, I figured I'd be ready for some ropa vieja.

After all the phone calls to update everyone, I looked around the office and decided I had done enough work for the day. So I grabbed my things and locked up to head home. When had I gotten such a large group of friends? I smiled a bit at that. It was unlike me, but I guess everyone had room for growth. An early dinner and evening on the couch sounded perfect. But first, I had to fulfill a promise.

I ducked back into Grounds to find the afternoon lull. There were a few college kids in the corner, but it was relatively quiet.

Mo glanced up, and when he saw me, he dropped his cleaning rag to come around the counter, concern heavy on his face.

"What the hell happened?" he asked, grabbing my shoulders to peer at my black eye.

I shrugged.

"Got kidnapped by the mafia. Got rescued by the mafia," I said, trying to make light of it. "Not the same mafia, though. That would be weird."

Maurice pulled me into a crushing hug.

"Good God, Mal! You've got to be careful!" he chided. "This job isn't worth your life."

"I know that, Mo." I shrugged. "I may have gotten in a bit over my head."

He gave me an eyebrow.

"Okay," I acceded. "But it's over now. And my next case is about stolen jewelry. No mafia involved! Scouts honor."

I raised my fingers in what I thought was the Girl Scout's salute. I wouldn't know; I was never a Scout. But it looked right from what I'd seen on television.

Maurice wrapped me up in another hug, gentler this time.

"Maybe it's a good idea to steer clear of the mafia altogether," he said.

"Well, that sounds like a good idea," I replied, thinking about Dom's offer. "I had a friend in some trouble this time. I had to make sure she was all right."

"Ever heard of backup?"

"Gee, sounds like a great idea." I rolled my eyes. "But it's not like I had any warning." Next time, I'll just tell them to hang on while I call in help, huh?"

"Well, I'm just glad you're okay," he said. "Come on, I'll make you a cup of coffee, and you can tell me more about it."

I grinned. "that sounds perfect."

I was feeling a lot more like myself on Tuesday morning when I headed out to the office. However, I pulled into the parking lot to find a Sentinel Security van parked outside. The guy inside nodded at me and pointed to my office building. *Not again.*

I hurried up the steps and opened the door. The hallway was empty again, and I rolled my eyes as I headed to my office door. The lights were on inside, and the sound of music rolled out from the door.

"Morning, Mal," sang Suzy's voice.

I stared at her in confusion, watching her sway in the receptionist's chair to music and Michael Bublé explaining how it was a marvelous night for a moon dance. She was at the desk with my laptop open in front of her, papers all over. Bills, receipts, and files were scattered around. I stood there for a few minutes, just staring when she finally said, "You all right?"

"Yes?" I answered her question with a question. Then blinked out of the haze. "What are you doing here?"

"I'm just helping out," she replied, a smug smile on her face.

"She's your new bookkeeper," came Sam's voice over her speakerphone, which was propped up next to her.

"You are, huh?" I asked, recovered enough to cock my head and lean a hip against the desk.

"Yep," she replied. "You said I could repay you with help."

"I don't recall us agreeing on anything."

"Well, you may or may not have been hyped up on morphine. I can't recall," she finished, continuing her work. She slid a small glance in my direction.

"Fine," I acquiesced, giving her a half smile. "But we're going to determine an hourly wage and how much is reasonable."

"Whatever." She laughed. She knew she had me. I mean, really, I never stood a chance.

"How'd you get into my laptop?" I asked.

She nodded to the phone, indicating the person on the other end, and grinned. "Sam's a whiz with computers."

I gave her an eyebrow. "I'm aware."

I told Suzy I had someone coming in later today, and she waved me off.

"I know. I found your calendar and synced it with mine." She pulled out a second computer from behind her. "I'll be done with yours in a sec, then you can have it back. I can do my work on this one."

I just shook my head.

"You have two more people scheduled this week. One more this afternoon and another tomorrow morning," she said. "I called them back this morning and lined it up. I also confirmed the appointment you set up for this afternoon. It's particularly interesting! What a sweet little old lady. Ms. Lamb says her son has been stealing her fortune. Poor thing, he even took her jewelry. Can you imagine?"

"We have to do a little fact-checking first to see if he's really even her son before we start digging," I let her know.

"I'm on it," came the disembodied voice over the phone.

I rolled my eyes. My job was never going to be the same again.

I walked into my office as a slow smile spread over my face. I just might be okay with that.

Epilogue

Two weeks later, as I sat at my desk, researching buyers for vintage jewelry, a dark shadow stepped in my door. I looked up to see Rhodes standing there, his keys in his hands.

I leaned to the right a bit to peer past him to Suzy at the desk out front. She hadn't told me I had a visitor, and I had been too focused on my new case to hear the door open. Suzy's face was radiating with a smile spread from cheek to cheek. She gave me two thumbs-up.

I rolled my eyes and straightened back up, looking up at the man. He was wearing a flannel shirt over a T-shirt, and he wore it well.

"Hi," he said. "I was just wondering how you were doing." His gaze was intense, even though his body language was relaxed.

"I'm doing fine," I replied, pushing back from the computer to give him my attention. "Feeling great, actually."

He looked at my face; the bruise had faded now to a bit of yellow-green around the edge and wasn't as noticeable. He nodded.

He looked back down at his keys, thoughtful. "Would you like to grab a coffee?"

"Have you met me?" I joked, rolling back in my chair. Then more seriously, I said. "That sounds great."

"You know," he said, glancing back at me. "You never did tell me your first name."

I let out a light snort and nodded. "No, I didn't." I regarded him, deciding to extend a bit of a peace offering. "It's Molly," I finally said.

He squinted his eyes a bit, considering, then grinned. "Molly Malone? Really? Your parents named you Molly Malone? Like the Irish song with the prostitute?"

I grimaced. "One and the same." I shook my head and grinned back. "Now you know why I go by Mal." I glanced into the other room, where Suzy was busily texting. Sam, I'd guess.

Rhodes let out a short laugh, his eyes lighting up. I smiled at that, happy to see it again.

I heard the faint strains of music through Suzy's phone.

"In Dublin's fair city, where the girls are so pretty…"

Groaning, I stood. Rhodes just glanced back at Suzy.

"You know, you never did tell me the rest of the story with the fire, either. Or what happened with, you know, the kidnapping." He looked back up at me. "I'd like to hear all about that."

I smiled at him. "I'd like that," I said and followed him out of the door. The research could wait.

From the author:
Thank you so much for reading my book. I sincerely hope you enjoyed it.

If you do, the nicest thing you can do is leave me a good review on Amazon, Bookbub, Goodreads, or wherever you review books.

If not, my name is Hal and I live in Egypt.

Connect with me online:
Website: **jenflanaganbooks.com**
Follow me on Amazon
Facebook: **@jenflanaganbooks**
Instagram: **@jenflanagan_author**
Bookbub: **@jen_flanagan**

Please visit my blog at **jenflanaganbooks.com** for upcoming books, comments, and minor musings.

What's Next?
Anxious to find out what happens next with Mal and her friends? Will Mal and Rhodes get a chance with each other? How will Suzy and Sam fit into her life in the future? Will she finally see Dessi behind bars?

Turn the page to read the first chapter of *Here I Go Again.*

Here I Go Again

A road trip with a failed romantic interest amidst a continued investigation against a criminal mastermind. At least Mal isn't doing it all on her own this time around.

Detective "Mal" Malone's life has turned upside down. Her office has been taken over by new friend and employee, Suzy, with her husband, Sam, persistently popping in like the techie-rockstar and wanna-be detective that he is. Around all of this, she's continuing to find a way to nail slippery Dessi behind bars and keeping up enough caseload to afford her new co-worker.

Discovering her new friend's strengths put a spin on how she does her job, including a new case of stolen jewelry. An unexpected visit from Rhodes, the fireman she has a fiery history with, sends her on a new journey with him out of state, in very close proximity, to find his estranged father. What could go wrong?

The new team comes together to devise a carefully laid plan that leads her directly into the lion's den. She's been caught in his web once before, this time, will she make it out alive?

Chapter 1

"Confirmed," I texted into my phone, attaching the incriminating photos and hitting the send arrow.

Sad, I slid my phone into my back pocket and eased away from the car I had been kneeling behind for a good shot inside the brownstone in Roscoe Village, a charming little burg in North Center, a larger neighborhood around Chicago.

It wasn't the kind of job I liked to do, honestly. Cheating spouses were the worst, but they also paid well, and well, it was easy work. My phone pinged in response, and I knew my client would be filing her divorce papers tomorrow, secure that her husband wouldn't be able to take her money.

See, she was the breadwinner and couldn't divorce him without him taking half of what was hers. Well, not without proof of disloyalty, as per their prenuptial agreement, or so she said. I tried not to get too far into the details with work like this. It was too emotionally draining.

Still, the occasional infidelity investigation would have to do. I had recently acquired a receptionist *slash* bookkeeper *slash* busybody who had wormed herself into my life in a way I wasn't upset about, oddly enough. What it meant, though, was that I needed to keep a steady flow of income. It was good filler work.

"Hey, you there!" came a booming male voice.

Just what I needed.

I took a quick right between two buildings. Apparently, the philanderer didn't want his photo taken. Maybe I had gotten his bad side… A snort bubbled out of me. Glancing behind my shoulder, I saw a shadow bounce against the brick wall.

"Stop!" The voice was closer than I'd like.

Yeah, right. My boots caught traction on the pavement. I easily made a left and cut through an alley, then took a sharp right into another. I knew this neighborhood; these were my stomping grounds. I jogged lightly up the path, made a quick right, and burst through the back door of the aptly named Grounds, my local coffee shop. Happily shrugging off the too-warm leather jacket and hat, I threw them on a barstool and took a seat in front of Mo, the owner.

"How's it going?" I beamed at him, breath only slightly faster than normal.

Raising an eyebrow, he glanced at the back door, but no one came in.

I smiled innocently.

He just huffed and went back to drying the coffee mug in his hands, lifting it in question.

I nodded. Was that even a question? I fluffed out my auburn hair, its waves having been smooshed by the ball cap.

Turning, he set it on the counter in front of him and went to work, weighting and tamping espresso powder. The air filled with the scent of freshly ground coffee, erasing any remainders of stress.

"Keeping out of trouble, Mal?"

I shrugged. "As much as normal."

"Any luck on the jewelry case?" he asked, frothing milk for the most beautiful creation in the world.

"Not really." I sighed. I had been approached, a few weeks prior, by a seemingly sweet little old lady, claiming her son was trying to steal her fortune, starting with her jewelry. "I've been keeping an eye on vintage jewelry sales sites but haven't seen anything matching the description she gave me yet. If he's after her fortune, he'd be after the money, right?"

"Unless he's trying to make her look incompetent and gain guardianship of her assets." He tapped the frothed milk on the counter and began to pour it into the espresso, making art.

"I thought of that, but since she doesn't want him to know she's on to him, I can't easily question him."

"So, your hands are tied."

"Yep." I sighed, sipping the slice of heaven he had slid my way. "I've got to wait for his next move."

I hated that part. My jobs often had an element of stealth. It added difficulty. I just hoped the guy would get greedy and try to make a buck on the jewelry.

"How's Suzy?"

"She's taken over things." I tried to look irritated.

"Nothing new, then."

"Nope."

"No sign of Dessi?"

"He hasn't been sniffing around her, but one of Wyatt's guys is still following her everywhere."

"I bet she loves that."

"I think she's just glad to be out of the house. For some reason, she likes bookkeeping." I shuddered.

"The horror." He grinned, turning back to his cleaning.

I lingered over my celebratory coffee for a few minutes. Then, finishing up, I nodded my thanks to Mo and paid my tab.

"Should we be expecting anyone looking for you later?" he asked, eyes sliding to the back door. "And if we do, do we know you?"

"Nah, you won't get any visitors." I chuckled, heading back out to the office.

Damn, it was good to have friends.

I waved at Brian, Suzy's bodyguard and driver posted outside the brick building housing my office, as I crossed the street from Grounds. The sounds of The Police greeted me when I walked in.

Not the actual police, the English rock band.

"Did you get it?" Suzy Mennon asked, swiveling in her chair to look at me, her stick-straight, mocha-colored hair swaying against her back, giving her a polished look in her professional wear.

"Yup." I held up my phone in confirmation. "And sent."

"Nice job!" she replied, already busily typing away on her computer. "And billed. She should be receiving the final invoice notification in a few minutes, paid with the credit card on file."

"What would I do without you?" I asked. Suzy was always way better at this part of the job than I had ever been.

"You don't want to know." She shook her head grimly.

The tablet on her desk buzzed, and she pressed a green button on the overly large smile of her techie-geek husband and aspiring PI. His brown hair looked especially curly in the photo.

"Did you get it?" Sam Mennon said as his actual face, eyes wide, replaced the contact avatar.

"Yup," I repeated, rolling my eyes. "Are you *still* tracking me?"

You get kidnapped one time by the mob, and everyone worries. It had been nearly four weeks.

"You were kidnapped only four weeks ago!"

Exactly.

I shrugged, not entirely irritated by their overprotectiveness. The event had set me back a little more than I liked to admit. Hence the boots. Regardless of the heat, I wasn't getting caught without them on a case again.

"You were moving pretty fast there for a minute. Were you being chased?" His voice raised in excitement.

"A bit."

"Oh boy."

"Any calls?" I asked, heading to my office in the back.

"Nothing from Rhodes," Suzy said sadly. "Didn't you call him? You said you called him."

"I did," I mumbled. It was a lie. I was going to call him after our last coffee date a few weeks ago. But I couldn't figure out what to say. Eventually, it felt like I had waited too long. Now, I wasn't sure what to do. "I meant work calls."

"No work calls."

"Great." I sat down at my desk, the coffee turning sour in my stomach.

I didn't like lying to Suzy, but it was easier than trying to explain everything that was going on in my head.

At least I had money coming into the bank. That part felt good. Opening my computer, I rechecked a few jewelry sale sites.

An unproductive hour later, I stood up to stretch. I felt bad Ms. Lamb was paying me for the fruitless computer time even though she'd assured me it was what she wanted. From the sound of it, the lady was loaded. I tried to brush off the guilt, but I felt like I should be doing more.

I had checked the local jewelry shops too, in case they had gotten loose stones in for sale. Most of her diamonds were certified and had been etched with a serial number. They had lists and would call me if anything came in with that number, but they informed me that if someone was hocking diamonds, they only had to recut them to remove the trace. *Great.*

If her son had any idea what he was doing, he wouldn't be dumb enough to simply sell a certified diamond.

Still, maybe he wasn't the sharpest tool in the shed.

Grabbing my keys, I decided to get a bite to eat. Suzy had already left, and there wasn't much else I could do today.

After grabbing a salad from my favorite salad bar at Mariano's, I drove by a few betting parlors, windows open to let in the warm late-June air. I'd have preferred a scone at Grounds, but I needed to keep in shape.

I scanned the neighborhood. I wasn't looking for anything in particular; I was just keeping an eye out for anything unusual. The same beat-up cars sat at the same betting parlors, with a few revolving ones thrown in for good measure. Nothing new.

They were all owned by Fabian Dessi, or so Sam's slick hacking skills said. He was the sleazebag who had ordered Suzy's death a couple of months ago and my kidnapping four weeks ago. We had gotten a few of the bad guys behind bars, but Dessi was the mastermind behind them, and we had yet to get enough evidence to throw the book at him.

It didn't help that he had ties to the Marchis, a known Chicago mafia family.

I swung through a drive-thru for a black coffee and pulled into my usual spot off to the side of Dream Time Furniture in Wicker Park, another of Dessi's holdings. He had several, and I kept my eye on all of them. Apart from the betting parlors and this place, there was a strange little video-gaming winery in Oakbrook. Honestly, I couldn't see him spending time in a place like that.

Checking for my baton, I found it in my door pocket. I wasn't going to get anywhere near Dessi's goons without having it at my side from here on out. I pulled out my salad and dug in, watching the traffic.

A couple arrived, one of a long list of regulars, dressed in trendy clothes and giggling as they made their way into the furniture store.

My watch showed 5:30 p.m. Brown-haired Guy pulled up and walked in. An attractive Asian-American woman arrived at 5:45 p.m. in a hurry. The door at the back of the building, that I could see from my vantage point, opened, and Apron Guy came out with a trash bag he deposited in the bin at the end of the building. It was the usual chain of events, and I had the pattern down by now.

Munching my salad, I watched the clock, waiting for the delivery that was due to arrive. Right on time, the truck pulled up and unloaded liquor bottles through the back door. In and out, like a choreographed dance of which I had the score.

A few other regulars arrived, only it wasn't the furniture store they were frequenting; it was the business within a business, accessible only through the Dream Time Furniture Store. A speakeasy and apparent office space for Fabian Dessi.

Correction, suspected speakeasy. I hadn't been into the building yet. I was taking my time, collecting facts, being careful. I wasn't fond of the idea of getting kidnapped again. But based on the intel Sam had dug up online—liquor license, business license, and address—plus my frequent surveillance, this was Red, a hidden speakeasy in Wicker Park.

It didn't look like Dessi was here tonight, and neither were any of the Marchi-related goons. Maybe they had other business around town. I wished I had a way to know what he was up to now that he wasn't spending his time at the Arlington Racecourse. But after we'd blown the cover of a doctor who was juicing the horses so he could win, he had found another hobby.

I needed to get in and find out what he was doing in there. Maybe I could find out which guests were new business partners and get more background on them.

It was time. I just needed to set a few things in order first.

Here I go again.

<u>Jen Flanagan Fiction Books</u>

Orca Cove Series:
Saltwater Cures
Uncharted Waters (coming 2024)

Books in the Detective Malone Series:
Bad Company
Here I Go Again
Under Pressure

<u>Willa Daniels Non-Fiction Books</u>

Stand-alone books:
The Art of Living Seasonally

The Natural Path Series:
An Introduction to Herbalism
An Introduction to Soap Making (coming 2024)
Home and Cleaning Solutions (coming 2024)
Body and Skincare Solutions (coming 2024)